His kisses were like hot rain

Luke stroked her back, and his hand drifted down. At the intimate touch, the clouds fogging Rosie's brain cleared. Suddenly she realized this was no dream and she was perilously close to repeating what had happened five years earlier.

She pushed him away. "No, Luke."

For a moment he resisted and drew her closer, then he finally released her and stepped back. The moment their bodies were free, she whirled around to face the ocean and wrapped her arms protectively across her chest.

Unable to control himself, Luke seized her upper arm and swung her toward him.

"Rosie," he gritted, "I want to talk to you."

She winced at his touch, but faced him. "Why are you here like this? What is this about?"

"Us."

"What do you mean, us? It's over. Five years ago it was over before it started. You told me that yourself."

"That was then, this is now. Rosie, I know the truth."

ABOUT THE AUTHOR

Clare Richmond lives in Maryland with her husband, three children, two youthful German shepherds and her Maine coon cat. She writes nonfiction, mysteries and poetry as well as romances. When she's not at her typewriter she can be found pursuing her various hobbies: swimming, snorkling, reading, photography and ice-skating.

Books by Clare Richmond

HARLEQUIN AMERICAN ROMANCE

174–RUNAWAY HEART
215–BRIDE'S INN
352–PIRATE'S LEGACY

CLARE RICHMOND

HAWAIIAN HEAT

Harlequin Books

TORONTO • NEW YORK • LONDON
AMSTERDAM • PARIS • SYDNEY • HAMBURG
STOCKHOLM • ATHENS • TOKYO • MILAN
MADRID • WARSAW • BUDAPEST • AUCKLAND

To our families

Published February 1993

ISBN 0-373-16476-9

HAWAIIAN HEAT

Printed in U.S.A.

Chapter One

Rosie Clarke snuggled beneath the sheets of the bed at Mrs. Weatherby's Bed-and-Breakfast. Her flight from Los Angeles had gotten in late and she was tired. Sleep, however, refused to come. One reason was the ominous plume of smoke she'd seen rising in the distance from Kilauea as her plane approached Hilo Airport. But that wasn't the only reason.

Well, here I am in Hawaii, she thought, focusing on the ceiling fan whirling gently overhead. *I did it. And there's no going back.* Restlessly she rolled over on her side. Through the open window she could hear the surf crashing against the Big Island's rocky coastline. Why did the sound, usually so soothing, make her shiver?

As she tried to empty her mind, an image arose—that of a dark-haired man dressed in white, leaning against a bleached pillar as he gazed out to sea.

Luke Devillers. His name summed up her answer.

Squeezing her eyes closed, Rosie curled up into a tight ball and concentrated on the thundering surf. At first it was a vain attempt to shatter the image of Luke that was crowding her mind. Gradually, however, the rhythmic ebb and flow of the sea did its job and carried her away into the darkness of sleep.

That night Rosie's dreams drifted into a collage—a field of orchids, tall green stalks of sugarcane swaying under island breezes, an alabaster cottage silhouetted against a black sand beach. And Luke Devillers on the porch. "I'm sorry," he was saying. "I'm sorry."

And then she was running, running through fields of purple orchids. Blinded by tears, she flinched from the small velvety blossoms that brushed her skin. As she tore through the flowers, trampling their delicate petals underfoot, all she could do was repeat over and over "I have to get away from here. I have to get away from here."

Gradually the pictures melded. Rosie's eyes darted, then refocused on a portrait of a dark-eyed island beauty, Queen Analani, Luke Devillers's great-grandmother. Then slowly, in a cascade of smoke, Analani metamorphosed into the figure of a wild-haired volcano goddess with blazing eyes. Pele.

In her sleep, Rosie clenched her sheet. She recognized who this apparition must be. Around the goddess's feet, flames sprayed against the midnight sky. The magnificent creature spread her arms, shooting sparks and red-hot ribbons that glowed and simmered. One of Pele's hands stretched forth and her eyes locked with Rosie's.

Pele aimed a slender finger at Rosie's heart, and Rosie felt herself tremble.

"What do you want?" Rosie cried out.

But Pele only shook her glorious fiery mane. Then the goddess shimmered and broke into a pinwheel of shooting lights.

Rosie awoke with a start, her hand pressed to her beating heart. Her skin was cold and clammy and her hands clenched into fists. "Pele," she whispered, "Pele."

"DID YOU HEAR what happened last night?" Mrs. Weatherby inquired as Rosie took the last empty seat at the glass-topped breakfast table. The tall, silver-haired innkeeper poured a cup of steaming coffee for Rosie and handed her a dish of fresh pineapple slices.

"Oh, it's awful!" an elderly guest exclaimed, shaking her permed curls. "To think that Henry," she said, nudging her plump husband, "and I scrimped for this vacation for ten years. Then we get here just in time to see the island burned to a crisp."

Rosie, remembering the ominous plume of volcanic smoke she'd spotted as she'd flown in yesterday, almost choked on the sip of coffee she'd taken. "Why, what's going on?" she asked, looking anxiously at Mrs. Weatherby.

The prim innkeeper rubbed her hands. "A fresh eruption," she began. "Lava is heading toward the Kawasaki Warehouse." Her voice wavered. "Frankly, we're all scared. It may even have reached the warehouse by now. And we're all wondering what's next."

While Rosie's mind raced, she took a bite of toast and a last gulp of coffee. Then she stood. "I'd better get down there and have a look."

The chatty tourist appeared startled. "I wouldn't go anywhere near that if I were you, dear. It's too dangerous."

Rosie smiled. "It's my job."

Everyone's eyebrows lifted. "Your job?"

"I'm a volcanologist," Rosie replied. Then, saying goodbye to forestall the many questions that always got asked whenever she admitted to her unusual profession, she hurried back to her room. There she grabbed her keys and purse, and rushed out the door to the car she'd rented.

Adrenaline pumping, Rosie drove down toward the Chain of Craters road to Hawaii Volcanoes National Park. An angry cloud of black smoke had begun to darken the already-overcast sky, and all around Kilauea's southern slope plumes of steam rose from simmering ropes of lava. The fresh flow was beating a sluggish path southeastward. She followed it until the road stopped, blocked by stanchions and, a hundred yards away, a creeping, hissing mass of magma. Pulling up behind the line of parked cars, she got out and walked up to where a thick blanket of magma had cut off the road years earlier. Her feet crunched on the solid black substance patterned like a crazy quilt of ropes, swirls and knobs. A crowd, held back by a park ranger, stood gawking.

"Awesome. That warehouse is history," a teenaged boy cried out as he peered through binoculars.

"Look at those palm trees burn," a woman said, shaking her head dolefully as her husband's video camera whirred away.

A wizened Asian man gazed at the spectacle with tears in his eyes. "My business, all those years," he kept muttering as a middle-aged woman, who looked as if she might be his daughter, patted his shoulder.

Grasping her own binoculars, Rosie threaded her way through the bystanders. Some were obviously tourists. But others, including the weeping Mr. Kawasaki, were islanders she recognized from the time she'd briefly lived on Hawaii six years earlier.

Suddenly she came up behind a tall, dark-haired man in khaki slacks and a white polo shirt. He was more than just familiar.

Rosie stopped dead, unable to move. All of a sudden she found it difficult to breathe. Her heartbeat accelerated and her legs felt weak. She had to get away before he saw her.

Before she could retreat, the man turned. It was as if he had felt her eyes on his back. Involuntarily she stepped back. Her mouth opened, but nothing came out. She stared, taking in ebony eyes, broad shoulders and lean, tanned features.

For a brief moment the man gazed at her as if she were a ghost. Then his eyes lit. "Rosie?" he exclaimed in a rich baritone. "Rosie Clarke?"

Hot blood rushed to Rosie's cheeks. She hadn't planned on meeting Luke Devillers so soon, and she felt totally unprepared. The way she'd envisioned this moment, she'd be meeting him under controlled circumstances—and she'd be calm, cool and collected. She'd know exactly what to say and what to do.

But it was too late for that now, she told herself. Stiffening her spine, she looked him in the eye and held out her hand. "Hello, Luke. How are you?"

He took her hand in his and looked her over. His gaze moved from her mane of auburn curls to her open-throated flowered cotton shirt, then dipped below her trim belted waist to her cream-colored linen shorts and sandals. Still holding her hand firmly, he cocked his head. "How long has it been?"

"Five years," Rosie said. And *forty-three days,* she added silently. She withdrew her hand, afraid that her fingers might start shaking at his touch.

"Has it been that long?" He shook his head. "Well, you look wonderful. As bright and beautiful as ever," he said with a smile.

Rosie felt another wave of heat rise up the back of her neck. Damn it, despite all her resolve, Luke was stirring up her emotions and turning them upside down, just as he'd always been able to do. What made it worse was that he didn't seem to know it. And what if he had known? Would he have cared, or would he only have been embarrassed? For a moment her temper flared, and she strengthened her resolve to keep her distance and hold on to her dignity.

"I'd heard you were coming back to the observatory." He gestured toward the hot gray clouds hovering over the volcano. "Well, Madame Pele has certainly got your work cut out for you."

Rosie's gaze followed his. She was glad to change the subject to one she understood better. "Madame Pele's latest tantrum will be a challenge," she said. *A challenge I'm more equipped to deal with than my feelings for you,* she added silently.

Luke grimaced. "As you might imagine, the new eruption has me and everyone else here mighty worried."

"Hey, Rosie, my girl," a familiar voice cried from the depths of the crowd. An islander of Chinese descent dressed in a brilliant yellow shirt and blue jeans shouldered past a knot of onlookers and rushed at Rosie with open arms.

"Mr. Fan!" she cried. They hugged, then stood back, surveying each other. "You look great," Rosie exclaimed.

"You, too." Mr. Fan winked. "Howzit?" he asked in the pidgin dialect so many of the islanders used.

"Everything's going fine."

"Hear you've been in Alaska all this time. You come back to take care of this angry lady?" Mr. Fan asked, looking toward the steaming inferno that oozed across the road, down the mountainside.

Rosie glanced at Pele's handiwork and nodded. "Yes, I was up in Homer studying Mount Augustine. Now I'm back here as a consulting volcanologist for the observation station at Kilauea."

Mr. Fan clasped his hands. "Now I sleep better." He turned to Luke. "You got a lot of moola invested in that Maile Gardens of yours, bruddah. You worried?"

Luke looked at the incandescent path of magma that was creeping toward the sea. "This one's going to miss us. But I think everyone's a bit nervous."

"Maile Gardens?" Rosie asked.

Mr. Fan reached up and patted Luke's shoulder. "This guy's one helluva architect. Building some very beautiful custom houses. Hate to see them become kindling for Madame Pele's barbecue."

"Me, too," Luke said, and brushed a hand through his thick hair. "But Pele's always smiled on my family. With luck, she'll stay friendly." He shot a dazzling white grin at Rosie and she found herself smiling back.

"My hope, too," Mr. Fan concurred. "Pele's always been like dat to me. She give us the black sand beaches and da kine park that looks like the moon. Brings in lots of tourists to my ice-cream shop. Can't believe she'd have a change of heart after we've been such good bruddahs."

"Well, I hope you are both right," Rosie said. She tore her gaze away from Luke and watched as a palm tree in the distance burst into flame not far from Mr. Kawasaki's warehouse. Was the adrenaline sizzling through her veins due to meeting Luke again or to watching this inferno? she wondered.

"You know, I'm not due at the station until Monday," she began. "But seeing this, maybe it would be a good idea to check in now. If Pele decides to shoot a few more fireworks in a different direction, I want to be prepared." Anyhow, Rosie thought, she wanted to get away from Luke and what he was doing to her pulse. Rosie excused herself and slipped away. Mr. Fan and Luke watched her walk back to the car.

"Still a beauty, that one," Mr. Fan commented. "Glad to see her pretty face again. No can understand why she go in the first place. Alaska," he said, shaking his head. "Why Alaska when you can be in paradise? Well, bruddah, I've got to get back to my ice-cream sundaes." With that he slapped Luke on the back, strapped on his helmet, climbed onto his big black motorcycle and roared off.

When he was gone, Luke returned his gaze to the spot where Rosie had been standing. He'd known for quite some time that she'd be coming back, yet it had shocked him to see her. In his memories, she had always been beautiful. But now he realized just how striking she was with her fine oval face, creamy skin, rounded breasts, long slim legs and magnificent red hair. And with a physical ache, he remembered how good it had felt to take her naked body in his arms. Unlike Mr. Fan, he had a pretty good idea why she'd run off to Alaska and why she'd beat a hasty retreat now.

"Hey, Luke." A voice broke into his fantasy. It was Jaimie Tong, his young associate. "We'd better get moving. Bob wasn't sure how to place those glass blocks on the west wing."

When Luke didn't respond instantly, Jaimie looked more closely at his boss. "Hey, you're really worried about this, aren't you?"

"Let's put it this way. We've got a lot to lose if Madame Pele up there blows her top in our direction." Then Luke chuckled. "Ladies are fickle, but I'll be damned if I let one run over me."

For the first time Jaimie looked alarmed. "That's *pupule* talk, boss. I know the ladies. They like you. But Madame Pele is something else. Don't say anything that might get her *huhu.*"

Luke rolled his eyes. "Now you sound like my grandmother. She was always telling me stories. She had all these rules about things that were *kapu,* things I couldn't do or I'd rile up Madame Pele. I'm not a superstitious man, Jaimie, but I guess you never outgrow certain beliefs. Don't worry. I'll watch what I say." He turned and, with the assistant architect trailing him, headed toward his truck.

ROSIE FROWNED as she looked in her rearview mirror. Ever since she'd left the observatory thirty minutes ago, the smoke from Kilauea had seemed to follow her. The news at the research center had been ominous. More than likely this was not going to be Pele's last spurt of anger. At this stage, there was no way of telling how many more eruptions were in store or what paths fresh lava flows might take. But for now, the immediate future appeared grim.

As Rosie's little car bounced down the familiar mountain road, she couldn't help looking around and remembering scenes from six years earlier. Back then she'd been an intern completing postgraduate work here and considered a job offer at the observatory. But because of what had happened between her and Luke, she hadn't accepted that position.

As she came up on a side road, Rosie slowed down. A sign at the entrance read Orchid Cliffs. How many times had she turned in at this road to visit Gretchen, Luke's late wife? she wondered. The left branch of the road went up a steep incline to Luke's sprawling family home. The right branch, however, went through the orchid fields, past the greenhouses and down to the beach.

Rosie shivered. Even so, she took the turn and then angled right toward the sound of the sea. She'd already come face to face with Luke Devillers. The sooner she met and dealt with those other ghosts, the better, she told herself.

At the edge of the fields, Rosie pulled to the side, parked and got out. For a moment she stood admiring the neatly staked small purple orchids. The nearby greenhouses, she knew, would be filled with lady slipper, buttonhole, comet and other varieties of the exotic blooms. Through the glass she could see the silhouette of the gardener with a watering can.

Then she started down a narrow, rocky path toward the edge of the cliff. When she reached the fringe of the palm trees Luke's Hawaiian grandmother had planted decades ago, she stood with one hand on a ridged trunk, looking down at the strip of black sand beach below.

To the left, half-hidden in the leafy canopy, sat a small white cottage. As she gazed at its roof, Rosie wrapped her arms around her chest and forced herself to remember. Painfully her mind went back to that fateful day when she'd gone down to this very cottage. She'd been delivering a tape she'd promised to lend Luke. Her intentions had been purely those of a concerned friend, for six months earlier Luke's beautiful wife, Gretchen, had drowned and he was still in mourning.

Before Gretchen's death, Rosie, Gretchen and Luke had socialized at parties, community gatherings and other functions on the island. But until lightning struck that afternoon, Rosie hadn't realized that her feelings for Luke ran deeper than friendship.

That fateful day, Mrs. Waneka, Luke's housekeeper, had suggested Rosie take the path past the main house at Orchid Cliffs, through the flower fields to the shore. When Rosie had come upon the old white wooden bungalow, it had stood open to the breeze. Filmy curtains had billowed through the side windows, seeming to float along with the melancholy sound of a Mendelssohn sonata.

Moments later as she'd come around to the small front porch, Rosie had found Luke sitting in a rocking chair, his hands folded pensively under his firm chin and his obsidian gaze fixed at the empty sea. He'd looked so remote that she'd almost turned and left, but just then, he'd glanced up.

"Rosie," he said, his expression brightening for a moment at the sight of her. He unfolded his six-foot length, stood, and ran a hand through the wavy black hair that swept his brow and brushed the edge of his collar. She could see by the expression in his eyes that he was pleased to see her.

She gave him the cassette, and after he'd put it into the tape deck, they'd sat on the porch, rocking in the wicker chairs. Rosie had always found Luke easy to talk to and as they'd chatted she'd studied his clean profile and smoothly tanned skin appreciatively. Though his last name and dark coloring were a legacy from his royal Hawaiian ancestors, it was clearly his aristocratic French forebears who dominated his looks and carriage.

While the lilting flute music had mingled with the rush of the sea, Luke had begun to reminisce about Gretchen. Once again, Rosie offered him her deepest sympathy and they'd shared some memories. Now, as she stood looking down at the cottage, she recalled how Luke had touched her hand and how a warm current of understanding had seemed to flow between them. Remembering this, she winced, still baffled at what had happened next. How had a sharing of sympathy between friends turned into lovemaking? Somehow when she'd curled her fingers around his to comfort him and they'd drawn close to offer each other solace, passion had ignited. An unacknowledged chemistry that must have been simmering beneath the surface of their relationship had flamed into something urgent and uncontrollable.

Later that night Rosie had awakened in the cottage's small bed alone. Immediately a horrible sense of foreboding had clawed at her. "Luke," she'd called gently. Getting no answer, she'd pulled on her sundress and sandals and walked out to the porch.

Clad only in his white slacks, Luke stood leaning against a porch pillar, his strong features bathed in moonlight. She knew he must have heard the door open, but he didn't respond.

"Luke," she said tentatively.

He turned toward her and the lines of his face were carved with remorse. "Rosie, I'm sorry. I'm so sorry."

Her heart sank.

"Can you ever forgive me, Rosie?"

"There's nothing to forgive," she answered bravely. Inside, she was shriveling and dying.

"This wasn't right." In the moonlight, his eyes were pools of darkness. "Rosie, you've been a good friend and I was using you to try to forget Gretchen. I had no right to do that."

She took a deep breath. "You have nothing to apologize for," she finally replied, just grazing his arm with her fingertips, then pulling her hand back almost immediately. "Maybe I should leave now.'

He nodded. "I'll walk you to your car."

Rosie had known she wouldn't be able to bear that. "No, I think it would be better if I go back alone." With that she'd kissed him lightly on the cheek, then turned and quickly headed up the path, her misty vision guided by the brightness of the full moon. Once out of Luke's sight, she'd begun to run. Tears streaked her cheeks and rough sobs tore from her throat. *I can't stay here another day,* she'd told herself. *This island is too damned small. I've got to leave Hawaii. I've got to leave.*

Now, half a dozen years later, listening to waves break on the same sandy beach, tears streaked Rosie's cheeks once again.

"Enough of this," she muttered. Then she turned away.

THAT NIGHT Rosie sat in the parlor of Mrs. Weatherby's guest house. Trying to distract her thoughts from the past, she was studying a report from the research station, when the phone rang out in the hall. A moment later the innkeeper stuck her head into the room.

"It's for you, Ms. Clarke."

Panic seized her. Who would be calling? Could it be Luke? Nervously she hurried out to the hall. When she heard her mother's voice on the other end of the line, she relaxed.

"Rosie, darling!" Mrs. Clarke exclaimed with her usual enthusiasm. "It's such a pleasure to phone you in Hawaii instead of Alaska. No more icicles on the line."

"Oh, mother!" Rosie moaned, picturing her mother's graying red topknot and vividly colored flowing clothes. Undoubtedly she'd be wearing dangly astrological stars and moons in her ears and a large crystal around her throat.

"I can almost feel the warm breezes through the wires," the older woman was saying.

"You'd just rather vacation on a beach than an ice floe."

"You got it!" Mrs. Clarke chuckled. "Anyhow, a certain young man and his stuffed monkey are going to appreciate the change. This morning I took Christopher to my Santa Monica beach. He's such a free spirit running around in his shorts, instead of being swaddled in all those oppressive layers of clothes he had to wear up in Alaska. Anyhow,'' she went on, ''I think you made the right decision.''

''I hope so,'' Rosie answered, thinking again of Luke Devillers. ''I hope so.''

Chapter Two

The next day when Rosie got back from signing the contract on a rental house, she found an invitation to a cocktail party on the rattan dresser in her room. Unfolding the crisp white envelope, she scanned the note. It was from the Big Island Citizens' Committee, a group of civic leaders mobilized to develop contingency plans for the latest threat from Kilauea. "The evening will be a get-together, as well as a work session to talk about the recent eruptions and to discuss contingency plans," the invitation read. "Civic leaders, concerned citizens, observatory staff and civil defense workers are invited."

Good idea, Rosie thought. This was exactly the sort of thing she was here to facilitate. She'd been hired by the observatory to act as a liaison between the scientists and the community, as well as to monitor the volcano. So any outreach like this fit right in with her job description.

Then, with a start, she noticed the address on the bottom of the engraved card. The gathering was to be held the next night at Orchid Cliffs.

Rosie sat down on the edge of the bed, where she read and reread the invitation. Mary Burns, another local rancher, had been her contact at the Citizens' Committee, but Rosie should have guessed that Luke would play some sort of role in the organization. She flopped back on the mattress and closed her eyes. Her heart pounded. When she'd climbed on the plane in Alaska she'd thought she was ready for all this. Her goals had seemed clear. Now she wasn't so sure.

"OH, DON'T YOU look pretty!" Mrs. Weatherby declared the following evening when Rosie came into the parlor to wait for her ride to the party. She'd dressed carefully, choosing a tailored sapphire linen sheath that buttoned off-center down the front. She'd wanted to appear business-like yet feminine. And despite her many fears and uncertainties about encountering the man who'd hurt her so badly, she wanted to look her best.

Moments later a white Lincoln pulled up to the guest house and an attractive, slender woman stepped out. "There's Mary Burns now," the innkeeper chirped.

Rosie thanked her hostess and went out to meet the woman whose letters and phone calls had convinced her to take the job. Though Rosie had never been formally introduced to Mary Burns, she recognized her from her intern days on the island. Mary, a tall, friendly dark-eyed brunette in her late forties, had been a rancher with her husband for the past twenty years. As a result, Mary had a good grasp of island politics as well as local gossip.

They greeted each other and Rosie settled herself into the plush leather of the passenger seat. Mary maneuvered the big white car along the shadowy winding roads through forests of ohia and strawberry guava. She turned to Rosie and said, "I won't give you my tour-guide spiel, since I know you've lived here before. But I will catch you up on what's happening with BICC."

"I'd like that."

"After Kilauea's last eruption destroyed the visitor center and several homes," Mary began, "a group of us realized we were going to have to be more prepared next time. Niha had an eruption come close back in the seventies, so we know it's possible our area might be struck again and we may not be so lucky the next time. That's why we're happy they've hired you. We want to work more closely with the observatory."

"I think it's a smart idea. Mother Nature—or Pele, in this case—can be fickle. It's good to be prepared for whatever she may fling our way."

They spent the next several minutes discussing BICC's aims and politics. Then Mary's car took a curve and the familiar gate to Orchid Cliffs loomed into view. "Luke Devillers has been quite a mover and shaker in BICC," Mary commented. "But I probably don't have to tell you that since he's the one who spoke so glowingly of you to the search committee at the observatory."

Rosie's eyes widened. "Luke?"

"Oh, yes, and it was he who put BICC onto you in the first place. Of course," Mary said, shooting Rosie a wide grin, "after we looked into your credentials, we were all sold—just as the observatory was."

Rosie took a deep breath. She'd never imagined that Luke had had anything to do with the job offer. Why had he recommended her? Given what had happened between them, she would have guessed he'd be relieved she was thousands of miles away. Or did he regard that afternoon when they'd made love as so insignificant that he'd discounted it?

Mary parked the Lincoln behind a Mercedes at the edge of the circular drive. "Looks like a good turnout, judging from the number of cars."

"Yes," Rosie answered automatically. Her mind was on meeting her host again and on the implications of what Mary had told her. Getting out, Rosie took a deep breath and smoothed her dress. She felt like a novice actress stepping onstage for a major performance before she'd had a chance to learn her lines.

Orchid Cliffs was just as she remembered it, a low, rambling, white stucco structure landscaped with palms, palmettos, ferns, blood-red anthuriums and torch ginger. In the softly scented twilight, the house's lights blazed out through the large Palladian windows. Behind them she could see clusters of informally dressed women and men talking.

Just before they walked through the carved wooden double door, Mary pulled Rosie aside. "I should mention, be prepared for Aunt Beatrice."

"Aunt Beatrice?"

"Luke's overbearing aunt. About a year after Gretchen died, the Queen Bea, as some of us call her, came to console Luke, or so she said. Then she decided she liked being lady of the manor and never left. She's a bit overwhelming. Forewarned is forearmed."

Rosie knit her brows. "I can't imagine Luke tolerating such an intrusion."

Mary laughed. "You haven't met Beatrice. I suppose Luke would send her packing if she got on his nerves as much as she gets on everyone else's, but I don't think he spends a whole lot of time in the house. The man's become a real workaholic. Maile Gardens, his spiffy new development, has become his obsession. And to be honest, the old lady does serve a function. She's thrown herself into managing the household. But it's a shame in some ways. Maybe if Luke didn't have her around he'd put less energy into work and more into finding another wife and continuing the Devillers dynasty."

"Oh?" Rosie asked curiously. "No new wife on the horizon?"

Mary shook her head. "Not that I know of. He dates sporadically, but no one in particular. And it's a shame, with all those wonderful genes going to waste."

On the other side of the door, the sounds of clinking ice cubes and buzzing conversation greeted them. In the foyer, Rosie stopped to glance at the grand oil painting of Queen Analani, Luke's great-grandmother and his family's link to their royal Hawaiian past. As always the queen stared down out of beautiful dark eyes that seemed to know all. Remembering her dream of Pele, the volcano goddess, Rosie had the uncomfortable feeling that the queen's enigmatic smile was directed at her.

"Oh, look. There's Luke," Mary cried. She took Rosie's arm and propelled her past the portrait of Queen Analani, through the arched entry and into the large, white living room with its splashes of bright contemporary art. The house, Rosie noticed, was just as Gretchen had left it—elegant and interesting in a spare, understated way. Had Luke deliberately made no changes, or was he just too preoccupied with his work to alter anything?

As they made their way into the crowd, Luke's tall figure came striding toward them across the polished wood floor.

Rosie caught her breath. Déjà vu. When she'd run into Luke the first time, he'd been dressed casually. Now, seeing him in his more formal clothes, the memory that had burned in her mind come to life once again. Luke, tanned and handsome, all in white, moving toward her. Unlike that night six years earlier, however, he was smiling, his dazzling teeth glinting against his bronze skin. For a brief instant Rosie wanted to shake loose from Mary and run toward him. But the crazy impulse faded. And suddenly she felt angry—angry at the thought of all the pain this man and her own foolishness had caused her.

"Rosie, we meet again," he said, taking her small hand.

As his ebony gaze traveled over her, Rosie realized again how vulnerable she still was to him. But just as she had the afternoon before, she'd keep her distance. "Luke, good to see you again." She gave him a firm handshake and then stepped back.

"Rosie, I was so surprised to see you the last time that I didn't tell you how much I'd been looking forward to having you back on our island." He favored her with another brilliant smile.

Involuntarily Rosie's hand flew to her chest. "You have?"

"Counting the days," he replied.

"We all have," Mary Burns chimed in, then turned away, distracted by a friend's greeting.

"Counting the days?" Rosie repeated, not sure what he meant by that. To her, it sounded like meaningless banter, something you'd say to be polite.

"Marking big x's on my calendar," Luke added. The conversation stopped for a moment and they both gazed at each other.

Drawing back into herself, Rosie dropped her eyes and then looked around the room. "A good turnout," she murmured coolly. His gaze remained fixed on her, and nervously she wondered what he was thinking.

"I'm not being a very good host, am I?" Luke finally said. "Here, let me introduce you to the cast of characters you'll be dealing with tonight."

So it was going to be all business between them, she thought, not sure whether she was relieved or sorry.

They walked a little way into the long, brightly lit room with its soft Persian rugs and impressive art collection. In front of a massive sculpture of Pele with her wild glassy strands of flowing hair, Luke paused to take two champagne flutes from the waiter's tray. While he was distracted, Rosie gazed at the sculpture and remembered her dream again. In her mind, Pele and the portrait of Luke's grandmother, Analani, had been confused. Now that she confronted the statue of the volcano goddess, however, she knew that it was Pele who had invaded her dream and had given her a warning. She shivered and then turned away, to find Luke observing her intently.

"I think a toast is in order." He raised his glass at Pele's statue. "To the woman who's inscrutable, dangerous and magnificent and," he added, turning again to Rosie, "who's brought you back to our island."

"Hear, hear," said Mary Burns, who'd returned with her husband, Bill, in tow.

"And," Luke went on, holding up his glass, "to Madame Pele's interpreter, Rosie Clarke."

Rosie shook her head. "I'm afraid you're giving me more credit than I deserve." Her eyes went to the statue with its Medusa hair. "It will take more than the likes of me to figure out that lady's whims."

"What's that about a lady's whims?" a throaty voice rang out.

Rosie turned in time to see an imposing gray-haired woman in a bright flowered caftan sweep into the room. Luke's aunt Beatrice favored the Hawaiian strain in the family. She was a solidly built six-footer with the imperious air of divine-right royalty. Rosie had only met her once previously, when the outspoken lady had been visiting from her home on Maui. Then she'd been memorable.

Now, as she bestowed a thousand-watt smile on Luke's guests, she dominated the room.

"Aloha. Aloha," she cried, giving Rosie a firm pat on the shoulder that almost made her sink to her knees. "Welcome to our island and our home. Luke," she said, turning to her nephew, "have you fed this young lady yet? She looks as though she could stand a little fattening up."

"I don't know," Luke replied. "She looks awfully fine to me."

Aunt Beatrice gave another throaty chuckle, patted Rosie on the hand and with a breezy "I'll catch up with you later" whooshed off to perform the role of gracious hostess to another set of guests.

For several moments, Rosie stood blinking. She felt as if she'd been swept by a tidal wave and left gasping on the beach.

"My aunt's seen too many old Loretta Young movies," Luke joked. "Her specialty is making dramatic entrances and exits. But let's get on with the introductions."

For the next hour Luke and Rosie circulated among the guests. As he introduced her to the mixture of Kilauea scientists, native Hawaiians, relocated mainlanders and descendants of nineteenth-century planters and missionaries, it was obvious to Rosie that he was even more respected and influential than he'd been six years earlier.

Most of his guests were members of BICC, and all were eager to discuss their concerns with the new volcanologist. "I just imported some sand for my beach," one wealthy socialite exclaimed. "Have I been dumping money into a lost cause?"

"It depends," Rosie replied. "Earth tremors could be a problem and make the tides much higher."

"And then there're always tsunamis," another guest chimed in, referring to the huge tidal waves that sometimes followed major quakes.

"Where exactly is your property?" Rosie asked.

"It's in Luke's new development, Maile Gardens."

Rosie glanced at Luke questioningly.

He frowned. "Maybe it would help if we looked at a map of the island. Why don't we go into my office, where I have a large one on the wall?"

The little group grabbed their drinks and trailed him through the house, out the back door to his office. It was a dramatic two-story structure with glass block walls and a winding stairway that cut through a series of landings. The main work area was on the lower level, where they had come in. A collection of geometrically patterned scatter rugs covered its oiled teak floor and three walls were lined with bookcases. The other wall was lined with handcrafted cabinets for storing plans and displaying three-dimensional models of houses Luke had designed. Atop two large work tables sat three computers, a fax machine, a copier and other assorted machines. Several drawing boards held architectural renderings in various stages of completion.

Rosie's eye went to a series of color photographs of houses framed on the display wall, but before she could study them Luke had raised a pointer to the large wall map behind his desk.

"There it is right there," the woman with the beach cried out, pointing a finger at a spot southeast of the observatory, near Mokuleia Black Sand Beach, not far from Niha. "We're the first house Luke built and we love it. I'd hate to think of anything happening to it."

Rosie studied the location. "Right now you're okay," she began. Nevertheless she knew she couldn't let any of her questioners be too complacent. "I hate to sound negative, but I don't think anyone living in this area can sit back and relax right now. I think we should all be making plans in case the lava spews in a southeasterly direction."

"Like what plans?" the woman asked anxiously.

Rosie glanced at Luke. He appeared troubled.

"Well, you've put a lot of money into your homes. Perhaps we should be looking at the possibility of having the houses moved in a hurry if necessary."

"Moved?" a man snorted. "Do you have any idea how difficult that would be and how much that would cost?"

From the reaction of the crowd and Luke's scowl, Rosie realized this wasn't the time to press the issue. She'd need facts and figures before she got into making any predictions or recommendations. "At this point it's just something to consider," she said soothingly.

Again she glanced at Luke, who was watching her closely. She wondered what was going through his mind—whether he resented her bringing up the possibility that his development might be in serious danger or whether it was just the situation in general that upset him. Her attention, however, was dragged back to the questions coming from the somber little group. For the next forty-five minutes, Rosie fielded queries about the eruption and the effect on the environment.

"What is this doing to my lungs?" a man asked. "And what about our cars?" another said. "This soot I'm cleaning off my Jeep every day can't be doing the engine any good. If nothing else, it's ruining the finish."

"It's not improving my skin," Mary Burns interjected. "Although Bill did suggest I should bottle it and sell it as a pore tightener."

"And what about the fish?" someone else interrupted. "Are they going to die off with all that hot lava pouring into the sea?"

Eventually the subject got around to future eruptions. "Tell me, bruddah, what can we expect?" said Mr. Fan, the ice-cream shop owner, who had joined the group. "How much chance of the flow swinging off in another direction, whatevah?"

"I wish I could tell you more," Rosie replied, "but I need a few days to study the situation. You should be aware, however, that things could get worse."

At that point Luke stepped in. "I'm sure we're all grateful to Rosie for being so candid. But before we all panic, let's keep in mind that we Hawaiians have slept side by side with Pele for centuries. By and large, she's been our friend. We're going to survive. We just need to keep on our toes."

A few minutes later the crowd began to wander back to the main house. Rosie started to follow, but Mary held her back. "I want to show you this. Luke's too modest to blow his own horn, but take a look at these designs." She led Rosie over to the wall of photographs.

"These are some of Luke's award-winning projects. This one," she said, pointing to a house that reminded Rosie of Frank Lloyd Wright's Falling Water, "is on Maui. This other one—" her finger moved to a striking plantation-style home "—is a renovation he did on Lanai. Look at how he blends the traditional architecture with an eye to the natural beauty of the land." She stepped back and admired the effect.

As Mary went on to explain the other projects and point out their many virtues, Rosie silently marveled. She'd known, of course, that Luke was talented, but she'd never realized how really creative he was. Five years earlier he'd just gone into business for himself; judging from this outpouring of fine work, it had been a wise decision. But, she thought, the unleashing of his creative energy seemed to have followed Gretchen's death. Was that his way of compensating for the terrible loss? If so, he must still miss her terribly. *No wonder,* Rosie told herself, *Luke rejected me so unequivocally.* Was recommending her to the search committee at the observatory a way of assuaging his guilt?

"The man's a genius at melding Hawaii's unique aesthetics with today's life-style," Mary was saying. "And Maile Gardens is really a godsend to the island. That property he built was targeted by a conglomerate wanting to build a big resort." She threw up her hands. "Golf courses. Tennis courts. Hundreds of rooms. Restaurants. Not to mention roads. Maybe it would have been good for the economy, but it would have been terrible for the ecology. And Luke saw that. That's what I like about him. He's as contemporary a man as you could hope to meet, yet his roots are deep in island tradition. He's a man who cares deeply about his heritage." She looked thoughtfully at a photo of Luke at the construction site. "Considering the roots the Devillers family has put down here," she went on, "it's a shame he and Gretchen never had a child to pass this legacy on to."

Rosie swallowed hard and then mumbled her agreement. "Do you think Luke would like to have a family?" she asked.

Mary considered. "Frankly, he seems lonely to me, Rosie. And I'm sure he'd make a wonderful father. And he certainly has a lot to offer," she added, casting an eye around at his well-appointed office.

Sure, he's rich, Rosie told herself. *But there's a lot more to being a good parent than having money and a pedigree.*

Rosie and Mary left the office and rejoined the group at the main house in time to fill their plates with *mahi mahi* and other island delicacies from the sumptuous buffet.

Again Aunt Beatrice made herself the center of attention. "Eat and enjoy!" she exclaimed as the guests stepped up to fill their plates from silver serving dishes bedecked with sprays of orchids.

Rosie couldn't suppress a smile as Luke's aunt placed another serving of roast pork on Rosie's already-heaping platter.

"You need some meat on your bones or you'll be swept out on the first tsunami," the woman declared.

After Rosie ate all she could, she discreetly hid her half-finished plate under an empty one on the serving tray. Then she wandered out to the moon-washed stone lanai overlooking the orchid fields and greenhouses. She was gazing over the sea of blooms, when Luke came to her side. He handed her a snifter filled with a liqueur made from coconut and chocolate.

"You make a very pretty picture with the moonlight gilding your hair," he said as he watched her take a sip of her drink.

Despite her resolve to remain cool with Luke, Rosie felt herself flush. For a moment they stood shoulder to shoulder, savoring the sweet drink, while Rosie tried to think of an appropriate response.

This was the moment, she told herself, to establish the kind of businesslike relationship between them that she wanted—no, needed. "I'm very glad you've given me the opportunity to talk to all these people here tonight," she began. "I have a lot to think about now."

"Well, you've given them something to think about, too. We'll all be feeling less complacent when we go to bed tonight."

Hearing Luke's deep masculine voice say the word "bed" set off a memory flash in Rosie's mind. The recollection was so vivid it was almost palpable. For an instant she could feel Luke's lips on hers just the way they had been that long-ago night as they'd lain entwined beneath the sheets. His naked arms had been so strong as they'd held her tight.

The dry note in his voice called Rosie back to the present, and pushing the memory aside, she turned to him. Perhaps more sternly than was necessary, she said, "I don't mean to be alarmist, but I have to tell it the way I see it. And frankly, Luke," she went on, looking him in the eye and trying to ignore the sensual memory that still hovered in her mind, "if once I get settled in the station and find the situation's even worse, I'm not going to mince words. I'm going to warn people if I think there's even a remote chance of danger."

Luke eyed her. "You've really changed in the past five years, haven't you?"

She smiled and took another sip of her drink. Yes, she really had, and indirectly, Luke was partially responsible for the tougher, more controlled person she'd become.

For a moment, they stood gazing out at the sea. Rosie's head only reached Luke's chin, and she was very conscious of his tall body mere inches from hers. Then Luke broke into her reverie by speaking again.

"Are you glad to be back?"

She turned to him. "Oh, yes," she said, her enthusiasm taking her by surprise. "I've always loved Hawaii. I've missed it." *There,* she thought, *now the door was open.*

He searched her face, and uncomfortable at the intensity of his scrutiny, she looked away. "Why did you leave?" he questioned softly. Then, after a pause, he added, "I guess I already know."

She fingered the round bowl of the glass, then met his gaze. It was best to be frank. "I guess you do."

His brows drew together. "Rosie, I've thought about what happened between us five years ago and I want to apologize. I know there's no excuse for my taking advantage of you the way I did, but all I can say is that it was a crazy time for me." He shook his head. "I just wasn't handling losing Gretchen very well. Rosie, I'm really sorry."

She nodded and swallowed, temporarily unable to speak. He was being honest and he'd apologized again. There was really nothing more she could expect. So why, all of a sudden, did she feel on the verge of tears?

When she spoke, her voice was shaky. "Luke, there's a question I have to ask you. Mary Burns tells me that you're the one who recommended me for this job." She tilted her head toward him. "Why?"

Luke wrinkled his brow and looked nonplussed, almost as if he didn't know the answer. Then he shook himself and said, "Why? Why not? You were the best person for the job. You were well liked and respected while you were here. You know and love the Big Island. And even without that, your résumé's pretty impressive."

She lifted an eyebrow. "How did you get hold of my résumé?"

He laughed. "Oh, I have my spies," he said evasively.

She flinched. If he had ferreted out her résumé, what else did he know? But surely if he knew the whole truth he'd have given some indication by now. Or maybe he was just playing Mr. Cool. A thread of fear wound through her. Before more game playing went on, maybe she should just lay her cards on the table.

"Luke," she began. However, her next words were drowned out by loud shouting from inside the house.

"What in the world?" Luke exclaimed.

The voices had risen and Rosie realized what they were saying. "Pele. Pele!"

Muttering an oath, Luke touched Rosie's shoulder. "I'm afraid I know what this is and I'd better go deal with it." While Rosie stared, he turned and strode quickly through the double doors.

"Uh-oh," one of the men standing on the opposite corner of the terrace mumbled. He and the rest of the guests who'd come outside to bask in the beauty of the moonlit evening flocked after Luke.

Rosie, curious, joined them. Breaking through the crowd, she stopped short and stared at the group of party crashers. Five tall, heavyset men and women, dressed in traditional loincloths and muumuus and dripping with leis of maile and orchids, circled the large statue of the volcano goddess, which dominated Luke's living room. As they performed a ritual war dance with forceful, menacing movement, a huge man, his face and body magnificently painted in war colors, beat a large drum. Round and round the statue the knot of newcomers went, brandishing clubs and chanting, "Pele. Pele. Pele."

Meanwhile Aunt Beatrice flew about the perimeter, trying vainly to push the protesters away from the prized artwork. "Stop this right now. Right now, I tell you," she shouted. "Do something, Luke!"

However, instead of interfering with the protesters, Luke clasped his aunt's fleshy arm and guided her out of the way. "Let's see what these people have to say," he told her.

At that moment, one of the dancers dashed a small smoke bomb against the floor, and the crowd, including Rosie, drew back in shock as plumes of red mist rose.

"The paintings, the statues!" Beatrice cried.

Luke restrained her. "It's okay, the smoke is only a stage prop."

At that moment a tall, voluminous woman with flowing black hair laced with silver emerged from the scarlet cloud. Crowned with a wreath of white and red flowers, the Junoesque vision was swathed in an ankle-length crimson-and-yellow muumuu. On her widely planted feet she wore woven sandals. It was if a portly goddess had descended to earth to shake an angry fist at her subjects. Glancing scornfully at the crowd and raising her arms toward the heavens, she commanded silence.

For an instant, everyone, including Aunt Beatrice, was struck dumb. Then, slowly and deliberately, to the steady beat of the drum, the woman spread her arms as her piercing gaze traveled over the crowd. "Pele, Pele," the protesters continued to chant as with deliberation, the woman raised her right hand and pointed a stubby finger at her audience.

"Pele waits," she intoned, her hand moving from person to person. She described almost a full half circle, passing up face after face, until finally her finger stopped on Rosie.

Involuntarily Rosie stepped back and her hand flew to her heart.

The finger came closer. "Pele. Pele. Watch for the flames. Do not stir the goddess's wrath, lest she spit her burning fury—and destroy us all."

Chapter Three

"All right, Liliana," Luke snapped as he stepped between Rosie and her assailant's accusing finger. "Just what is this little sideshow all about?" Abruptly the music stopped, and he and the heavyset intruder faced off.

"If anyone should know why we are here, it's you, Luke Devillers." The woman's eyes blazed. "We are Pele's Partisans. We have come to speak for her."

"Well, I never!" Aunt Beatrice muttered in the background. Her fingers gripped the strand of fat pearls that hung knotted between her large breasts.

"We all wish you'd never," Liliana retorted, without looking in the other woman's direction. Keeping her gaze on Luke, she continued, "We warned you about building Maile Gardens." She stamped her foot. "It's an insult to Pele to dig holes and pour cement near her sacred ground. See how she reacts to the insult?" Liliana made a dramatic gesture in the direction of Kilauea.

Luke put his hands on his hips. "Liliana, you're an intelligent woman. You know very well that's all superstition. Besides, we're a good five miles from the *heiau.*"

Rosie recognized the reference. The *heiau* was a holy temple or place of worship. The one that Liliana and Luke were discussing had been dedicated to the volcano goddess by early Polynesian settlers. To violate that ground in any way was strictly *kapu*.

"Too close, too close!" Liliana was shouting, emphasizing the words with her flattened palm. She thrust her moon face into Luke's chiseled one and harrumphed. "Five miles! That's not enough! What kind of Hawaiian are you? Your great-grandmother, Queen Analani, would rise from her grave," she said, lifting her hefty arm to the sky, "if she could see what you're doing. All you care about is building houses for rich *malihini*," she added, indicating the wealthy newcomers who were taking up residence on the island.

"Enough!" Beatrice, who was enough of an Amazon herself to match Liliana like a bookend, drew herself up and glared at the feisty party crasher. "You just take your silly theater troupe and get out of here!"

Swiveling, Luke frowned at his aunt. Obviously, Rosie thought, he didn't like her outburst any better than he'd liked the show put on by Pele's Partisans. As Liliana continued her tirade about disturbing the sacred ground, Rosie listened and tried to make sense of what was really going on. But she was still feeling shaken by the way she'd been singled out. The whole episode was too much like the warning dream she'd had about Pele. Suddenly Rosie wondered if she hadn't made a terrible mistake in coming back to Hawaii.

"Unless you stop construction," Liliana was insisting, "Pele will destroy us."

Luke shook his head. "We've already been through this, Liliana. We hashed this out way before I began the construction. I've helped you preserve the ancient fish ponds at Niha and restored the *heiau*. Before we got there, the whole thing was crumbling into the dust. I built Maile Gardens because I had a dream of sharing our island with people who would appreciate it. And at the same time I wanted to protect it and make sure when we said 'Welcome to paradise,' we were telling the truth."

Liliana crossed her arms over her ample bosom. She was not to be appeased or argued down, even by the strong-willed Luke. "I repeat, Luke Devillers, you must stop your construction, or we will lose our beautiful island." With that, she heaved her bulk around and signaled her followers. Then, entourage in tow, she swept out of the room with her voluminous muumuu swirling around her legs.

As the last of the protesters disappeared, the guests stood around awkwardly.

"That woman is impossible!" Beatrice declared. "Pele's Partisans, bah! Just a bunch of crackpots!"

"They're not crackpots, Aunt Beatrice," Luke interjected briskly. "But they are a little fanatic about this one subject and it doesn't help that Kilauea's putting on a show right now."

"Well, I understand their point of view about not wanting to harm sacred lands," Mary Burns argued, "but it's unfair to blame Luke for an act of nature."

"Frankly, I think she and her group are just upset about the new eruptions, and Luke is a convenient scapegoat," another guest declared.

Luke shook his head. "Sorry, folks, this isn't what I had in mind for the evening. But it certainly presents another point of view. Everyone who builds on this island—whether it's a hotel, house or store—takes a risk. We all live in the shadow of the volcano and its legends."

"Don't worry about it no more, Luke," Mr. Fan said heartily. "Liliana, she's a regular Sarah Bernhardt with her causes."

Several other guests chuckled and murmured assent. Then the party settled down to quiet groups finishing their dessert and talking under the cold eye of Pele's statue.

Luke took Rosie aside and put his arm lightly on her shoulder. "Are you okay?" He searched her face. "I don't know why Liliana picked on you that way. I guess you were just a convenient target."

"Maybe she knows I'm a volcanologist and thinks I have more power than I really do," Rosie speculated. She gazed up at Luke curiously. "Apparently, you two have crossed paths before."

Luke smiled and shook his head. "I'll say. Liliana's a distant cousin of mine. There's nothing like family to keep you on your toes. Anyhow, Liliana wants to preserve our past, which I'm all for, but not at any cost. The Pele Partisans see Maile Gardens as an intrusion."

"And how do you see it?" Rosie asked.

"Look," he declared, raising a large hand and chopping it emphatically, "any builder out for a quick buck could have scarred our landscape by putting up a ticky-tacky tract. I've tried to design a community tied to our land in a positive way, and I have to say I resent Liliana's implication that I'm some sort of turncoat Hawaiian out to make a quick buck."

"I can't imagine you ever being that, Luke." And she meant it. Whatever criticisms Rosie had of Luke, she didn't doubt his integrity.

He cocked his head. "I appreciate your confidence, Rosie, considering how long it's been since we've seen each other. However, I'm sure there's a lot we don't know about one another."

Rosie dropped her eyes. That was certainly true, she thought.

"I'm looking forward to our getting reacquainted," Luke went on. He took a step toward her and she fought the urge to step back. "If you like, I can take you out to Maile Gardens and show you what I'm doing."

"Why, yes," Rosie started to agree, then she hesitated. When it came to Luke, she wanted to take things slowly and cautiously. Right now the chemistry between them was too potent for her comfort and she needed time to reassess. "But I'm going to be pretty busy for the next few days," she added. "I've got to get set up at work and next weekend I move into a cottage I've rented." She listened to herself rattling off excuses and knew that was how Luke was hearing them, too. "Let's take a rain check on Maile Gardens—maybe the end of the month," she finished, putting an end to her awkward recitation.

Luke's only reaction was a faint lift of his eyebrows. "Busy woman."

Just then Mary came up and tapped Rosie on the shoulder. "Ready to take off?"

"Yes." Rosie turned to Luke. "Thank you again. It's been an interesting evening." Luke captured her hand and held it longer than was necessary. The heat of it seemed to radiate through her.

"Yes, it has," he agreed with a wry grin. "Very interesting."

AFTER THE LAST of Luke's guests had left, he went back to his office and climbed the stairs to the second floor. Unlatching a wall unit, he unscrewed a bottle of Scotch that he kept for those rare occasions when he had time alone just to think.

After pouring the pale golden liquid over ice, he slid open the door and went out to a small triangular deck that overlooked the fields and the sea beyond them. He settled into a canvas chair, propped his feet on the railing and took a thoughtful sip of his drink. It had certainly been one hell of an evening, he mused. Rosie looked gorgeous. And he was impressed by the way she'd handled herself that evening. She was smart, professional—and, he had to admit to himself, a lot more distant than he wanted her to be. Obviously she hadn't forgiven him. He'd have to make it up to her somehow. Until he'd seen her two days earlier, he hadn't been certain he wanted to break down the barriers that had grown between them during her absence. Now he knew he did and he knew he could do it. It was just going to take a little time and effort.

Then Luke's thoughts turned to Liliana and his expression darkened. What did she want from him, blood? He'd always had a soft spot for the woman, but tonight she'd gone too far. Yet even as he told himself that, he glanced back at the pall of smoke staining the night sky and clenched his glass.

ROSIE DUMPED the last of the cartons on the floor of her kitchen. After a week of living like a tourist, she'd finally gotten into her house at Black Crescent Beach. The pink cottage she'd rented was simple but charming, with two airy bedrooms cooled by ceiling fans, a cozy living room with wicker furniture plushly cushioned with chintz, a kitchen with a breakfast nook painted butter yellow and a lanai bedecked with wooden rockers. The best part was that the beach, one of Hawaii's remaining black-sand retreats, was only a short stroll away.

She was crouched on the sisal rug in the living room, unpacking a book carton, when she heard the rap on the door. Straightening, she wiped her dusty hands on her jeans and pushed back a stray lock of auburn hair from her forehead. "What can that be?" she wondered aloud.

Her question was answered when she was within five feet of the screen. Through it she could see a tall figure who made her heart skip. It was Luke. He wore old denim shorts and a T-shirt that showed off his lean body. In his hands, he carried a spray of orchids and a bottle of champagne.

"Aloha!" he exclaimed, grinning at her through the mesh. "This is the residence of the famed volcano chaser, Ms. Rosie Clarke, isn't it?"

After a moment's pause to collect her wits she said, "The very same, though I don't know what I'd do if I caught one. To what do I owe a visit from the infamous architect who's thumbing his nose at Madame Pele?"

Luke made a face. "You're on dangerous ground."

"In more ways than one," Rosie said, casting her eyes toward the floor.

"Are you talking about earthquakes?" There'd been several tremors since the party at Orchid Cliffs.

"What else?" Actually, she'd been thinking about their shaky relationship. But she didn't want to say so.

"Oh, I don't know. Thought there might be something else." He studied her. "If the earth isn't moving beneath your feet, how about inviting me in?" He held up the bottle of champagne. "A housewarming present."

With a self-conscious smile, Rosie opened the door and stood aside. So much for keeping her distance. "How did you find me?" she asked.

"Spies again."

"I can see you're good at undercover work," Rosie said, then almost bit her tongue at the Freudian slip. Good going, Rosie, good going, she told herself.

"Easy stuff," he told her, ignoring the double entendre. "I just picked up the phone and called Mary." He handed her the flowers. "For you, mademoiselle."

Rosie looked down at the pink and white orchids. They were lovely, but they conjured up the image of herself running, sobbing, through fields of flowers. She suppressed the memory as quickly as it sprang up.

Meanwhile, Luke was looking around. "Cute little place. Just right for one person."

Rosie stroked a velvety petal. Another opening. Her heart raced and her palms suddenly felt damp. Perhaps this was the time to tell Luke she wasn't planning on living here alone.

But he'd already strode to the kitchen to put the champagne in her empty refrigerator. She followed, cradling the delicate blossoms in her hands.

"This is awfully nice of you, Luke."

He closed the refrigerator door. "Well, I thought you might need a big, strong man around here." He laughed as he flexed his muscles. "Perhaps to move some boxes or furniture?"

"Hmmm." Rosie decided to put off the conversation she'd been dreading for months and surveyed the pile of boxes in the next room. "Well, since this job is only temporary, I've stored my own furniture along with my winter clothes. But there is the little matter of bookcases. I bought some of those knock-down jobs that take a Ph.D. in engineering to assemble."

"That's what I like—something that really challenges my machismo." He marched into the living room and glanced at the instructions that were lying on the floor next to the carton. "They seem to be printed in Swahili and Armenian but not English. Well," he said, sailing the instructions toward the floor, "no problem—I'm an architect. I should know something about construction—well," he added, picking up a strange-looking part and eyeing it dubiously, "maybe."

Rosie smiled and handed him a hammer. She hadn't been pretending to need help with the bookcase; it really had baffled her when she'd tried to make sense of the diagrams. For all his jokes, however, Luke didn't appear to be having a problem.

She grimaced. She hated to admit it, but it looked as if there was a male gene for putting together break-down furniture. The work went quickly. Like a doctor doing surgery, Luke called for parts while she scrabbled through the boxes, matching items with his descriptions. While they assembled the pieces, they exchanged island news. Kilauea, like a monster brooding over its next attack, had been strangely quiet that week and Pele's Partisans had retreated, as well.

"But," Luke said, hammering a shelf into parallel slots. "I suspect we haven't heard the last of them."

"Nor of Kilauea," Rosie added. "All these tremors and all our readings indicate more eruptions are on the way."

Luke frowned and tightened a bolt. "Then let's enjoy the island while it's still here." He pushed a bookcase against the wall and they both stood back to admire. When the other three were done, they unpacked the books and loaded them onto the shelves.

Then Luke broke down the boxes and carted them out to his truck. Rosie followed with the rest of them and watched the ripple of his muscles through his T-shirt as he stacked the flattened containers in the bed of the vehicle. When he was finished, he clapped the dust off his hands. "I'll make sure those boxes get recycled."

"Thanks. And thanks for all your help." Suddenly she was feeling awkward again and all too aware of the unfinished business between them. As easily as they had chatted, she hadn't told him what was really on her mind, and she wasn't ready to, she realized. He'd just done her a favor and by rights she should reciprocate with an invitation for dinner or to stay and sip a glass of the champagne he'd brought. But that would begin the sort of involvement she didn't want.

Instead she held out her hand to say goodbye.

Ignoring it, he lifted a tarp propped against the side of the truck bed. "Oh, you can't get rid of me that easy," he joked. "I didn't bring my sailboard all the way out here just to cart it back home again without even getting it wet."

"Your sailboard?" Rosie withdrew her hand and watched while he lifted a sleek white polyurethane board off the truck bed. Then he slid out the blue-and-white sail and aluminum mast that had been rolled up next to it.

Rosie put her hands on her hips.

Grinning wickedly, he looked at her. "I bet you didn't do much windsurfing in Alaska."

"You're right about that. Too many polar bears and not enough ice floes."

"Polar bears in Homer? That's where you were, wasn't it?"

Rosie was startled. "What did you do, memorize my résumé?"

"Of course. Go ahead, quiz me on it." He hefted the board and started walking down the path toward the beach. "You do want a lesson, don't you?" he called back over his shoulder.

Rosie hesitated while she conducted a quick debate. What was the harm anyhow? She smiled and shook her head. "Oh, why not?"

"Good, you look as if you could use a little R and R. Get into your suit and meet me down by the water."

Ten minutes later Rosie pulled up the strap of her aqua maillot, then studied her reflection. Though she'd been back on Hawaii for a week, she was still pale. *Just why am I doing this?* she asked herself. Searching her mind, she finally came up with a reason. Maybe the way to get into the conversation she needed to have with Luke was to reestablish her friendship with him first. That way they'd be more likely to see eye to eye. Reaching for a plastic bottle, she began slathering on sunscreen. No sense turning into a lobster.

After pulling on a T-shirt and donning her sunglasses, she headed to the beach. As she came down the hill, she spotted Luke. He'd taken off his shirt and his bare back was to her. For a moment, she stopped and sucked in her breath. What a magnificent man he was! His skin was smooth and brown, sculpted with muscle and sinew. As she watched, his hands went to the front of his jeans and in one motion he slid the denim down over his narrow hips, revealing black bathing trunks.

Below the trunks, his thighs were deeply tanned. For a crazy instant, she wanted to reach out and stroke the hard curve of his narrow waist. He turned, spotted Rosie and shot her a smile. Flushing, she waved and hurried down to the gritty black sand.

Luke was a great teacher. He began the lesson on land, instructing her on the basics: wind direction, the parts of the craft and the seven steps of getting underway. Then he showed her how to lower and hoist the sail.

"It's tricky when it's heavy with water," he said, "so I'm going to fill it with sand and teach you how to handle it that way first." Deftly she learned to maneuver the sail so the sand slid off. "Great! You'll make Neptune's daughter jealous."

She beamed, absurdly gratified by his compliment.

When they finally got the sailboard into the water, all of Luke's preliminary instruction paid off. For an hour, Rosie worked on the steps and practiced her balance. Several times she tumbled off the board, but Luke was always there to help her up and start over again. At first his hands around her waist made her skittish, but it wasn't long before she succumbed to the pure joy of accomplishment and of his company. Finally with Luke cheering her on, she managed a short solo flight.

"I feel the way Amelia Earhart must have the first time she got behind the controls and soared," Rosie said as she helped Luke load the sailboard back into the truck. "But I feel bad. You didn't get to ride the board at all."

"I get to sail whenever I want, Rosie. It was fun for me to watch you. And," he added with a wink, "if you have to drag someone out of the water who's just tumbled off a board, it might as well be a beautiful redhead."

Rosie blushed. The flesh where Luke's hands had touched her still felt warm. She was glad she'd worn the T-shirt over her aqua suit. Even though the cotton was thin, it had made her feel protected from the hot light of his admiring gaze.

She cleared her throat and searched for a way to change the subject. She was really thirsty from all the saltwater and probably Luke was, too. "You've been so patient. How about I reward you with a glass of iced tea?"

"I thought you'd never ask."

After Luke had packed up the boat, they strolled back to the house. Rosie put a pot of water on the stove to make the tea. Then she found towels and they took turns showering. Afterward, clean and refreshed, they sat on the porch, sipping the cool minty drink.

They chatted for a while. Rosie described the situation up at the station. "Some of the people I'm working with were there before. George McCall, for instance."

"I know George," Luke said. "He's a good guy. He's been on the island for ten years at least."

Rosie nodded. "They're going to be a good group of people to work with," she said, "but right now they're all under such stress, just waiting for Kilauea to make up its mind."

Luke nodded. "We're all like that. You go around the island and you can feel the tension. The tourists don't feel it so much, but boy, the natives do. It's a lot different from the last time you were here, isn't it?"

"Yeah, things were pretty quiet back then. And my position was very different. I was very junior—still a student, really. And I wasn't responsible for any major decisions. That makes a big difference."

He looked at her consideringly. "I remember the first time Gretchen brought you out to see us. You were so enthusiastic."

Rosie smiled. Gretchen Devillers had worked as a marine biologist for the research station. She had been a beautiful, elegant woman from a midwestern family and Rosie had taken an instant liking to her. The feeling had been mutual and they'd seen quite a bit of each other, both socially and professionally. Naturally Rosie had gotten to know Luke in the process. She'd liked him, but until that fateful night, after Gretchen's death in a diving accident, she had never thought of him as a lover. Now, under her lashes, she glanced at his strong profile. Was it possible they could be just friends again? Rosie asked herself.

"Gretchen was a lovely lady, Luke. I know you must still miss her very much."

"Yes, I do miss her. But I've learned that life goes on." He sipped his tea. "You're like her in a lot of ways, you know."

"Me?" Rosie was startled.

"You're both smart ambitious women. Both scientists in a male-dominated field. I admire that."

"Well, I'm flattered. Not every man holds such respect for career women."

Luke sighed. "I guess the only thing I didn't like about Gretchen's devotion to her work is that it didn't leave her time to start a family."

Rosie's eyes widened. This was the first she'd heard about that. Gretchen had been a very athletic person, and always absorbed in some new project that fascinated her. Rosie supposed it would have been hard for her to give up on that, even for the few months that pregnancy made a woman awkward.

"I didn't realize you wanted a family," she said aloud.

"Oh, yes. We Devillerses are a dynastic lot, I'm afraid." The expression in his eyes intensified. "For years starting a family was the one thing Gretchen and I argued about. The irony is that I'd finally convinced her to have a baby, when she had the accident. She was two months pregnant when she died."

"Oh, Luke, I'm so sorry." Rosie touched his hand and then drew back quickly. It was the same gesture of sympathy that had gotten her in trouble the last time she'd been alone with him in Hawaii.

"I didn't even know she was pregnant until after she died. I'm not even sure she knew." Luke gazed out at the breaking surf. "When I lost Gretchen, I lost not only her, but all the promise that our baby held."

He sighed again and looked at Rosie. "I know it's no excuse, but I'm apologizing again for my actions. When we made love that day, I was just still crazy with grief and loss." He held up his hands. "I should have called afterward, Rosie. I should have tried to stop you from giving up everything here and leaving. But I was sunk in my own misery until it was too late."

"Tell me something, Luke," Rosie said carefully. "Is that why you arranged for me to be offered this job? Because you were feeling guilty all these years?"

He glanced down at his hands, which lightly clasped the empty iced-tea glass. "In some ways, yes. I needed to make amends to you. But, Rosie," he said, looking her way again, "I meant everything I said about you being the best person to hire. I wouldn't have recommended you if you hadn't been so well qualified."

Rosie supposed she should feel grateful. After all, the man had really gone out of his way to atone. He couldn't know just what the consequences of that night had really been. As far as he was concerned, his actions had just been rude and thoughtless. But it didn't do a thing for Rosie's ego to be told that he was now, in a sense, paying her off with a job recommendation.

"Well," she said uneasily, "it's all water under the bridge. It happened a long time ago."

Luke was impressed with her self-possessed attitude. "Alaska must have been a good experience for you." He continued to study her speculatively.

She grinned to herself. "Yes, it was. A real learning experience."

"What was it like up there?"

"Cool, sometimes cold, and breathtakingly beautiful," Rosie said absentmindedly. She was turning over whether this was the moment to bring everything up. How could she talk about her life in Alaska without opening a Pandora's box?

Luke swirled the last ice cube in his drink. Then he stood and leaned against the porch rail. "Getting close to dinner time,'' he murmured, shooting her a mischievous look. ''And your refrigerator is pretty empty.''

Am I about to be asked out on a date? Rosie thought. How ironic. If only he knew. But maybe the time to get it all out would be over dinner.

At that moment, the purr of a motor distracted their attention.

Luke turned his head. ''Expecting company?''

Rosie looked puzzled. ''No,'' she said, standing.

The car had come to a stop out front, and she could hear the doors opening. Hurrying off the steps, Rosie walked around the front of the house with Luke at her side. Just as they rounded the corner, a familiar little voice split the silence.

''Mommy, Mommy!'' said four-year-old Christopher Clarke. Clutching his stuffed monkey, he came running up to Rosie and threw his arms around her hips.

Rosie hugged her only child. ''Oh, darling, I'm so glad to see you!'' she exclaimed, kissing his forehead. Then, for the briefest instant, she glanced fearfully at Luke.

He looked thunderstruck.

Chapter Four

"I tried to call," Rosie's mother said as she rounded the corner behind Christopher.

"Oh, Mom, I'm sorry. The phone's not connected yet," Rosie explained. With one hand on Christopher's silky head, she put her free arm around Mrs. Clarke and gave her a hug. "I thought you were staying on Oahu all this week with your friend Lucy."

Denise Clarke patted her gray-red hair, which was caught behind her neck with a leather clasp and hung down her back almost to her waist. She had been a hippie in the sixties and had never changed her style of dress or her flower-child outlook.

"Oh, Lucy was feeling under the weather and my horoscope recommended travel. So," she said airily, lifting her palms, "here we are." Her gaze strayed to Luke, and brightened. "Really, Rosie, who raised you? Aren't you going to introduce me?"

Rosie's fingers flew to her cheeks. "Oh, I'm sorry." She looked over at Luke, who was staring at all of them with a fascinated expression. Quickly Rosie averted her eyes. What was he thinking?

"Mom, this is Luke Devillers. He's one of the people responsible for my return to Hawaii." Briefly she described how Luke had recommended her for the job at the observatory. "He has quite a lot of influence on the island," she added, giving her mother a brief explanation about BICC and its work in civil preparedness.

Mrs. Clarke stuck out her hand and pumped Luke's. "Well, I'm delighted to meet the man who helped persuade my daughter to abandon snow and ice for sun and sand. I do my grandmotherly duties much better without an overcoat." She smiled fondly at Christopher. The little boy still clung to his mother's skirts with one hand, while he clutched his monkey with the other. He stared up at Luke with shy but interested brown eyes.

Luke looked back with equal curiosity. "And who is this young man?" He squatted, then held out his hand.

There was a weighty pause while Rosie gathered her forces. "This is my son, Christopher," she said. "Chris, shake hands with Mr. Devillers."

Shyly the four-year-old put his small hand in Luke's. Solemnly Luke shook it. "Pleased to meet you, Christopher Clarke," he said. "And your friend," he added, pointing to the monkey.

The little boy dangled the animal by one arm. "That's Kong."

"As in King?"

The boy nodded and grinned. "Only he's a nice monkey, and he's not all grown up yet."

"I can see that." Luke grinned back and then straightened. He turned to Rosie, who was standing with her feet frozen to the ground.

While he studied her speculatively, she met his eyes defiantly. At the same time, she could feel her mother watching them. Unspoken questions seemed to be flying around the air like snow in a blizzard.

"I didn't know you had a child," Luke finally said.

"Well, I do. Christopher's been visiting with my mother while I got settled. But now he's here to stay," she said, giving her son a protective squeeze. "Honey, what do you think of your new house?"

"Mommy, I haven't seen it yet."

"I think it's just darling. All that pink—sort of like cotton candy!" Mrs. Clarke exclaimed, gazing up at the blue shutters and gabled roof.

"Well, c'mon," Rosie said, grasping Chris's hand, all too happy to have something to do. "I'll give you a tour." As she spoke, her mind raced. This had to be one of the most awkward scenes in recent history. With luck, Luke would be polite and just go home. She could talk to him later in private when she'd had a chance to figure out what she wanted to say. She cast him a hopeful look. *Please go away,* she thought.

But there was a bemused expression on his face and a stubborn set to his shoulders that told her he wasn't going to take the hint. "It's a great little house," he said to Mrs. Clarke as they climbed up the front steps. "Chris, do you like the beach?"

"He loved playing in the sand near my house in Santa Barbara," Denise Clarke told Luke cheerfully.

Luke gave the older woman his most charming smile and mused that Rosie was full of surprises today. Mrs. Clarke, with her long, loose flowered skirt, gauzy shirt and dangling crystal earrings was nothing like her willowy outdoorsy daughter. How had such an apparently free-spirited woman who obviously espoused New Age theories produced a no-nonsense scientist offspring? And how had that redheaded daughter come to be the mother of a dark-haired little boy? As he followed behind the Clarkes, Luke decided he wouldn't leave until he'd had the last question answered.

"Laura Ashley would be right at home here," Mrs. Clarke said, squishing one of the plump turquoise flowered pillows. She kept up her admiring comments as Rosie led them into the kitchen. "It's like sunshine."

"The minute I saw this room, I could picture myself eating breakfast here. Look out the window, Mom, and you can catch the sunset."

"I'm hungry, Mommy," Christopher suddenly announced, bored with the *House Beautiful* talk.

"So am I!" Mrs. Clarke headed for the refrigerator and pulled it open. Her face dropped. Except for the champagne bottle, the shelves were empty.

"Oh, I haven't had a chance to go shopping yet." Rosie glanced at the clock over the stove and wondered aloud if any stores would be open this late. "Maybe we should go out to a restaurant."

Frowning, Christopher plopped down in the middle of the tile floor and Mrs. Clarke groaned. "We've been dragging around all day, dear. And we're beat. Isn't there some carryout that delivers?"

Smoothly Luke stepped in. "I know the perfect carryout place," he said. "I'll call and order on the car phone." He turned to Mrs. Clarke. "Any particular preferences or dislikes?"

"Brussel sprouts—I hate them." She wrinkled her nose. "And no red meat or milk products or anything that contains animal fat. Potatoes, tomatoes or anything else in the nightshade family is definitely out. And I really try to stay away from shellfish—a lot of it has a high mercury count." She shrugged. "Otherwise I'm easy."

Luke blinked and glanced at Rosie. She looked as though she was having trouble suppressing a grin.

"I want chocolate milk and a hamburger," Christopher piped up.

"You got it, buddy. And you, Rosie?"

Rosie waved her fingers. "I'm really easy. Anything."

"Will do." With that he headed out to his truck, with Christopher's voice echoing in his ears and Rosie's defiant expression troubling his mind.

MOMENTARILY RELIEVED, Rosie watched as Luke stroke out of the room. Wanting to avoid her mother's inevitable cross-examination, she bent down and pushed a lock of Christopher's dark hair off his forehead. "Want to see your room now, honey?"

"Yeah! Yeah!" Christopher thrust Kong in her face. "Kong wants to see it, too!"

She picked up the stuffed monkey and held him up to the light. "I think it's time Kong had a bath. Maybe we'll do that tomorrow. Okay?"

"All right," the little boy replied, and they headed down the hallway.

For the next few minutes, Rosie busied herself talking to Christopher, showing him his white painted bed and dresser and pointing out the built-in shelves for his toys. She was deliberately not giving her mother a chance to assuage her curiosity.

But Mrs. Clarke was up to the challenge. "Luke Devillers is quite a hunk. What a bod" she could hear her mother saying. "What does he do for a living?" she persisted as she trailed behind her daughter. "Rosie, are you listening?"

"Well, Mom, Luke Devillers is single and available, if you want him."

Denise fluttered her eyelashes. "How old is he anyhow?"

"About thirty-six."

"Hmmm. If I were ten years younger I'd take you up on that. But you're a little closer in age. And frankly I think he's more interested in you than in me."

Rosie smoothed a wrinkle out of Christopher's bedspread. "We're just friends, Mom."

Mrs. Clarke cocked her head. "Well, friendships develop. When I get back home, I'll draw up an astrological chart for you. Let's see," she went on, putting a finger to her cheek, "you were born at 1:00 p.m. when the sun was in the ninth house. I think that means..."

Rosie rolled her eyes.

"FRUIT SALAD with the snapper will be terrific," Luke was saying to his housekeeper, Mrs. Waneka. "Sounds like a safe choice," he added, thinking of Mrs. Clarke's caveats. "Oh, and don't forget, a hamburger for the little boy." Luke untangled the cord on his car phone. "When do you think Shun will be here with it? Half-hour? Great!"

Luke hung up the receiver and sat back in the leather seat of his truck. For several seconds he stared through the windshield, thinking hard. Denise Clarke was really a trip, but it was her daughter and her grandson who intrigued him most. How old was the boy, anyhow? Three, four, five? No, he couldn't be five. Rosie hadn't had a son when she'd last lived here. Unless he was adopted. With his dark hair and brown eyes, Christopher didn't really look much like Rosie. Was there an ex-husband lurking somewhere in the background? Or perhaps a husband?

The question hit Luke with disconcerting force. He hadn't seen a ring on Rosie's finger, but that didn't mean she wasn't married. He was surprised and disturbed to realize how much he didn't like the idea of Rosie with another man. No, he didn't like the idea at all.

Back in the house, he followed the sound of voices to Christopher's bedroom, where he announced, "Rescue is on the way. Our care package should be arriving shortly."

"You're a hero!" Mrs. Clarke exclaimed brightly.

Rosie, Luke noticed, looked a good deal less thrilled. In fact, there was a tight cast to her mouth that suggested she was either nervous or angry or both. Now, why was that? he wondered. He knew she wanted him to leave. But he was damned if he was going to. Why all the secrecy about her son? Just what was going on here?

Luke turned his attention and his charm on the receptive Mrs. Clarke. "How about I get your bags from the car?"

She beamed. "Oh, you sweet man. You're a moon child, aren't you?"

Luke looked blank.

"Mom's asking about your birth sign," Rosie injected. "She wants to know if you're a Cancer."

He shot Mrs. Clarke a devilish grin. "No, I'm a Taurus. But when I'm not being bossy, I'm a pussycat."

"I just bet you are," Mrs. Clarke retorted with a girlish trill of laughter. "A forceful man with a soft side..." She sighed and glanced at Luke's naked ring finger. "Some woman is going to be very lucky. I'm surprised no one has roped in a treasure like you already."

Rosie felt her stomach lurch. *You're really laying it on, Mom. Next thing you know you'll be opening a dating service.*

Fortunately Luke handled the situation with aplomb. "Well, I'm a widower," he replied. "My wife died almost five years ago."

"Oh, dear, I'm so sorry." Denise Clarke clasped her hands in a sympathetic gesture. She turned to Rosie. "Was she the friend you wrote me about? She died not long before you left the island, right?"

"Right," Rosie answered stiffly. Inadvertently her mother had raked up everything Rosie didn't want to think about. She had never explained who Christopher's father was. Of course she and her mother had had several discussions about the problems Rosie would face as a single parent. But when Mrs. Clarke had pressed, Rosie had made it clear that marriage to Christopher's biological father wasn't an option. Luckily her easygoing mother hadn't made an issue of that, but it didn't mean she wasn't curious. Nor did it mean she couldn't put two and two together, Rosie thought.

Just then Shun Lo, Luke's Chinese houseboy, pulled up in a station wagon bearing two large picnic baskets. When Luke and Rosie brought them in, the fragrance of fresh bread, fruit and just-baked snapper perfumed the air in the little cottage.

"Mmm, this smells marvelous!" Rosie exclaimed as she carried one of the baskets over to the table she and Mrs. Clarke just finished setting. Though she hadn't wanted Luke to stay for dinner, she was grateful for this banquet he'd provided. Anyhow, Luke and her mother seemed to be hitting it off so well; maybe they'd keep each other entertained and things wouldn't be as awkward as she'd feared.

Soon everyone was gathering around the glass-topped table. Rosie picked up a round shape encased in foil and unwrapped it on her son's plate. Still clutching Kong, Christopher was already wriggling onto the chair.

"Mango, papaya, pineapple—wonderful," Mrs. Clarke declared, holding each fresh fruit up and admiring it before she set it in a pottery bowl on the center of the table.

"I hope my selections were okay," Luke said.

"Marvelous, just marvelous. And that makes it perfect," she cried as Luke sat the spray of fresh orchids he'd brought earlier next to the fruit bowl.

A few minutes later they were all seated, their plates heaped with fish, saffron rice and fresh pineapple. While Christopher bit into his hamburger, Luke popped the cork on the champagne and filled the wineglasses Rosie had unearthed at the back of a cupboard. "A toast," he said, holding up his drink and looking from Rosie, to Mrs. Clarke, to Christopher. "Aloha. Welcome to our island."

"May the force be with us." Mrs. Clarke sipped happily. "To a comfortable civilized tour of duty."

"Mom, with all your New Age proclivities, I'd think you'd be a little more open to adventure," Rosie teased affectionately.

"Dear, I had all the adventure anyone could ever want when your father was alive. Brad was a volcanologist, too," she said, leaning toward Luke. "We spent our honeymoon peering into bubbling craters in Indonesia. And Rosie here was born in Costa Rica. I almost didn't make it from the site to the hospital in time."

"Sounds as if your life has been full of escapades," said Luke. He smiled at Rosie, who, despite all her misgivings about the evening, smiled back. Though she was tense, she couldn't stop herself from responding to the warm light in his eyes.

"It was fun growing up with gypsy parents," Rosie admitted. "I got to see so much of the world and meet so many interesting people."

Denise Clarke clapped her hands. "It was a great experience for us all. But," she added slyly, "I didn't have a grandson then. I want to see this little boy," she went on, patting Christopher's arm, "more than once every decade."

The youngster's mouth was full of French fries and chocolate milk. "And I want to see my grandma," Chris replied after hastily swallowing most of his food.

Luke returned his attention to Rosie. "I always wondered how you chose your profession. I gather you followed in your father's footsteps."

"Actually, not at first. When I was in school, I was a geology major." She shrugged. "I liked rocks."

"So do I," Christopher interjected. "I have a big collection."

"You do? You'll have to show it to me sometime."

"I'll go get it," Chris said, scrambling off the chair.

When he was out of the room, Luke switched his attention back to Rosie. "What changed your mind about geology?"

A look of pain crossed Rosie's face and she glanced questioningly at her mother.

"It's all right, dear. I don't mind your talking about it. It's been more than ten years."

"I decided to go into volcanology after Dad died. He was studying the Mount Saint Helens eruption and, fanatic scientist that he was, he just didn't get out when he should have. He was photographing the dust cloud above the central vent when his helicopter went down." She moved a piece of fish around with her fork. "After he died, I realized I wanted to carry on his work. This earth we live on is still a mystery to most of us. I want to learn more about it and help people cope with its dangerous forces."

"Is that why you toasted us with 'may the force be with you'?" Luke questioned Mrs. Clarke.

She giggled. "Absolutely." Then she patted the younger woman's shoulder. "Rosie, and Brad before her, have wrestled with the most incomprehensible forces of nature. And I'm very proud of my daughter."

Luke gazed at Rosie. "I can certainly see why."

Flushing and avoiding Luke's gaze, Rosie smiled at her mother. "Thanks, Mom."

"I found it," Christopher exclaimed as he trotted back into the kitchen with a shoe box. "It was next to my teddy bear." Carelessly he pushed aside the plates, tore the lid off the box and set it down in front of Luke.

"A very fine collection," Luke said, holding up each rock and marveling at it. "Where did you collect them all?"

"In Alaska and at my grandma's."

"Well, maybe you'll find a few interesting specimens here."

Christopher nodded happily.

"Okay, Christopher," Rosie said, "time for your bath now."

"Oh, let me do it," Mrs. Clarke insisted. "You have company."

Before Rosie could object, Mrs. Clarke led the little boy away down the hall.

Over Rosie's protests, Luke insisted on helping her with the dishes. Stepping up to the sink, he began to run warm water. "Any soap?" he questioned.

"Oh, I think I've got some somewhere," Rosie said, rummaging through an unpacked box.

"That's a great kid you've got there," Luke said as he dipped a plate into the soapsuds. "How old is Chris?"

Rosie picked up a towel and dried the clean silverware. "Four." Though she was intensely aware of Luke's tall athletic body within inches of hers and his eyes on her profile, she kept her gaze on the forks she was wiping.

"He's got your nose," he said, scrutinizing her. "But you and your mother are both redheads. Where did he get those dark eyes and hair?"

"From his father." This conversation was going exactly where she didn't want it to, and despite the meal she'd just eaten, the pit of her stomach felt hollow.

"I didn't even know you were married."

Rosie took a deep breath and dropped her dishtowel. "I'm not." She started across the room.

"Divorced, then?"

"No, Luke," she replied, turning and meeting his inquiring gaze with boldness. "I'm a single parent. Now, if you'll excuse me, I think I'll go check on Christopher." With that she strode out of the kitchen.

LUKE STARED after her. He'd obviously struck a nerve and he was a bit ashamed of himself for pressing her. But he had to know. Rosie apparently didn't think much of the father, whoever he was. Or maybe she was still in love with the cad.

Luke began to twist the dishcloth between his hands as if he were throttling the delinquent father's neck. Whoever the guy was, Luke didn't have much respect for him. Who would abandon a woman like Rosie and a child as sweet as Chris? Luke grew angry just thinking of some irresponsible character seducing Rosie, getting her pregnant and not appreciating all she had to offer. But maybe he had it all wrong. Maybe not marrying had been Rosie's choice. Maybe she was even more independent than he had realized.

When had it happened? It must have been not too long after she had left Hawaii. He thought back to that time when he'd been in such confusion over Gretchen's death and the loss of the child she'd been carrying. With a wince, once again he remembered how badly he'd treated Rosie, making love to her and then turning his back on her.

Even now he could feel the blind rush of need and desire that had overcome him when he'd taken Rosie into his arms that day. Her beautiful body had welcomed him and eased his pain. The passion between them had been so explosive, so overwhelming, that the guilt, when reason returned, had been twice as great.

Had she been so hurt by the unreasonable way he'd turned on her that she'd conceived Christopher on the rebound? How ironic if that was the case. How he'd envied the Clarkes' little family tonight as he'd sat at the table with them. Their togetherness had pointed up all that was missing in his life. He'd been thinking a lot about that lately. What did it take to make a life worth living? Satisfying work? He had that, and for the past five years it had been his solace. But work couldn't be everything.

There was an emptiness at the core of Luke's existence, and he knew it well. He also knew what would fill that emptiness. A woman to love, a son to be proud of and watch grow. But it had to be the right woman and the child had to be his. He pictured Rosie and Chris as they'd smiled across the table at each other and his eyes narrowed pensively.

"I THOUGHT he'd never leave," Rosie muttered an hour later. Mrs. Clarke, who'd been flipping through an island guidebook, pushed her bifocals back up the bridge of her nose and looked surprised.

"Don't tell me you're talking about Luke. Goodness, Rosie. What have I raised? He's the most gorgeous thing I've seen since Tom Selleck in *Quigley Down Under*. And he was here in the flesh and not charging admission."

At that moment, Chris came out of the bathroom.

"All done?"

"Yep."

Ignoring her mother, Rosie took Christopher by the hand and led him into his bedroom. Barefoot, in pajamas, he sleepily climbed into bed. "Do you want me to read you a story," Rosie asked as she tucked him in.

Christopher clutched Kong. "Don't you like Luke?"

She really had to be careful what she said within earshot of Chris. He was like a little sponge soaking up information. "I like Luke fine."

"Then why did you want him to go?"

"Because we've all had a long day. Besides, I want to have some time alone with you," she added, giving Christopher a kiss. "Now, which story is it going to be—the one about the kangaroo with too many pockets or the one about the polar bear who forgot how to fish?"

"The polar bear."

Christopher nodded off to sleep halfway through the story. For several minutes Rosie sat looking down at his face in the circle of warm light from the bedside lamp. Tenderly she traced the fans of long dark lashes. His cheeks were plump as ripe peaches now, but she had no doubt that someday they'd be angular like Luke's.

Maybe his short straight nose resembled hers, but everything else about him—his thick dark hair, his sturdy well-made body, his brown eyes and his bright questioning mind were like his father's. Had Luke seen any of that tonight? And if he had, what would the repercussions be? It was a question she'd been asking herself ever since she'd first considered this job. With a sigh, she dropped another kiss on her son's forehead, closed the book and switched off the light. Now for the next round, she thought as she headed out to face her mother.

Mrs. Clarke had settled on the lanai in one of the wooden rockers and was gazing out over the moon-streaked ocean. She didn't look up when Rosie came out. "So that's Christopher's father," Mrs. Clarke said simply.

Well, that didn't take long, Rosie told herself as she settled into a chair next to her mother. "Yes."

The older woman turned and looked at Rosie. "I knew it the minute I saw them together."

Rosie nodded.

"He doesn't know, does he?"

"I hope not. But Luke's no dummy. If it's that obvious to you, he'll probably figure it out soon."

Mrs. Clarke stared into her daughter's troubled eyes. "Don't you think it's time you told me about it?"

Rosie shook her head. "There's not much to tell, Mom. It was a one-night stand. It didn't mean anything to him and I was a fool."

Denise Clarke fingered her crystal. "Now, wait a minute, Rosie. A one-night stand—that doesn't sound like my daughter. The girl I know leads with her head, not her heart. You were always so sensible—sometimes when you were growing up I felt as if you were my mother instead of the other way around. I do declare you were born cautious."

"Well, when it came to Luke Devillers all my common sense seemed to fly out the window," Rosie said dryly. "Certainly I find Luke very attractive—any woman with eyes would. But I swear, Mom, I never thought of him romantically while Gretchen was alive. Even after she died, I considered him only a friend. Then one night it just happened." She threw up her hands. "Maybe the moon was out of phase. Maybe Venus was cavorting with Taurus. I just can't explain it."

Mrs. Clarke nodded wisely. "Well, you're the scientist. But I know enough about chemistry between men and women to know when it's there. And it was very obvious to me tonight that it was there between you and Luke."

Roughly Rosie shook her head. "No, it isn't. And it's not going to be. Once was enough."

"But," Mrs. Clarke said emphatically, "Christopher has a right to know his father and Luke has a right to know his son."

Rosie put her face in her hands. "That's one of the reasons I came back to Hawaii. I felt I had to straighten this out. But now that I'm here I'm afraid I've made a terrible mistake."

Mrs. Clarke gazed at her daughter in amazement. "How can it be a mistake to introduce a son to his father—especially when the father seems like such a good man?"

"Oh, Mom. You don't know what the Devillerses are like. For generations, they've been a rich powerful family on this island. When they've wanted something, they've gotten their way. Luke joked with you about being a Taurus, but that really does describe him. He can be bullheaded and determined to get his way no matter whose toes he steps on. Look at Maile Gardens. He's even risked the wrath of the island gods to do that."

"Maile Gardens?"

"It's a fancy development Luke has built despite protests from some of the other islanders." Rosie went on to explain what had happened the night of the party at Orchid Cliffs. "As I said, Luke's stubborn. When it comes to something he wants, he stamps it top priority and he charges ahead. Luke doesn't back down easily, Mom.

What if once he learns Christopher is his son, he decides to take him away from me?''

''How could he do that?''

Rosie lifted her tear-filled eyes. ''I don't know. I'm just afraid.''

Chapter Five

Mrs. Clarke got up and dragged her chair around so she faced Rosie directly. "Okay, sweetie, I can see you're upset, but I'm not sure that what you're saying makes sense." She hesitated and then rolled her eyes. "I can't believe this. Here you're the one who's being emotional and I'm talking 'let's be analytical.'" As she spoke, she pulled a tissue out of her pocket and handed it to her daughter.

With a sniff, Rosie wiped her eyes and blew her nose. "You're right, Mom. I've overreacting. But I can't help it. A lot's at stake here."

"Certainly. But is that everything you're afraid of?"

The night wind from the ocean ruffled Rosie's hair as she shook her head. A little way off, the gentle rolling surf was a soothing counterpoint to her troubled thoughts. "Obviously Luke and Chris hit it off together tonight. And I'm happy about that. But what if Luke should decide he wants equal custody—or, heaven forbid, full custody?"

"Oh, now, honey, really! Why would a judge give it to him? You're of good moral character."

"I'm a single mother, Mom. And I don't have a lot of money. I'll probably never be able to offer Chris the kind of stability that a rich man like Luke can."

"Nonsense. In this day and age—"

Rosie broke in. "I hadn't planned for them to meet this way. I'd wanted time to assess the situation before I decided whether to introduce them."

"What is there to assess?"

"For one, just how the Devillers family would take knowing that their only heir is an illegitimate child. It's very possible they might think I'm a gold digger trying to cut myself in on their fortune. The thought gives me the creeps, and I don't want Christopher in the middle of a mess like that."

Mrs. Clarke waved her hand dismissively. "Rosie, you can't be serious."

"It's not so far out. Wait till you meet Luke's aunt Beatrice. The blood runs bluer in her veins than in Queen Elizabeth's." They rocked for a moment while Mrs. Clarke absorbed that. "And another thing," Rosie finally continued. "The job here on Hawaii is only temporary. I don't expect to be here for more than a year. Suppose the Devillers family embraces Chris. What happens when I try to take him away to my next assignment?"

Denise Clarke sighed. "Okay, I see your point, but Luke seems reasonable to me and I think he and Chris both deserve to know the truth about each other."

"I think so, too. I want Christopher to know his dad. I wouldn't have come here otherwise. But I'm just not as prepared as I thought I was. I don't want to make the announcement until I feel the time is right."

"Honey, much as you'd like, you can't control the whole world."

Rosie rubbed her forehead. "I just need to think. I'm sure there's a logical way to do this. It's just that seeing Luke has jumbled my emotions. Look what happened the last time my heart overruled my brain."

"Yes, you had a wonderful little boy named Christopher. Surely you don't regret that."

"No, of course not. Christopher is the best thing that ever happened to me. But I want to be careful. As Chris gets older he'll ask more questions. What if he's angry with me for not living with Luke as a family—not that Luke has asked me... or ever will. But kids aren't always rational. What if when Chris is older he decides he'd rather be with Luke than me? Luke can offer him a whole lot more than I can."

"He can't offer him a mother's love."

But Rosie's churning thoughts kept turning to the dark side of things. "Okay, what if Luke rejects him outright? How would that make Christopher feel?"

"Be reasonable, Rosie. In that case, you wouldn't tell Christopher," Mrs. Clarke said gently.

"No, but I don't know how I'd deal with the resentment I'd feel." She sighed heavily. "I'm sorry, I guess I just have cold feet."

Mrs. Clarke studied her daughter. "I understand, dear. All right, give yourself time. Reestablish a relationship with Luke—it doesn't have to be romantic, but it should at least be friendly. No matter what, don't wait too long. They'll both end up angry with you if you do."

"THERE," Rosie said, putting down her hammer and dusting her hands off on her khaki slacks. She had just driven a series of stakes into the steaming blackened earth close to Kilauea's crater. Since the explosion on the day she'd arrived, the volcano had been quiescent. But Rosie knew it might just be the calm before the storm.

For the next two hours she made careful measurements, which she would chart and compare over the next few days to determine whether the ground near the volcanic vent was swelling. If it was, it was the harbinger of another explosion. But Pele was a quixotic deity. She could just as well go back to sleep and leave her islanders at peace for the next ten years.

Just as Rosie was stowing her gear in the observatory's Jeep to head back to the station, she noticed a small crowd gathering a short distance away at one of the steaming vents. Curious, she locked the Jeep and wandered over.

As she approached, she realized the tourists were watching a lone woman standing at the edge of the vent. The woman was stately, her tall, stout figure wrapped in a purple-and-lavender muumuu that brushed her sneakered feet. Layers of white flowered leis hung down her ample bosom and her long dark hair was loose, flowing over her broad shoulders down past her waist.

Rosie squinted and strained her ears. The woman was chanting something in Hawaiian. From time to time she raised her hand in a graceful arc, plucked a berry from a branch she held and tossed it into the pit.

"What's she doing, Dad?" a young boy asked his father.

"I think it has something to do with placating the volcano," the man answered.

Rosie fixed her attention back on the woman, who looked familiar. She was turning in a slow circle now. Rosie recognized the leaves on the branch. The father was right. The woman must be tossing sacred ohelo berries, Rosie thought. She was about to tell that to the little boy, when the woman turned in her direction. As Rosie had already guessed, it was Liliana, the leader of the protesters who'd invaded Luke's party at Orchid Cliffs.

She glanced over the crowd to see that several of the tourists were taking pictures. Calmly Liliana went on with her ceremony and ignored them. A moment later that changed. Liliana's face darkened and she went rigid, her hand poised midair. With a scowl, she began to rumble. At first her Hawaiian words were incomprehensible and the tourists stared at her with their mouths open.

She launched herself off the rise where she'd been standing and pushed her way into the small crowd. Startled, several of the tourists backed off. Involuntarily Rosie stepped back, too. Was the woman going to point a threatening finger at her again? She was edging toward the Jeep, when she heard Liliana shout "Stop!" Rosie froze in her tracks and turned. But the command wasn't for her.

Liliana had planted herself in front of a tall young man in denim cutoffs. With great disdain, she pointed at his bulging pockets.

"What?" the tourist yelped. "Hey, what's the idea?"

"Empty your pockets!"

His hands went over them protectively. "Hey, take it easy, lady. I haven't stolen a wallet or anything. They're only a few souvenir rocks. Nobody's going to miss 'em."

Liliana's scowl deepened and her dark gaze bored into him. She seemed to grow larger and he seemed to shrivel before her. "It is forbidden to take lava rocks. They are sacred to Pele. By stealing them you will bring a curse down on us all."

The young man glanced sheepishly at the other tourists and then shrugged. "Okay, okay. Here're your stupid stones," he said, tumbling them out on the ground. "Sheesh!"

Liliana stared him down until he had emptied his pockets completely. "Anyone else?" Her gaze then encompassed the crowd.

People murmured and shuffled their feet. There were small clinks as others dropped their contraband souvenirs on the ground.

Rosie stopped a little way off and watched in fascination. She knew that native Hawaiians believed it was unlucky to take lava rocks, and with Kilauea so active, emotions on this subject would be running high. She remembered visiting one of the sacred sites years ago. At the time she'd been struck by a slew of handwritten letters on display in the visitors' center. They'd been penned by penitent tourists who'd tempted fate and stolen a rock. All told tales of monumental bad luck, illnesses, accidents, investments gone sour. In hopes of stemming their ill fortune, the letter writers had returned their stolen rocks in everything from Styrofoam hamburger containers to egg cartons to old shoes and glass jewelry boxes.

As Liliana stared balefully, the tourists headed en masse to their cars. Rosie pushed back her impulse to leave, as well. The image of Liliana's pointing finger had haunted her dreams. Though she was wary of Liliana's obvious anger, she wanted to understand just what all that was about.

Gingerly she walked over to where the woman stood with her arms akimbo. Rosie regarded herself as average size, but next to Liliana's imposing bulk, she felt like a Lilliputian.

"Excuse me, but I'd like to introduce myself. My name is Rosalyn Clarke. I work up at the station." She gestured with her head and held out a hand.

Liliana's fierce gaze swiveled to Rosie's face and she stared her up and down. For a moment Rosie felt her knees quake and debated withdrawing her hand.

She was about to do that, when the woman's face softened. Her arm came out and she swallowed Rosie's hand in her meaty palm. "Liliana Aina."

"Perhaps you recognize me," Rosie ventured. "Last week when you came to Orchid Cliffs, you chanted about Pele and pointed at me."

"Yes, yes. I remember you well."

"It's been bothering me. Why did you single me out?"

"Because of your hair of fire," Liliana answered.

"Only that?"

"No. We know that you have come to do research on the volcano."

"Yes, but what did your actions mean?" Rosie persisted. "I'm not doing anything to harm you or your cause. I'm only trying to understand and prevent lives and property from being lost."

Liliana began to pace back and forth with heavy feet. "Perhaps your intentions are good, but we, the *kama'aina*, are worried. The tourists who come to our beautiful island bring good things—an appreciation of its beauty and, of course, money that keeps our economy going. But along with good comes bad." Liliana raised her hands. "Hotels spring up, the water gets polluted. More building means more electricity, so they have to cut down the rain forest to build a geothermal plant. Then more people can live here, so they build more houses that crowd our *heiau*. It is all too much. Pele is angry and so are we."

"Well, I can understand your feelings," Rosie said. "I hope you're not angry with me, though. Believe me, I only want the best for Hawaii."

As they talked, they found themselves walking slowly through the blackened moonscape. Lengths of hardened lava lay coiled beneath their feet like braided rock. The clinky *a'a* lava crunched under their soles. Other patches resembled chocolate pudding brought to a boil and then flash-frozen. Here and there slits in the stone steamed like spouts of overheated teakettles.

For an hour, Liliana poured out her anguish and Rosie listened sympathetically. Clearly Pele's Partisans were upset about the burgeoning development. They were deeply concerned people worried about disturbing Hawaii's delicate ecological balance. Their conviction was tempered by superstition and a strong desire to preserve the old ways. Naturally the past few years of significant change frightened and upset them.

Liliana's frequent references to the ills of development encouraged Rosie to bring up Luke's name. "You seem to be particularly upset with Luke Devillers."

Liliana's brows snapped together. "The royal blood of King Kamehameha flows in Luke's veins. He, of all people, should know better than to risk offending Madame Pele. But he is so taken up with his project that he's lost sight of what's most important. Many times I have tried to reason with him, but he is bullheaded."

Privately Rosie thought Liliana was a bit that way herself. Nevertheless she found herself liking the woman. Liliana had a passionate love for her island, and she was honest and forthright. She also agreed with Liliana's assessment of Luke. Luke had always been a take-charge person. She remembered from her earlier days here how he'd spearheaded many of the island's civic projects—a youth club, a recreation center, an expanded medical clinic—and he wasn't used to opposition. His dynamism and assertiveness were part of what attracted Rosie to him. They were also what made her afraid.

Suddenly Liliana smiled at Rosie, and it was as if the sun had broken through a cloud. "If you want to learn more about the true Hawaii, come to my village. Next Friday we have a luau. Bring your family."

Rosie was pleased by the invitation and quickly agreed. It would be a wonderful way for Christopher and her mother to get to know the island.

"Wow!" Christopher's brown eyes lit up. He, Mrs. Clarke and Rosie were strolling down from the narrow dirt road where they'd left their car.

The "wow" was for the ruins of the sacred site near Maile Gardens. On the way to the luau in Niha, Rosie had decided to make a little detour so her mother and Christopher could see it.

"Oh, boy!" Christopher exclaimed as they walked the rough path down toward the sea. A ring of carved wooden gods glared down from the courtyard that surrounded a thick stone platform. "They look mean."

"They're just warning you and everyone else to respect the sacred ground." Rosie thought of Liliana's feud with Luke.

Mrs. Clarke walked up to one and clasped her hands as she studied its menacing face. "Well, this guy would certainly convince me."

"In ancient times, everything was run by a set of taboos," Rosie explained. "For instance, women couldn't eat the foods reserved for offerings."

"And men could?"

Rosie nodded. "And women couldn't prepare meals for men or even eat with them."

"Well, I pretty much like the first part. I'm not so sure about the second."

Rosie laughed. "When a taboo was broken," she went on, "the penalty was death."

Christopher's eyes widened and he put his hands around his throat and made playful gagging sounds.

"But you were safe if you could take refuge at a sacred site. It was sort of like a home-free zone in tag."

"I'll have to remember that if I ever get in trouble," Mrs. Clarke said.

"You mean if you get here you're safe no matter what?" Christopher asked.

"That was the idea," Rosie replied. She looked out at the ocean, where the last rays of sun were sinking below the horizon.

Behind her she heard her mother admonish Christopher "Oh, don't pick up those. They're dirty."

"What's that, Mom?"

"Just stones." Mrs. Clarke waved her hands in dismissal. "Don't worry about it."

"It's getting dark," Rosie said, turning. "We'd better get on." Together they walked back along the *pahoehoe* shelf, a safe distance from where the sea crashed and blew up through the rocks, to the path up to the car. On the way back she noticed the sign for the turn-in to Maile Gardens. Another time she'd have to go take a look, she thought.

A few minutes later when they arrived at Niha, they could see a man in a loincloth running along the edge of the fish ponds, swinging a wand of fire. As he lit a ring of torches, their reflection shimmered on the dark surface of the still water.

Rosie riffled the top of her son's hair. "Pretty, isn't it?"

"It's spectacular!" Mrs. Clarke exclaimed. "Look at those carved figures. They all look like they've had a particularly bad day." She pointed at a set of carved wooden idols bleached by centuries of sun and salt air. Shadows played over their course features eerily.

The village itself was only a collection of small wooden houses painted white. In the torchlight the colored lanterns strung on poles and the villager's bright flowered garments, fragrant leis and happy ukelele music made it all seem very festive.

As Rosie and her little family approached the center of activity, she glanced around. Several picnic tables had been arranged in a U-shape. They were covered with oilcloth and lit with candles. Off to the side, a pair of men wearing red-and-yellow shirts were tending an open pit.

"Look at that, Mommy!" Christopher exclaimed. "They're cooking a whole pig."

"They certainly are," Rosie answered. She sniffed the air appreciatively. The smoke from the *imu,* the earthen pit lined with *kiawe* wood and lava rock, permeated the warm night air. "Roast pork is called *kalua* here and is a traditional Hawaiian dish. And so is poi," she added, spotting a heavyset man pounding the taro root with a pestle in a bowl. She tapped her mother on the shoulder. "You'll have to try some poi tonight."

"I like poi," Mrs. Clarke declared. "I am a woman of the world, after all."

Rosie wrinkled her nose. "It tastes like liquified cardboard to me. You can eat it for both of us."

As Rosie spoke, she studied the other guests. Liliana and the Pele Partisans were using this feast to lobby their cause, so they'd invited all the members of the Big Island Citizens Committee. That meant Rosie was likely to be seeing Luke.

Knowing that, she'd dressed in a turquoise-, fuchsia-and-white sarong. Though it flattered her figure, she told herself it wasn't just for Luke's benefit. It was also a way of showing her respect and admiration for the Hawaiian culture.

Apparently Liliana thought so, too. When she spotted Rosie, a big smile spread over her face and she came rushing forward. In her hands, she carried a dozen leis made from many colored island blossoms. "Aloha," she called, wrapping Rosie in her large arms and kissing her on the cheek. After Liliana dropped several flowered wreaths on Rosie's neck, Rosie introduced her to Mrs. Clarke and Christopher. Beaming, Liliana squatted and smothered the boy in a warm hug. After that she bestowed her perfumed necklaces on him and his grandmother.

"These leis are made from *lehua,* blossoms of *ohia* tree—they are the flowers of Pele," their hostess proclaimed.

While Christopher fingered his and Mrs. Clarke exclaimed in delight, Liliana led Rosie and her party farther into the torchlit circle. "The luau will begin after the Kahunas have performed the ceremony of apology for disturbing the bones of our ancestors. I hope," Liliana said, looking around, "that the bullheaded developer of Maile Gardens will be here to see it." Then she focused on the fish pond, where a group of new arrivals were strolling out of the darkness into the torch light.

Rosie turned around and Christopher cried out, "Look, there's Luke!"

An expression of triumph crossed Liliana's face and she clapped her hands. "Now we will have a truly fine ceremony."

Meanwhile Christopher had broken away from Rosie's hand. He ran across the packed earth to the spot where Luke stood talking with Mr. Fan. Next to the wizened little man, Luke was a vision of masculine splendor. He wore a dark blue flowered shirt tailored to fit his wide shoulders and slim waist. Beneath it, a pair of white jeans cupped his tight derriere and encased his long legs like a second skin. He, too, like all the other guests, was wearing a lei made of *lehua*.

Rosie watched as Chris tugged at Luke's pant leg. An odd feeling came into her chest as Luke scooped her son up into his strong arms and punched him playfully on the chest. They looked so comfortable with each other—and so well matched—the little boy with his mop of dark brown locks and the tall, lean man with his thick black hair and obsidian eyes. Usually Chris was shy with people he'd met only once or twice. But he was behaving with Luke as if they'd known each other for years. And Rosie wasn't sure how she felt about it.

Mrs. Clarke nudged her daughter. "Look at that! Aren't they a gorgeous pair. They've really taken to each other, Rosie."

"I can see that, Mom."

Denise patted Rosie. "Don't worry so much, dear. This is a good thing."

Rosie didn't answer. Inwardly she was wishing she could be sure of that. She trailed behind as her mother hurried over to Luke and Chris.

"Luke, it's wonderful to see you again," Mrs. Clarke chirped. "Rosie said you might be here."

Over Denise's shoulder, Luke's eyes met Rosie's. There was a light in his gaze that hadn't been there the last time they'd seen each other. What was going through his mind?

Carefully he set Chris back down on the ground and put what looked to Rosie like an ominously proprietary arm around the boy's shoulder. "Yes, good old Liliana is doing some lobbying for Pele's Partisans. Otherwise I'd probably be persona non grata at this shindig."

"I think she's trying to make peace with you, Luke," Rosie said.

He chuckled. "I doubt that. Have you seen the kahunas?" He gestured toward the group of tattooed priests that had begun to assemble at the far end of the compound. "Liliana's idea of compromise is my putting a wrecking ball to my development. But I'm here. That should say something."

He bent his face toward Christopher's. "I'm thirsty. How about you, *keikikane?*" he said, using the Hawaiian word for little boy. "Want to go over and get ourselves a soda?"

While Chris chattered happy agreement, Rosie's eyes narrowed. Maybe she was behaving like an idiot, but the way Luke was taking over her son and the fact that Christopher didn't seem to mind it gnawed at her.

"That sounds like an excellent idea," Mrs. Clarke was saying. "If we're going to see a ceremony, it's best to be well fortified."

Again Rosie found herself trailing after Luke, Chris and her mother. It was almost as if she were the outsider and they were the family unit. *Now stop this nonsense,* she told herself. *You're being paranoid.*

To give herself something else to think about, she allowed her gaze to wander appreciatively over Luke. As he strode along with Christopher's hand tucked into his, he moved with an athletic grace and assurance that made him stand out from all the other men.

A table at the far end of a pair of tall totemlike carvings had been set up with a bar. After getting Chris a soda, Luke offered Rosie and Denise cups of passion-fruit punch served in a fat coconut.

"Oh, how delightfully authentic!" Mrs. Clarke exclaimed.

Rosie smiled and shook her head. Her mother was incurable. Then her eye caught Luke's. He was grinning, too. "I think if I'm going to get through this particular ceremony, I'll need something a little less authentic," he said, and ordered Scotch on the rocks.

At that moment, a group of stern-faced older men paraded solemnly into the clearing. Ankle-length sarongs wrapped their waists and necklaces of braided tea leaves adorned their necks. Elaborate tattoos of constellations covered their bare arms, bellies and shoulders. As the priests arrived all the other guests parted before them, moving to form an outer ring.

Meanwhile, half a dozen young men with drums carved from logs had dropped down on the ground. Soon they were pounding a hypnotic rhythm while another kahuna lifted a nose flute made from a bamboo cylinder to his nostrils and produced a high thin sound.

"Oh, my," Mrs. Clarke murmured. "What's happening?"

"They're priests," Luke explained. "That staff they're all carrying represents Lonomakua—the god of fertility."

"Remind me not to get too close to that one," Mrs. Clarke declared, putting a hand to her flat stomach.

Good advice for me, too, Rosie thought, shooting Luke's handsome profile a surreptitious glance.

"Maybe we should take some seats," Luke was saying as he led them to a picnic bench. "This is likely to go on for a while."

"I want to sit next to Luke and my mommy," Christopher announced as he scrambled between them.

"Of course you can sit wherever you like, Christopher, dear." Mrs. Clarke beamed at the three of them.

Rosie squirmed but made no comment. "Just what's this ceremony going to be about?" she asked distractedly as she settled herself on the wooden seat.

"To beg the gods' forgiveness for disturbing the bones of our ancestors," Luke replied.

"And have they been disturbed?"

"No, they're still resting very much in peace." Luke's chin jutted. "Maile Gardens is far enough away that the spirits of our ancestors probably don't even know it's there."

Obviously, Rosie thought, there was a big difference of opinion on this point. She couldn't believe that Liliana would go to so much trouble and make such a fuss if she didn't honestly believe that Maile Gardens was in some way arousing the ire of Pele. Of course, it was all superstition, but sometimes deeply held beliefs could have far-reaching effects. She knew, for instance, that at one time on the islands a person could have been burned to death or buried alive for letting his shadow fall on the house of a lawmaker-chief.

Rosie glanced down at Christopher, who was staring at the ceremony with his mouth open. She smiled. Whatever else the kahunas were, they were engrossing and compelling, and they certainly had a sense of the dramatic.

After they'd finished chanting, the priests offered a symbolic sacrifice of ti, taro and gin for the goddess Pele. Then they chanted a prayer to the four most powerful gods of Hawaii—Ku, Kane, Lono and Kanaloa.

"Who's Kanaloa?" Mrs. Clarke whispered in Rosie's ear.

"I think he's the god of thunder. I believe the idea here is that all the island gods are upset about this ancestor-disturbing business, so the kahunas are going to make a big deal of appeasing them."

She stole a furtive look at Luke, who was watching the ceremony with his arms crossed over his broad chest. There was an ironic expression in his dark eyes. How was this affecting him? Sure, he was a highly educated twentieth-century man, but Hawaiian blood ran deep in his veins. Was he really unmoved by this appeal to the old gods?

The other seventy or so guests who ringed the arena seemed impressed by the chants and ritual gestures. Mr. Fan looked solemn, as did Mary Burns and her planter husband. Even George McCall and Joe Masters from the research station, who'd arrived moments before the kahunas began, appeared fascinated.

The emotion was so intense, Rosie wondered if people would be able to relax and enjoy themselves during the dinner. But as soon as the kahunas made their exit, the atmosphere magically turned festive again. Village maidens with wreaths on their shiny dark straight tresses came out bearing platters heaped with roast pork, chicken, salmon, poi, pineapple, coconut pudding and other island specialties. Rosie's family and Luke twisted in their seats to face the table when Liliana waddled over to join them. The other villagers had spread themselves among the tables and Liliana, it was obvious, intended to make a point of sitting at theirs.

"Ah, the antiprogress lobby is thundering our way," Luke muttered.

"Be nice," Mrs. Clarke hissed, and poked him in the ribs.

Undaunted, Liliana plopped her meaty thighs down on the bench across from Luke. "Now that we've had a good ceremony, it's time for good *kaukau,*" she announced in her rich throaty voice.

Christopher grinned at the heavyset woman, who reached over and patted him on the head. "I like the kaka... hookas!"

"You mean the kahunas," Rosie corrected.

"Yeah, they have great drums. Bam. Bam," he said, thumping the table.

The adults laughed. "I have some drums at home I could show you, and some other good stuff, too," Luke told Christopher. "Would you like to see a canoe buster? That's a hammer the old Hawaiians used to smash enemy canoes."

"Yeah!" Christopher exclaimed.

"Oh, that reminds me," Liliana proclaimed. "I have something for you." She took out a small carved jade tiki that had been strung on a leather thong and ceremoniously placed it around the boy's neck. "This will bring you luck as it did for our ancestors when they first came to this island."

While Christopher examined the gift with delight, Liliana turned back to Luke. "Perhaps the ceremony you just saw will quiet our volcano." She shot Luke a dark glance. "Tell me, my cousin, what will you do to appease Madame Pele?"

Rosie looked with interest at Luke.

"Well," he said, "I could always throw her a virgin."

"What's a virgin?" demanded Christopher.

"Never mind, dear," Rosie said, putting an arm around him. "Try the roast pork." She dished a small sampling of all the different foods onto Christopher's plate and her own. As they circulated the platters, hunger and the tempting fragrance of the hot delicacies preempted conversation.

After Rosie was full, she gazed with awe at Liliana, who was shoveling a third mammoth pile of food onto her dish. Even Luke couldn't keep up with her. The conversation turned to Mrs. Clarke's departure.

"When are you going back to Santa Barbara?" Luke asked.

Mrs. Clarke scooped up poi with two fingers and licked it off. "Next weekend," she replied. "I'm leading a tarot-card reading seminar."

Liliana pointed a forkful of chicken at Christopher. "Who's going to take care of the little one?"

Rosie sighed. "Well, I'm still looking. As a matter of fact I'm interviewing several people next week."

Liliana chewed thoughtfully. "I'm available."

There was silence while Rosie stared at her in surprise. "You are?"

"There was a fire in my craft store last month," Liliana said between mouthfuls. "It will be at least two months before I can open it again. Meanwhile, I can sit for the boy."

Christopher's head swiveled to his mother. "Liliana's nice. I like her."

Rosie felt flustered. She didn't really know Liliana that well. She shifted the leftover poi on her plate with her knife. "Well..."

"Think of the advantages. Christopher would certainly learn the local culture," Mrs. Clarke chimed in.

Suddenly Luke added his deep voice to hers. "No matter what political differences my cousin and I have, I can vouch for her honesty and integrity. When Liliana sets out to do a job, she does it right." He laughed at himself. "I should know."

Luke and Liliana grinned across the table at each other. As Rosie looked at the two faces, she saw that Luke and the large Hawaiian woman were really friendly adversaries.

Rosie had been worried about finding someone reliable for Christopher. And all the people she was interviewing were strangers. Luke and Liliana knew each other well. *A bird in hand,* she thought. Reassured, she finally said, "With a recommendation like that how can I say no? Liliana," she declared, holding out a hand, "you're hired."

Chapter Six

After the feasting wound down, Christopher scrambled off the bench and wandered over to the fish ponds with Rosie in tow.

"Did you like the luau?" Rosie asked.

"Yeah, but it went on too long," Christopher replied. He swung the tiki around his neck. "Liliana sure can eat."

"She sure can," Rosie said, concealing a smile and wondering how she'd keep her refrigerator stocked when Liliana came to the house. She glanced over her shoulder at the picnic table where the Hawaiian woman and Luke were still tossing off cheerfully barbed remarks. When she looked back, she was just in time to see Christopher skim several stones across the still waters. "Oh, no, no," she exclaimed. "The fish in the pond don't like that."

Christopher, who held another rock in his fist, looked frustrated. Quickly, so Rosie didn't see, he pocketed the stone on top of others he'd picked up back at the sacred site.

"Let's go back now," Rosie said, taking his hand. "It's time to get you home to bed."

But as they returned to the table, a group of voluptuous young women in ti-leaf shirts, lei-smothered bandeaux and flowered wreaths had come out to dance. Rosie bent down to Christopher. "Do you want to stay and watch this?"

He shook his head and rubbed at his eyes.

"Oh, you look tired." She ran gentle fingers through his hair.

"He does," Mrs. Clarke agreed. "And so am I." She got to her feet and stretched. Then she took the little boy's hand. "Let me take him home, dear, and you watch the dancing. I'm sure Luke will give you a ride back."

Irritated by her mother's obvious matchmaking, Rosie opened her mouth to protest, but Luke broke in. "Certainly I'll take you home."

"You must not miss our dancing," Liliana exclaimed. "Our girls are wonderful." She clicked her tongue in approval.

"Yes, dear," Mrs. Clarke said, giving Rosie a little punch in Luke's direction. "Do stay."

I'm beginning to feel like a marshmallow, Rosie thought. She was too accustomed to being in charge of her own life to appreciate being manipulated by other people. On the other hand, after so much fuss, it would be rude to insist on leaving. What's more, she really did want to see the dancing.

After kissing Christopher, she watched Mrs. Clarke lead him away to the car. Turning back after it pulled away, she saw that Luke had been watching the boy's departure. Something in the intent expression on his face as his eyes followed the rental car gave her a moment's disquiet. But then they were both distracted by the reappearance of the drummers.

While setting the rhythm for the kahunas the drummers had been solemn. Now, as the beautiful wahines began to sway their hips in languid circles, the muscular young men sitting behind them looked more relaxed. Three ukelele players in white pants and Hawaiian shirts came out and stood in front of the drummers. To complement the sinuous motion of the dancers' lithe bodies, they started off with the slow strains of "Lovely Hula Hands," followed by "Blue Hawaii" and "Sweet Leilani." The girls' faces had taken on a dreamy, romantic appearance that was a counterpoint to the sultry motions of their undulating arms and hips.

As Rosie watched, she thought of other hulas she'd seen. There'd been commercial exhibitions at hotels and impromptu performances at parties, but none had moved her like this one. Maybe it was the torchlit setting, the moonlight reflecting on the fish ponds and the gentle clattering of the wind in the tall palm trees. Or maybe it had more to do with her own emotional riptide and the man whose thighs were within inches of hers on the picnic bench.

She was all too aware of Luke leaning back and putting his arm on the table behind them both. As she sensed his motion and inhaled the fresh, healthy scent of his skin, the hairs on the back of her neck lifted and she suppressed a faint shiver. The hula, among other things, had been a fertility rite. Since before recorded time young men and maidens had come together in the dancing circle to display themselves to one another.

The female with the driving motion of her hips and her half-naked beauty promised the mysterious secrets of womanhood, and the drummers, as they pounded out their hypnotic rhythms, promised the vigor of the responsive male. Inevitably the frenzy of the dance had led to passion. Now, as the age-old rite gathered energy, Rosie could feel its potency.

As if her head had a will of its own, it turned and she found herself staring into Luke's eyes. For a moment, as she seemed to sink into their depths, she had the uncomfortable feeling that he'd read her erotic thoughts. Quickly she looked away, suddenly aware of the heat of Luke's body and the energy that seemed to emanate from it and surround and capture her like an invisible net. They were sitting too close, she thought, yet she felt self-conscious about suddenly scooting away. Even though she wasn't looking at him now, his expression haunted her. All the while the throbbing beat of the drums hummed through her veins. Clenching her hand in her lap, she fought the primitive tides of feelings flowing through her.

LUKE'S GAZE LINGERED on Rosie's averted profile. Out of the corner of his eye he was very aware of the dancers and their sensual invocation.

What was she thinking? Was she remembering the night they had made love? Lately he'd been remembering it with disturbing frequency. And when he'd tried to sort it out in his mind, he'd only come up against confusion. Luke was a man who rejected confusion and he'd taken that rejection out on Rosie that night five years earlier.

Now he was beginning to think of what had happened very differently. He and Rosie had never had a chance. The circumstances had been against them. He'd been too close to his grief and so had she.

He shifted slightly so that he could look at her without seeming to stare. Her long red tresses gleamed in the moonlight. His fingers itched to touch the shiny strands. She had such a neat, clean profile. Her eyebrows were smooth wings over her wide, intelligent blue eyes. He liked her slightly retroussé nose, and suddenly had the crazy impulse to reach out and run his forefinger gently down its bridge. His gaze dropped to her mouth. It was delicately cut, yet with an underlip full enough to be temptingly kissable. He had a sharp memory flash of taking her in his arms and sealing her lips with his and then pulling her pliant body against his taut one.

Luke felt a throbbing tightness in his slacks. Ruefully he crossed his legs and shifted his thighs away from Rosie's. The combination of her nearness, his thoughts and the erotic storm being brewed up by the performers had inflamed him more than he cared to reveal.

A sharp jab to his back brought Luke's head around. Liliana's grinning face was three inches from his. Instinctively he drew back.

"You like the dancers, huh?" Liliana asked.

He cleared his throat. "They're terrific."

She gave him a throaty chuckle and a knowing wink.

When the young women were finished and the formal part of the evening had ended, the ukelele players broke into a lively version of "My Little Grass Shack." A few Pele's Partisans coaxed out some of the guests and together they began to do their own impromptu versions of the hula. Grinning broadly, Mr. Fan gyrated like Elvis tanked up on mai tais. Mary and Bill Burns faced each other, their leis bouncing, as they shimmied like palm trees in the wind.

Liliana clapped her hands. She leaned across Luke and tapped his and Rosie's shoulders. "You watch me. I'll really show you how it's done."

Leaping from the bench so quickly that it quivered behind her, she barreled out into the center of the dancers. Despite her bulk, when she began to sway she looked graceful. A mysterious smile lit her generous face. Her hands made wavelike beckoning gestures to the men who watched her appreciatively on the sidelines.

Liliana would never win a beauty contest, yet Rosie could see the earthy attraction she possessed. Liliana's smile broadened and a gleam came into her eyes. Her hips still rolling, she drifted toward the table where Rosie and Luke sat mesmerized.

The music changed to a more enticing, suggestive rhythm, and reaching out, Liliana grabbed Luke and Rosie by the hand and pulled them up and onto the dance area with her. "You both have hips," she said, bestowing a mischievous sideways glance at each of them. "Show me how you can shake them."

Rosie blushed and might have sat back down, except that Mary and Mr. Fan were urging her on. And she knew if she tried to escape Liliana would yank her right back out. Rosie glanced over at Luke. His dark eyes glowed between his long black lashes.

"You heard the lady. We'd better oblige."

His gaze never leaving her face, he began to rotate his narrow hips in a slow circle. His white jeans were tight in all the right places, and Rosie found she didn't need much imagination to picture what was beneath them. Feeling herself go warm all over, she lifted her gaze and looked over at Liliana and Mary and made a feeble attempt to imitate their choreography.

"Here, let me show you," Luke said, coming around behind her. Then his hands were on her hips and he began slowly but firmly rotating them. "It's all in the knees," he whispered in her ear.

His warm breath feathered the sensitive lobe. As Rosie turned her head and caught the wicked glint in his eyes, she felt a tide of hot blood surge through her.

"Watch me," he suggested with mock innocence, and circled around in front of her again. Then he proceeded to demonstrate that despite everything he was a real *kanaka,* a son of Hawaii. He definitely knew what to do with his body. He moved with a graceful athleticism, yet there was an unmistakable provocativeness in his slow, sinuous grind that vividly called up the sexual act to her overheated imagination.

As if her body was answering its summons, her hips began to sway in a mirror image. Heat radiated from her legs and suffused her skin. Though she tried to look away from Luke, her eyes kept returning to his. A silken cord seemed to be spinning out between them, its threads twining and coiling, drawing them together ever more tightly. A thought wove itself into her consciousness. If Luke were to reach out and take her into his arms right now, she wouldn't be able to draw back.

At last the music ended and the dancers sank back exhausted onto the picnic benches. People stood around chatting and the hedonistic spell invoked by the music began to dissipate.

As the villagers and Pele's Partisans gathered up leftover food, Liliana began lobbying her cause. Plodding from group to group, she thanked the BICC members and her other guests for coming and pressed her view that construction anywhere near the sacred grounds should be stopped immediately. "Otherwise," she kept repeating almost like a chant, "Madame Pele will punish us all."

She saved Luke for last. "Well, my bruddah," she said, seizing his elbow, "I hope this feast has reminded you of your heritage."

"It certainly has," he replied.

"Your family is *kama'aina.* Generation after generation, the Devillerses have received the gifts of the island gods. But," she said, lifting a warning finger, "gifts can be taken away. You must think not only of yourself and your ambitions, but of your unborn *keiki.*"

"I'll take that into serious consideration," Luke was saying. "I care about this island very deeply, Liliana. I feel I've built on it responsibly. And I'm not only thinking about the moment. I'm thinking about my legacy to my heirs, as well. If I ever have children I would want them to live at Orchid Cliffs and uphold the Devillers's tradition on this island with honor."

"You must have children to carry on our traditions. And you will," Liliana pronounced.

As Rosie listened to their words, alarm shook her heart. There was nothing casual in the way either put their comments. If Luke really meant what he said it would have unsettling implications for Christopher. She'd been flirting with the idea of telling Luke the truth about their son tonight, but now she drew back.

While Rosie and Luke had been dancing, she'd forgotten her fears. Caught in the heat of the native rhythms, once again she'd let herself be captivated by the strong sexual attraction between them. Now she regretted that and kicked herself for not listening to her first practical impulse. If she'd gone home with her mother, she wouldn't have the prospect before her of driving alone through the night with Luke. No matter what, she vowed, she wouldn't let herself get lulled again.

Luke and Liliana lingered for another few minutes, debating enthusiastically. Finally the Hawaiian woman turned to Rosie. "We must make arrangements for me to care for your little one."

Rosie nodded.

After they'd exchanged telephone numbers, Luke took Rosie's arm and guided her along the rim of the torchlit fish ponds. Moonlight glittered on their smooth dark surfaces. Every now and then the mirrorlike patina was broken by the leap of an orange *koi*.

"The fish seem active tonight," Rosie commented, feeling the need to break the tense silence between them.

"The music must have stirred them up."

Rosie shrugged. "Maybe. Or perhaps it was Christopher. He was skipping stones across the pond earlier. The poor fish probably thought they were caught in a meteor storm."

"They're probably used to it. All small boys like to toss rocks—it's the Y chromosome. In fact," he added after a weighty pause, "Chris reminds me a bit of myself when I was his age."

Rosie's stomach lurched. Great, she'd stepped right into it. Why had she brought up the subject of Christopher? "Why? Were you a troublemaker when you were small?"

"Yes, and I still am." His eyes glinted. "Don't pretend you don't know, Rosie."

Her eyes narrowed. "Know what?"

"That I was trying to stir up a little trouble back there when we were dancing."

"Trouble?"

He took her chin in his hand and grinned roguishly down at her. "Rosie Clarke, you like to pretend that you're so prim and proper, but I know all too well there's a hot-blooded woman beneath that cool, scientific veneer. Quite appropriate for a volcanologist, I might add."

Rosie pulled away. "I think I'd better get home." Her voice was husky, even to her own ears. And as Luke's gaze drifted over her, she knew he'd caught the quality to it, as well.

"YOUR WISH is my command," Luke answered. But his tone was ironic. Home was where he wanted to take her, but not to her cottage. He was incredibly aroused by this beautiful woman, and he wanted nothing more than to find some quiet place where they could be alone together. He let his gaze skim her figure and imagined himself slowly peeling away the sarong from her soft curves. How would she react?

Tucked in the more rational part of his mind, however, was another question. Just who was Christopher's father? Ever since he'd seen the boy, that had been a burning issue in his mind. And he was determined to get an answer to his question.

As Luke guided his truck up out of the valley and along the winding coastline road, another uncomfortable silence settled between them. Rosie had run out of energy for chitchat. She looked over at Luke's strong profile and felt the sexual tension that had been growing all evening between them. It was obvious that he was brooding about something. Was it the erotic spell of the dance floor? Perhaps it was something safer—the arguments between him and Liliana, maybe.

"I know you and Liliana disagree, but you seem to like each other," Rosie ventured.

Instead of answering, Luke rounded a curve and pulled the car into a scenic overlook. He switched off the ignition and for a moment sat looking down at the crashing waves below them. Beneath the bodice of her flowered sarong, Rosie's heart thumped.

He turned to her and stroked her hair, then he leaned forward to kiss her. Hungrily his lips sought her mouth and she felt herself yielding to him. Then suddenly she was pushing him away, flattening her hands against his chest to hold him at bay.

"Rosie, what is it?"

She leaned her back against the passenger door and shook her head. "I'm not ready for this, Luke. This isn't what I came back to Hawaii for."

Luke was silent for a minute. "What did you come back for, Rosie? Was it the job? Or was it something else?"

"The job, of course," she replied. "What else would it be?"

Leaning his left arm on the top of the steering wheel, Luke studied her. "Rosie," he said, "I think there's more to why you're here. We need to talk."

She closed her eyes tightly and let out a sigh. Here it was—the moment she'd been dreading ever since she'd arrived on the island. She opened her eyes but couldn't look at him. Taking the coward's way out, she said, "Luke, it's late. Whatever it is, can't it wait?"

"No, Rosie. It can't."

"All right."

If they were going to have this conversation, she didn't want to have it in the close confines of the truck. Before Luke could say anything more, she opened the door and stepped outside. The wind off the ocean had picked up. It lifted her hair, sending cool ripples of sensation along her bare shoulders. She leaned her hands on the seawall and gazed down on the moonlit flecks of white foam flung up from the rocks below.

Luke had followed behind her. She could feel his body looming inches from hers as he came up alongside her and curled his large hands over the edge of the stone barrier.

"I've been doing a lot of thinking about that night we spent together," he began.

Rosie said nothing.

"I even went back and checked the calendar to be sure of the exact date."

"You want to celebrate the anniversary?" she said with so much bitterness she surprised herself.

"Hardly." He faced her. "You have every right to be angry, but it did happen. On November 4, to be precise."

Rosie's heart began beating rapidly.

"Rosie, when is Christopher's birthday?"

"You want to celebrate that, too?"

"Rosie," he said, grabbing her shoulders and pulling her around to face him. "I want to know who Christopher's father is. You've been very evasive about it."

She had been avoiding his gaze. Now she tossed up her head and looked at him through narrowed eyes. "Maybe it's none of your business."

"I think it might be. And I'd like an answer."

As Rosie studied Luke, she saw that he was anything but the charming dance partner he'd been at the luau or even the seductive lover who'd kissed her a few minutes earlier. His chin looked rock hard and so did his eyes. He appeared as forbidding as the dark cliffs surrounding them. An animal threat radiated from him that made her want to draw back and protect herself. Yet at the same time, Rosie felt irrationally angry about his demand for information about the child she'd borne, protected and supported alone all these years.

"You said you were never married."

"That's right."

"Fine. But unless you've accomplished an immaculate conception, Christopher must have been fathered by somebody."

As she lifted her chin, her adrenaline pumped fiercely. Like a mama bear backed into a corner, she was prepared to fight to defend her cub. "How do you know I haven't had dozens of lovers? Or for that matter, I might have been artificially inseminated. It's not so unusual these days, you know."

"So soon after you left the island? Somehow I doubt it." Luke eyed her ironically. "You're beautiful enough to have attracted a fleet of lovers, but I can't imagine you sleeping around with just anybody."

"You surprise me. After all, I did go to bed with you."

"But we know how that happened, Rosie. You and I had known each other for months. We were close and we were vulnerable. And we were also, as I remember, too caught up in the moment even to think of using birth control." Tightening his grasp on her shoulders, he drew her face up close to his and looked searchingly into her eyes.

Rosie tried to resist, but his forceful grip controlled her easily. "I want to know if Christopher is my son."

Another tide of anger surged through Rosie and in that moment she threw aside all the considerations that had persuaded her to come back to Hawaii in the first place. What right did this man have to treat her so high-handedly? He was behaving with her as if he were the lord of the manor and she were some kitchen wench he could command at will. How could she have forgotten Luke's arrogance? He really was the king of Orchid Cliffs and all it surveyed. Here on the Big Island, his sprawling estate was a fiefdom. He was used to commanding and having his way. If he was to decide that Christopher belonged to him, how could she fight him? It had been a terrible mistake to come back.

When Rosie remained stubbornly silent, he shook her. "Tell me the truth, damn it."

With all her strength, she tore away from him. Then she whirled, faced him and spat out, "The truth is that Christopher is my son and nobody else's." She let that sink in. "I don't know who his father was. It could have been the shipboard romance I had on the way to Alaska," she improvised. "It could have been the trapper I took up with when I first got to Homer. Or maybe it was the artist up on China Poot Bay."

"An artist?"

"Why, yes," Rosie went on, feeling a pang at her deception, yet determined that if she was going to tell a story it would be a good one. "He lived in a cabin overlooking Cook Inlet and he painted wildlife and wonderful landscapes of the Alaska range."

"I suppose he was a wonderful lover," Luke snapped.

"Terrific."

"But not interested in fatherhood."

"Maybe I was the one who wasn't interested in settling down."

Momentarily silent, Luke clamped his hands on his hips.

"Well, it hardly matters now, does it?" she added.

"I don't believe you."

She shrugged. "Your choice."

"That's right. It is my choice. And I'm going to do something about it. If you won't tell me the truth I'm going to find out for myself."

"You just do that," she shot back with far more confidence than she felt. "You've always been able to buy everything you wanted. Let's see if the truth is for sale, too."

Chapter Seven

"Let's call a truce," the note read. "Can we start peace negotiations soon? Luke." Rosie crumpled the paper and tossed it alongside the spray of blossoms the delivery boy from Orchid Cliffs had brought ten minutes earlier.

"How lovely!" Mrs. Clarke exclaimed as she danced through the kitchen door with Christopher at her heels. "From Luke?"

"Yes," Rosie said between her teeth. She hadn't mentioned anything to her mother about the ugly confrontation after the luau. Her mother would be appalled at her behavior, at the lies she'd told and the way she'd dodged Luke's cross-examination. After all, he did have a right to some answers.

All day long at work she'd felt guilty. She'd fretted that by her deception she'd made an even bigger mess of the situation. As she'd worked in the lab, charting Kilauea's upheavals, she'd held an inner debate. But no side had won. She just wasn't sure what to do. Finding this peace offering from Luke the minute she'd gotten home hadn't helped.

Mrs. Clarke crossed to the table and fingered the striped pink-and-white throat of an extravagant bloom. "How romantic."

"Mom, Luke has a ranch carpeted with these things. It probably didn't take much to tell a houseboy to pluck an armful and trot them here."

"Yes, dear," Mrs. Clarke replied patiently. "The important thing, however, is that Luke thought of it. We'll have to remember to thank him when we go to his house Saturday."

"His house? Saturday? What are you talking about?"

"Don't you remember? Luke promised Chris he could see his collection. You know, the canoe buster and shark teeth. In fact, we had a nice little lunch today with Luke, didn't we, Chris?"

"Yeah, hot dog and milk shake," Chris interjected. The little boy was sitting on the floor making Kong, his beloved stuffed monkey, climb the back of a rattan chair.

"You did?" Rosie kept her voice even and tried not to frown.

"Afterward he went with us to the barbershop when Chris got his hair cut," Denise continued. "Wasn't that thoughtful of him?"

"Yes, very."

"That's when he reminded us about coming to see the canoe buster. Not that Chris needed reminding. He was talking about it all morning."

"Yeah, yeah," Christopher chanted to Kong.

"Now, don't ask me what a canoe buster is," Mrs. Clarke rattled on. "It's some sort of old weapon—you know the kind of thing that would fascinate boys. Just the thing for male bonding," she added with a knowing wink.

While Rosie stared in consternation, Christopher scrambled off the floor and jumped up and down. "Canoe buster. Wham. Wham," he said, making ramming gestures with his arms.

Rosie had completely forgotten Luke's promise, but obviously Christopher, Luke and her mother hadn't. *Oh, Lord,* she thought. *The last thing I need is a visit to Orchid Cliffs.* But with Christopher in such a fever of anticipation, how could she back off?

THE NEXT FEW DAYS passed quickly. Everyone up at the observatory was nervous about the evidence coming in from Kilauea. Calculations indicated that the slopes of the shield volcano were swelling ominously. The work schedule had been unusually frenetic. Emergency plans for possible evacuations were being revised daily.

At night, driving home to Black Crescent Beach, Rosie could see the foreboding plume of smoke that hung over the area. It really seemed as if Pele was gathering herself for an all-out fire storm. Meanwhile, buried in her work and concerned about the potential disaster that loomed over the island, Rosie had allowed some of her anxieties about Luke's threat to recede to the back of her mind. There was no way he could be absolutely certain of Christopher's parenthood, she told herself.

Friday night Kilauea rumbled like an old man with sinus problems. And Saturday dawned with a hazy red sun.

"Oh, dear," Mrs. Clarke said that afternoon as she, Rosie and Christopher walked out of the house to the car. "If only I could take some window cleaner to that sky. It just looks as if everything is covered with a smudge of smoke."

"That's because it is," Rosie said, gazing up toward the mountains with knit brows. The windshield was proof of the reality of the smoke. Before they could set off, they had to wash away the grit Kilauea had dusted over it.

"I'd be concerned about you and Christopher staying here after I leave," Mrs. Clarke allowed after they'd settled themselves in the car. "But I know you'll be sensible and get off the island if there's any real danger. Won't you, dear?"

Rosie patted her mother's hand reassuringly. "I'd never take any chances with Chris, so don't worry."

They both glanced at the back seat, where the little boy sat safely belted next to Kong. Oblivious to their conversation, he was making motor sounds as he ran a toy truck up and down the seat cushion.

Turning back to the steering wheel, Rosie started the car and they headed out to the main road. She hadn't seen or talked to Luke since their argument, and she braced herself. This afternoon on his turf was going to be awkward.

"What a beautiful house!" Mrs. Clarke marveled as they pulled into Orchid Cliffs's circular driveway. As Rosie nodded her agreement, it suddenly occurred to her that one day, if the truth was known, Christopher might preside over this lavish estate. Did she have the right to interfere with that?

Five minutes later they were inside the big front hall, being greeted by Aunt Beatrice in a flowing caftan. With a fulsome show of hospitality, she led them past the ancestral portrait of Queen Analani in the hall and then into the huge living room, where they came face to face with the statue of the volcano goddess Pele.

"So that's the troublemaker," said Mrs. Clarke, shaking her finger playfully at the statue.

"You'd better watch out, Mother. That lady doesn't have much of a sense of humor," Rosie warned.

Neither did Beatrice. She looked slightly offended. "This is an original Makahaka," she said.

"Oh, a Makahakaka," Mrs. Clarke answered. "That's different."

Behind her mother Rosie cringed slightly and rolled her eyes. It was going to be a long afternoon.

At that moment Christopher tugged at Beatrice's skirt. "Where's Luke?" he asked.

Beatrice stared down. "Oh, he'll be here in a minute, dear."

Was it her imagination, Rosie wondered, or was Luke's imposing aunt giving Christopher an unusually prolonged scrutiny?

Beatrice's gaze went from Rosie to Mrs. Clarke and back. "What an adorable little boy. Where did he ever get such dark hair and eyes? You two are so fair. Was he adopted?"

Rosie colored. "No. He's all mine."

Christopher looked at her oddly and for a crazy moment she felt like gathering her son protectively in her arms and rushing him back out to the car. Though the subject of his father had come up before, she'd always been able to maneuver around it. But soon his questions were going to become more insistent. Hopefully Beatrice's inquiry hadn't planted the seed.

At that moment Luke came in from the back of the house. As he saw Rosie and Christopher together in his home, he experienced a surge of male satisfaction. This is where they belonged, he found himself thinking, and this is where they would be if he had anything to say about it. For a moment, his and Rosie's eyes met and he knew she was remembering his last words to her: "If you won't tell me the truth, I'll find it for myself." He didn't regret what he'd said, but, at the same time, he didn't want her running for the hills because she saw him as a threat. He smiled warmly.

With easy grace he dropped down into a squat before Christopher. "Well, buddy, what's it going to be first? Ice-cream sundaes or shark teeth?"

The little boy's eyes widened in delight and he hesitated like a puppy torn between two meaty bones. "Both."

"We can't do both at once, honey. Which do you think Kong wants to do first?" Rosie asked.

Christopher pretended to consult his monkey and then played ventriloquist. "Ice cream!"

Luke chuckled and once again his eyes met Rosie's. "This is a boy who knows what he wants. I like that."

"Just like another little boy I used to know," Beatrice chimed in.

"Let's go out to the lanai," Luke suggested, ignoring the knowing look that had come over his aunt's face, which he suspected Rosie had noticed, as well.

They followed him through the French doors onto the flagstone patio. Seconds later, Mrs. Waneka wheeled out a glass serving cart. It was covered with blue-and-white china dishes brimming with whipped cream, cherries, pineapple, chocolate shavings, walnuts, hot fudge, butterscotch, macadamia nuts and sprinkles. Three molded plastic containers held chocolate, vanilla and strawberry ice cream.

"I'll be the soda jerk," Luke offered, picking up a scoop. "No comments, please."

"We didn't utter a word," Rosie joked. She had decided to try to put the best face on things that she could. It wasn't lost on her that Luke was giving a show for her mother's and Christopher's benefit. She couldn't believe that he'd go to so much trouble for just any child. This ice-cream extravaganza had been carefully orchestrated to win a little boy's heart.

While Christopher cheerfully gorged himself on a banana split, the adults ate smaller sundaes and chatted.

"The orchids you sent were so beautiful," Mrs. Clarke said. "Tell me, how did your family get started in growing them?"

"It's a fascinating and romantic story," Beatrice began. "As you came into the house, you probably saw the painting of Queen Analani. The queen was Luke's and my ancestor," she said importantly.

"Yes, watch how you hold your spoon," Luke interjected with a grin. "You're in the presence of hallowed royalty."

"You can joke about it all you want," Beatrice declared with great dignity, "but you should be proud of your family's heritage."

"I am proud of it, but I'm also getting very tired of hearing about it," Luke muttered.

Ignoring him, Beatrice turned back to Mrs. Clarke. "Luke's great-great-great-grandfather was a French planter who came here in the 1700s. It was he who married Analani and founded our line. And it was he who brought the first orchid to our shores."

"'French planter' is a euphemism for 'reformed pirate,'" Luke cut in.

Scowling at her irreverent nephew, Beatrice huffed, "Luke, you know quite well Guy Devillers was French aristocracy. That story about his being a pirate was just a tale your grandfather told to irritate your poor grandmother."

"Worked, too," said Luke. He ladled another spoonful of butterscotch onto his vanilla ice cream.

"Despite my nephew's flippancy," Beatrice declared to Mrs. Clarke, who was listening attentively, "I believe, and

I think Lucas really agrees, that family is important. Blood will tell, you know."

"Blood lines may be important, but so is what you've done in your past lives," Denise countered with perfect composure.

"Oh?" Beatrice looked taken aback.

Rosie swallowed a smile. *Beatrice is in for a real treat,* she thought.

"For example," Denise continued, "I happen to know that I was a gunslinger with the James gang back in Dodge City in the late 1800s. Before that, I was a maharani in a northern Indian province. I used to ride in a jewel-encrusted howdah on the back of a big white elephant in the Himalayas." She made an extravagant gesture with her hand. "And I was a battlefield nurse in the Civil War. All of it has contributed to my karma in this life."

Beatrice's mouth had dropped open. "What?"

Rosie sneaked a look at Luke and saw that the corners of his lips were quivering. Obviously he, too, was trying to swallow a grin.

"Now, Rosie here," Mrs. Clarke went on, "has been resisting all my efforts to explore her past. I'm working on her, though. One of these days, I'll get her to do a past-lives regression. What insight she'll have into her present then!"

Rosie said nothing.

"And how about you, Beatrice? With your interest in history and family, wouldn't you like to know who you've been and what you've done?"

Beatrice put down her spoon. "Sounds interesting, but perhaps another time." Deliberately she craned her neck in Christopher's direction. "I see our young man has finished his ice cream. Lucas, I think we should all go look at the canoe buster now."

"Yes, indeed," Luke said. Putting down his dish, he got up, and so did everyone else. Taking Christopher's somewhat sticky hand, he led him over to the sink and helped him wash. Then the group went back into the west wing of the house and down a long corridor.

"I'd need a road map if I lived here," Mrs. Clarke whispered to Rosie.

"Or at least some bread crumbs," Rosie whispered back.

Luke's collection of Hawaiian antiquities had a large room to itself. Ancient carvings, a four-foot wooden idol, pottery and spear tips, fishing traps, a magnificent feather cape, chunks of coral, and other artifacts were all on display.

"We've donated most of our collection to the historical society," Luke said as he led the little party along a wall of glass display cases. "But the family wanted to keep some items to pass down. I suspect eventually everything will wind up in a museum."

Chris had paused in front of the spear tips, which Luke then took out and let him handle. When they came to the weapons case, Luke unlocked it and withdrew a large stone mallet. Carefully he held the heavy weapon so Christopher could cup it in his hands.

"Let me tell you how these things were used. Just picture two warring canoes out at sea. They'd bash each other's boats with something like this until one got so splintered it sank. There are only two canoe busters in existence now."

"And a good thing," Mrs. Clarke murmured.

Chris reached out to grab the strange object. "Oh, boy, wow!"

"It's very, very heavy," Luke told him. "But we can hold it together."

As Rosie watched, she couldn't help but be impressed with the way Luke was handling himself with Chris. Once again a stab of fear shot through her. With Luke's imperious aunt towering over her on one side and Chris staring adoringly at Luke on the other, she felt more threatened and confused than ever. And it didn't help that her own mother was acting like a cheerleader for family unity.

A few minutes later, they moved on to the next display, where Luke pulled out a shark's jaw encased in a Plexiglas cube about a foot square. "I caught this little fellow when I was about ten, and my dad cleaned it up and had his business end mounted."

Clearly awestruck, Christopher held out his hands and Luke placed the large cube in them.

"Careful now." Luke made sure Christopher could hold it before he took away his own hands.

Nervous about Christopher breaking such a valuable memento, Rosie guided the boy over to a table, where she had him set it down. "It's eye level now, so you can still see it and not worry about dropping it."

"Did the shark put up a fight," Chris asked, peering at the rows of razor-sharp teeth.

"I'll say."

"Wow! Can you take me to catch a shark someday?"

"I'd love to, if your mom gives me permission."

Eagerly Christopher turned to Rosie. "Can I? Can I?"

Her eyes met Luke's and registered the challenge in them. "Maybe when you're a little older, dear."

Christopher started to pout, but Luke patted his shoulder. "I've got an idea. Until you're a little bigger and we can go out shark hunting together, why don't you take this home with you? You can keep it until you've caught a shark's jaw of your own."

Rosie's mouth dropped.

"Oh, that's so sweet of you!" Mrs. Clarke exclaimed, surreptitiously nudging her daughter. "I'm sure he'll treasure it."

Rosie was sure Chris would treasure Luke's gift, too. However, she didn't like being manipulated this way. Perhaps it was paranoia, but she was beginning to feel like a fly caught in the web of a very large and clever spider.

"What do you say, Mom?" Luke asked.

What could she say but "Sure, why not?"

"JUST HOW OLD is that boy?" Beatrice demanded soon after the Clarkes walked out the door.

"Four," Luke replied.

Luke's statuesque aunt fingered the fat trademark pearls at her breast. "And how long ago was it that you knew this Rosie Clarke?"

"About five." He busied himself returning the artifacts to the cases.

"Hmm." Beatrice eyed her nephew. "She is a very pretty girl for a *haole.*"

"She's a very pretty woman period." He turned the lock on the display case that held the canoe buster.

"I was surprised when you gave the boy the shark jaw. That's not something you'd hand over to any little boy."

"Chris isn't just any little boy."

"I can see that. And I'm curious." She paused. "Just how well did you know his mother?"

"She was a friend."

"I find it quite interesting that your friend has a child who looks just like you did when you were that age."

"I've been thinking the same thing," said Luke. He glanced out the window to where Rosie's car was just disappearing around the bend in the drive.

"Hmmmph. You know I don't like to pry, but is there any chance he's a Devillers?" Beatrice slid in.

Luke clicked the last case shut and then turned to confront his aunt. "Aunt Beatrice, you do a fine job overseeing the household, but I don't need a manager for my personal life. I'm going to my office to do some work now." With that he strode from the room before she could say anything more.

Ten minutes later Luke sat with a business card before him and dialed the number printed on it. Two phone calls later he'd connected with a man named Jake Edwards in Alaska.

"You've come highly recommended," he said to Edwards. "I want you to do a job for me. I want you to investigate a young woman named Rosie Clarke who worked as a volcanologist out of Homer until a few weeks ago. In particular, I want you to find out who the father of her son was. The boy's name is Christopher Clarke, and he was born four years ago."

After Luke had conveyed the rest of the necessary information to the detective and they'd discussed fees, he hung up. For several minutes, he sat contemplating his next move. Decisively he opened his desk drawer and took out an envelope. Inside it was his trump card. Now to play it.

Chapter Eight

Four days later shafts of late-afternoon sun were filtering through the tall arched windows of Frieda and Jack Hall's new home in Maile Gardens. The house was a cantilevered contemporary, with rounded walls and glass block towers. Its clean lines and graceful curves were a trademark of Luke Devillers's architectural style.

"We'll start on this list tomorrow," said Ky Mahoto, the builder, referring to the list of tasks that needed to be done before the house was finished.

"Don't forget the leak in the kitchen skylight," Luke reminded him firmly as they stood in front of the wraparound glass wall in the living room. "That should be taken care of right away."

"Will do." The builder tucked his pencil behind his ear and closed up the notebook he was writing in.

Frieda Hall, an athletic woman with sparkling green eyes and short gray hair, smiled gratefully.

"And while you're at it, plug up that volcano, too," Jack Hall, Frieda's retired stockbroker husband, added with a laugh.

"I wish." Luke grinned at the couple. They were two of his favorite clients. He wanted everything just right for them. If it were only possible, stopping Pele from making trouble would have been on the top of his list.

Frieda clasped her hands and surveyed the bleached wood floor and cathedral ceiling. "Bravo, Luke and Ky. I'm so thrilled with this house. All our lives Jack and I have dreamed of retiring to a place like this. It's like coming to live in a palace after thirty years in our cramped condo in New York." She gazed out the window at the ocean, spread like crushed blue silk in the distance. "I feel as if all our years of hard work have paid off with a permanent vacation in paradise."

"You're going to love living here," Luke answered, "just the way we all do. And it's my pleasure to welcome you. If there's anything you need after you've settled in, you can give me or Ky a call."

After the Halls had left to go back to their hotel, Luke walked out of the empty house and paused in front of his truck with Ky.

"Nice couple," the builder said.

"Exactly the kind of people I designed Maile Gardens for," Luke said. "They've worked all their lives to retire in a place like this and they really appreciate it. What's more, they're big environmentalists."

"I figured that with all the energy-saving stuff we've installed for them."

Luke nodded. "It cost a little more money up front, but over the long run it'll save them money and keep their conscience clear."

"Speaking of natural resources . . ." Ky murmured. For a moment, they stood looking up at the volcano, registering the pall of smoke that had thickened around its crown.

"I don't like the looks of that," Luke said.

"Me, neither. In all the years I've lived here I've never had such a bad feeling about Kilauea." Ky shook his head. "Well, can't do much about it."

The two men parted, Ky driving off in his pickup and Luke climbing into his car. Switching on the ignition, Luke picked up the car phone and dialed his answering machine. Most of the messages were routine business calls, but the last one made him lean forward and tense his shoulders.

"This is Jake Edwards here," the detective's gruff voice told him. "I have the information you wanted. I'm leaving for the day now, but you can reach me at home after 8:00 p.m. your time." When he gave the number, Luke jotted it down in his pocket calendar. *So I'll be getting some answers before the day is out,* he thought.

MRS. CLARKE LOOKED UP from her mystery novel. "My goodness, they certainly work you hard up at the observatory." She took off her reading glasses and peered at the wall clock. "Good grief, it's 9:30. Have you had anything to eat, child?"

Rosie dropped her briefcase on a chair and plopped down on the cushioned wicker couch. "A salami sandwich."

"Very nutritious."

"Mother."

"Just think of the fat and the nitrates." She made an exaggerated shudder.

"I'll do penance and eat a salad tomorrow."

"Well, I should hope so. Problem is, I won't be here to supervise. It's been a wonderful week for me, but it's time I got back home. All play and no work make Denise a dull old girl."

Rosie laughed. "What time do you want to leave for the airport, Mom?"

"Seven sharp." Mrs. Clarke closed up her novel and put it over by her large straw purse on the table near the door. "Liliana called. She's coming over to sit at 6:30. So everything's taken care of."

"Chris go to bed okay?"

"Just fine. I tucked him and Kong in at 8:00."

"He's going to miss you, Mom."

Mrs. Clarke's eyes got teary and her lips quivered as she smiled. "I'm going to miss him and you, too. And until this volcano business is cleared up, I'm going to worry about both of you." She held up her palm as if giving an oath. "That's a promise."

"Oh, Mom. Maybe you can counteract Kilauea with crystals or something," Rosie replied lightly. Though she didn't want to let her mother know, she was very worried herself. There wasn't yet enough information to call for a general evacuation, but signs pointed to the good possibility of a large eruption. If it did happen, she was certain they could move residents in time to avert any injuries. Still, she worried about the possible damage to property. So many had moved here and built in the past few years and some of those newcomers were probably going to find that their houses and businesses stood in the path of a hot lava flow.

A few minutes later Mrs. Clarke gathered up her things and went to Rosie's bedroom, where she'd been sleeping. Rosie followed her in and grabbed her nightgown, pillow and blanket. After brushing her teeth and washing up, she undressed, slipped the white silky night dress over her head and returned to the living room. While her mother was visiting, Rosie had been camping out on the couch.

Sighing and then stretching, Rosie walked into the kitchen and poured herself a half-inch of Kahlua. Then she padded outside to the porch, where she settled into a rocking chair.

It was a beautiful night, warm with a heaven full of stars and a crescent moon. The soft swish of the waves lulled her and she let her mind wander. She hadn't seen Luke since that afternoon at Orchid Cliffs. Indeed, she'd spent a lot of her week pushing him out of her thoughts.

That hadn't been difficult up at the research center, where the pace of work had been frantic and shifts doubled to try to handle the crushing work load. At home, however, it hadn't been so easy. Chris had enshrined the shark's jaw in the place of honor on his dresser. Each evening when Rosie had returned from work, the little boy had treated her to constant chatter about Luke. He made up amazingly inventive stories about the killer fish, whose needlelike teeth grinned from the Plexiglas cube.

Chris's fascination with Luke and all things Hawaiian wasn't surprising. Over the past two weeks, while she'd been hovering over seismographs, Luke had been courting Chris and Mrs. Clarke, taking them out sight-seeing to the Parker Ranch, the Painted Church, Puuhonua o Honaunau National Historical Park, waterfalls and the botanical garden. It was nice to know that her mother and son were being entertained during the day while she was gone, but the tour director made her very nervous.

Suddenly restless, Rosie put her drink down on the railing, got up and walked off the porch toward the sea. Once she reached the black crescent shore, the sand felt warm and gritty beneath her bare feet and the breeze cooled her shoulders, exposed beneath the thin straps of her gown. The beach was small and private, so she didn't worry about meeting anyone in her night dress. Besides, her silk shift, except where it clung to her curves, looked like a sundress.

For several minutes she stood at the edge of the surf on the hard-packed sand. The moonlit water rolled in from the vast sea with a mesmeric beauty. The whisper of the rush and retreat was soothing. Experimentally she dipped one toe in the water. It felt warm. The breeze whipped her hair around her face, and she pushed the fiery red strands back. Then she walked a little way into the water so that it foamed up around her ankles. She was standing there enjoying the sensation, when a larger-than-usual wave churned up around her calves and wet the hem of her gown.

Stepping quickly back, she hiked the night dress up around her knees and shook it free of droplets. Then she turned toward the shore and froze. A tall, dark silhouette stood planted on the beach. The tousled hair and wide shoulders were unmistakable. It was Luke. How long had he been standing there watching her?

LUKE'S GAZE WAS FIXED on the vision in the water. Moonlight silvered Rosie's long hair and gilded her slim figure. Her damp gown was molded to her body, accentuating her high rounded breasts, curved hips and long slender legs. She looked like a goddess walking out of the sea.

For a long moment a spell seemed to spin itself between them and he couldn't find the angry words that had brought him down there. All he could think of was her beauty, and how much he wanted to stride toward her and take her in his arms.

Giving way to his impulse, he kicked off his sandals and closed the distance between them. Cupping his hands over her naked shoulders, he pulled her soft body against his. His mouth came down on hers and kissed her roughly. Ignoring the surf that rushed and pounded around their legs, he cradled her face between his hands and brushed her brow and then her closed eyelids and cheeks with his lips.

"Rosie," he murmured gruffly, "Rosie."

LUKE HAD TAKEN Rosie by storm. As she stood frozen by astonishment, his kisses fell on her like hot rain. "Luke," she tried whispering in protest, but another kiss silenced her.

Suddenly, long repressed feeling welled up inside her, and a swell of passion swept away her reason. With a will of their own, her fingers went to Luke's broad chest and fanned over his firm muscles. She could feel the rapid thrum of his heart beneath his cotton shirt. As his kisses went on, burning and devouring her, she closed her eyes and reveled in the sensations swirling within her.

With the moonlight shedding its radiance over them and the hypnotic rush and retreat of the sea around them, the scene seemed unreal—more like a dream than something that was actually happening. Luke stroked her back and then let his hand drift from her waist to her rounded bottom, shaped now by wet silk. At the intimate touch, the clouds fogging Rosie's brain cleared. Suddenly she realized that this was no dream and that she was perilously close to repeating what had happened five years earlier.

Stiffening, she pushed him away. "No, Luke."

For a moment he resisted and drew her closer. But at the continuing pressure of her hands, he finally released her and stepped back. The moment their bodies were free, she whirled around to face the ocean and wrapped her arms protectively across her chest.

Behind her, Luke stood clenching and unclenching his fists. Then he pivoted in the opposite direction and stroke up the beach. Ten yards off he stopped and looked back at her. While he struggled with his frustration and longing, he remembered the anger that had propelled him there in the first place, and it returned full force.

Heading back to her, he seized her upper arm and swung her toward him. At the fierce expression on his face, her eyes widened.

"Rosie," he gritted, "I want to talk to you."

As he dragged her out of the water, she yanked her arm away. "If it's talk you want, you certainly have a strange way of going about starting conversations."

Luke's brows snapped together. "I'm sorry. But I swear, Rosie, you make me crazy. You really shouldn't stand around half-naked in the water."

"I wasn't expecting company." She stopped and faced him. "Why are you here like this? What is this about?"

"Us."

"What do you mean, us? It's over. Five years ago it was over before it started. You told me that yourself."

"That was then. This is now. Rosie, I know the truth."

She stared at him, her eyes flaring in the moonlight. "What truth?"

"Chris is ours. Yours and mine. He's our son."

His declaration fell on her like a lead weight. Her eyes slid from his and for a moment, her resolution wavered. Then, determined to fight for her own, she drew in her breath and met his gaze. "Chris is mine, and that's it."

The groove between his black brows deepened. "Stop playing games, Rosie. Chris is ours. When you stonewalled me, I hired a detective to check things out."

Rosie blinked, thinking fast. What could a detective have found out, she asked herself. "Oh?" she finally said with false bravado. "And just what proof do you have, might I ask?"

"At the moment, only that no other man's name is on Chris's birth certificate, and according to it, he was born exactly nine months after we made love. It didn't take a detective to discover that he looks like me. It's obvious that he's a Devillers."

"Little boys with dark hair and brown eyes are as common as—"

Luke dismissed her rationalization with a brusque wave of his hand. "Rosie, there's more. I have tangible proof."

"What are you talking about?"

"DNA. I had a sample of Chris's hair analyzed."

"You did what?" Rosie's jaw dropped.

"I had his hair analyzed. I sent a sample to a lab in Honolulu, along with a clipping of mine. I haven't got the results but in a matter of weeks I will. Rosie, I know they're going to match."

Rosie tried to speak, but she could only make inarticulate sounds. That Luke would do such a thing had never entered her mind. "His hair? You took a piece of his hair" was all she could say.

"It was when he had his haircut. Don't look at me like that. I had to do something."

Throwing her hands up in the air, she turned away and walked up the beach. Buying time and aware of Luke following at her side, she gazed down at the sand. What should she do? She'd come to Hawaii to tell him about Chris. It was only after she'd arrived that she'd begun to think she'd made a mistake. Now it was too late to go back.

He put a hand on her shoulder and stopped her. "Rosie, let's not drag this out any further. I want to hear it from your lips. Tell me the truth, Rosie."

"All right," she said, facing him defiantly, "you fathered him. But that doesn't make him yours."

"The hell it doesn't." Luke's eyes burned.

Rosie swallowed, but her throat was so dry the effort was merely painful.

"All these years I had a son and you kept him from me. You had no right to do that."

"Stop acting like a tiger with a thorn in his paw and be reasonable. There was nothing between us except a mistaken moment of passion, Luke. Afterward we both regretted it. You more than me. Anyhow, I didn't discover I was pregnant until I was in Alaska. What was I supposed to do? Toss aside my life and my pride and come begging to you for help?"

"What about my life, Rosie?" He thumped his chest. "You never gave me the chance to see Chris's first smile, his first step, hear him call me 'Daddy.' What's your pride to that? You cheated me, Rosie. And I'm pretty damn mad about it."

Bitterness in his voice struck her like a physical blow, and she took a step backward. "Look, you provided nothing for Christopher but the sperm. To you his conception was nothing but an emotional fluke. I'm the one who dealt with the consequences. I bore him, cared for him, loved him. All these years I've done what was best for him."

"Oh, really? How can it be best for him not to know his father or his heritage?"

"His heritage?"

"Orchid Cliffs, this island, it's all part of his legacy and he shouldn't be cheated out of it."

Rosie's heart rattled against her ribs. "It was an impossible situation, and I did what I thought was right."

Luke's jaw hardened and his eyes were unreadable dark pools. "Let me ask you another question. If you really believed you'd done what was right, just why the hell did you come back here?"

"I was offered a job."

"No, Rosie. It's more than that. You came back because you knew you *hadn't* done the right thing. You know what I really think? You came back here to come clean with me. Then for some reason I don't understand, you got cold feet."

She took a deep shuddering breath and clenched her hands at her sides. "Suppose you're right. If I got cold feet, it was for a good reason. I didn't want to be bullied the way you're bullying me now."

Luke stuck his hands in the pockets of his slacks and did a quarter turn. "If I'm angry, it's with good reason. I could have helped you, Rosie, in a lot of ways."

"You're talking about money, I suppose."

"Yes, money. It certainly doesn't hurt. But I could have helped in other ways, too. Why couldn't you trust me, Rosie? I could have been there for you emotionally. And who knows, with Christopher between us, we might have even gotten married and made a real family for him."

Rosie's stomach tightened. "Oh, really? You're telling me you might have been willing to marry me if you'd known I was pregnant? Well, that's very kind of you, Luke. But the last thing I would want is a loveless marriage."

He shot her a long look. "What makes you so sure it would have been loveless," he said more gently.

"Isn't it obvious? That night you dismissed me as if you were some imperial lord and I were a serf. You were sorry about what we'd done, even ashamed."

He shook his head and looked up at the sky. "God, Rosie, won't you ever get past that? My emotions were so mixed up, I didn't know what I thought or felt. Maybe if

I'd been in my right mind," he said, fixing his gaze on her, "I would never have let you go."

She let out a half gasp and then shook her head in disbelief. "That's not good enough, Luke. I don't want your pity."

He took a step toward her. "Damn it, Rosie, it's not pity that I feel when I look at you. Did that feel like pity back there?" he asked, pointing at the spot in the water where they'd embraced so passionately a few minutes earlier.

"You're right. It wasn't pity. It was lust."

Luke went very still, his strong face carved in shadow. "Rosie, I've thought a lot about that afternoon Chris was conceived. It may have had the appearance of a one-night stand, but it was a lot more than that. We were friends—good friends. And, if nothing else, I'd like us to be good friends again."

She looked at him dubiously. Did he really mean that? After all, that's what she'd hoped for when she'd decided to come here. She'd wanted to establish some sort of rapport with Luke that would allow a mutually satisfactory relationship with Chris to develop. It was only after she'd seen Luke with Chris that her emotions had gotten the better of her and she'd convinced herself that she'd made a mistake. Now her only option was to try to work things out so they could all be happy.

"Okay, Luke," she conceded warily. "If you think we can be friends, I'm willing to give it a try."

For the first time that evening he smiled. "Okay. I have a suggestion. There are a lot of things I'd like to know about Chris. Why don't we go back to your place and talk over a cup of coffee?"

She shook her head. "Mom has ears like a Doberman pinscher and I don't want Chris overhearing any of this—

at least not yet. I'm going to have to figure out how to tell him about you."

"Yes, you will. Soon."

When Rosie didn't answer, Luke smoothed a spot on the sand. "Well, then let's have our tête-a-tête here, madame." He swept his hand and bestowed on her another charming smile.

For a moment, she paused, wondering if she was being manipulated. Luke could be irresistible when he chose. The sensible part of her wanted to put this off for a later time when her emotions weren't so jumbled and when she was wearing something more than a damp, silk nightgown. But if she faced the dilemma now, she'd get past the hardest part. And Luke did seem ready to be accommodating. If she put him off for too long, he might be less reasonable.

Nodding, she settled herself on the sand, folding her legs beneath her and smoothing her skirt modestly over them.

He dropped down beside her. "Cold?" he asked, glancing at her bare shoulders.

She rubbed them. "It is getting a bit cooler."

Before she could say anything more, he had unbuttoned and removed his shirt and draped it around her.

"Oh, I didn't mean..." She gazed at his broad shoulders, sculpted by the reflected radiance from the sea.

He shrugged. "It's okay. I'm fine."

For several seconds they watched the moonlight play on the water. Then Rosie felt his eyes on her.

"Tell me how it was when you found out," he said. "I know it couldn't have been easy."

Shifting her weight, she drew her knees to her chest and hugged them. "No, I was really scared. There were so many questions. Would I be able to keep my job? What would my mother think? What would my co-workers and friends think? I'd only been in Alaska for a short while. How would I manage so far away from home?"

"How did you manage?"

Rosie let her mind drift back to that harrowing period. "Luckily I didn't have much in the way of morning sickness and I really didn't show until my sixth month, so that bought me some breathing space. By then everyone knew me a whole lot better and I was lucky. The friends I'd made were so supportive."

"I'm not surprised you found people to help you. You're a person who's easy to care about."

She shot him a sideways glance and picked up a handful of sand, allowing it to sift through her fingers. "Let me back up and start from the beginning." For the next half-hour she described as best she could everything that had happened since she'd fled the island five years earlier—her work in Alaska, her struggle to be a good mother to Chris and to provide good care when she had to work in the field and couldn't be with him.

Listening intently, Luke took her hand, and as his palm closed around hers, she felt how strong and warm it was. The temptation to lean against his shoulder was almost overwhelming.

"You've been through a lot."

"Well, it was difficult at times, but at least Chris never doubted that I loved him. That just came naturally."

"Still, it must have been tough on your own."

She nodded.

"Rosie, there's something I'm curious about. A beautiful woman like you—I would think there'd be men standing in line for you."

Her throat worked. "To be honest, after what happened between us it was a long time before I was interested in a relationship with a man again. And then, though I dated, I just never seemed to meet the right one. Maybe I was just too wary."

He stared at her. "Oh, Rosie, I really did hurt you, didn't I? I'm so sorry. God, I wish so badly that it had all happened differently."

His deep voice sounded so sincere that she gazed up at him in astonishment. "What do you mean? How do you wish it had happened?"

"If we hadn't made love that afternoon, if we'd let more time pass, more time for healing..." His voice trailed off, then he resumed on a stronger note. "Rosie, we made love because all the ingredients for it were there. We liked and respected each other and we were physically attracted. If you'd stayed on in Hawaii and we'd kept seeing each other, it's inevitable that we would have come together eventually. Our timing was just off. If it had only happened a few months or even a year later..."

"Maybe it was bad timing that created Chris, but I can't be sorry for that."

"No, of course not. And it doesn't do any good to be sorry. But why should the past doom the future?" He took her shoulders and drew her toward him. "Why can't we see if there isn't something worth saving?" His hands stroked her hair back from her face and as his warm fingers touched her skin, she began to tremble. "Rosie, Rosie," he murmured, and lowered his mouth to hers.

A few minutes earlier she would have resisted. But the seductive starry night, the hypnotic rush of the incoming waves and the warmth and understanding Luke was showing her all had their effect. How could she be indifferent to his kiss when every time she saw him her heart turned over? At night she dreamed of him and each day, when she looked at her son, she saw Luke's face.

At first Rosie merely submitted to the kiss, closing her eyes and savoring it without committing herself to a response. But as she breathed in Luke's male scent, and as his strong arms went around her and drew her close, she couldn't go on pretending indifference. An aching need bloomed inside her and her lips softened against his.

Soon her mouth parted, accepting the invasion of his tongue and meeting it with a foray of her own. Their tongues entwined and their breaths mingled. Her arms went up around his neck. As her thumbs caressed the curve of the back of his head, she closed her eyes and tipped her head back. "Oh, Luke," she whispered, "we shouldn't—"

"Why not?" he whispered back. He smoothed her hair from her face. "Rosie, I want you so badly."

He kissed her eyelids and then her jaw and then the beating hollow of her throat. As his lips burned over her skin, she shivered with rising excitement. Her breasts were crushed against his naked chest, with only the damp silk of her gown between their flesh.

The shirt he'd draped around her shoulders had fallen off into the sand. Reaching behind her, he spread it flat and then tipped her back. At the same time, one of his hands went beneath the crook of her knees and straightened her legs so that he could gently lay her down on the shirt. All the while she clung to him, bringing him down with her. When they both lay flat with their bodies pressed close, his lips sought her mouth again and they kissed passionately.

Caught up in the heat of Luke's kisses and the feel of his strong, hard body against hers, Rosie had forgotten her caution. His hand stroked her thigh and then moved up higher to caress the smooth curve of her hips. Then, lifting his mouth from hers, he slipped a strap of her gown down over her shoulder and caressed the sensitive strip of skin that had been covered.

"So lovely," he murmured. "Your skin is like satin."

His mouth moved over the curve of her breasts. When she felt his tongue tasting the valley between, she moaned and moved against him in feminine invitation. The velvety night seemed to close around them so that they were sealed in a private world of sensation, of sighs and whispers. For Rosie, Luke's arms and lips and urgent, compelling kisses on the sensitized tips of her breasts were all that existed.

When his warm hands lifted her silk shift from her and she felt the ocean breeze on her naked body, she sighed and kissed him passionately. As he returned her fervor even more ardently, his hands went to the snap on his shorts. A moment later he, too, was naked. As inevitably as the sea just beyond them rushed in to meet the shore, they came together.

With a gasp of satisfaction, Rosie felt Luke thrust deep into her and wrapped her thighs around his lean hips. Together, they strove to make their union perfect.

THE NEXT MORNING Rosie woke up alone in her bed and remembered what had happened the night before on the beach. She groaned and turned her head on the pillow. She didn't exactly regret making love with Luke. How could she regret an experience so beautiful? But she wasn't at all sure that it had been a good idea. Not that much thinking went into it, she conceded. "It's five years ago all over again," she said aloud, "only even more complicated."

Later that morning as Rosie drove her mother to the airport, she looked up at Kilauea. The pulsing unstable volcano seemed to mirror her own confused passions. Could it be that she and Madame Pele were actually soul mates?

Chapter Nine

"I wonder how many surfers this fella chowed down," Liliana said, clicking her strong white teeth at the shark jaw on Christopher's bureau. While the little boy giggled, she made a face like a fish and pretended to chomp a path up his arm.

Chris broke away and waved his monkey at her. Pumping her arms in a mock swimming motion, Liliana chased the two of them around the bed.

"Shark attack, shark attack," Christopher yelled.

"What's going on in here," Rosie asked, peering around the door.

"Save me, Mom. Save me." Giggling all the while, Christopher grabbed his mother's knees and buried his face in her skirt.

Rosie grinned at Liliana and patted Christopher's head. "Look, look, Chris, the shark is all gone. Now Liliana is a lovely mermaid who's going to get you ready for your nap."

With a toss of her long dark hair, Liliana scooped up the little boy and lifted him high. "Time for little fish to go beddy bye."

Smiling, Rosie watched as Liliana carried Christopher over to the mattress. Having Liliana care for Chris had been an inspired decision. The two of them obviously enjoyed each other's company. Sometimes when Rosie stopped in from work to check on things, as she'd done today, she even felt like an intruder.

After she'd kissed Chris and Kong, she left while Liliana was reading a story. Heading to the kitchen, she pulled open the refrigerator to make herself a sandwich. Her break this afternoon was a godsend. Her nerves, like those of everyone else watching over the volcano, were wound tight. She'd worked more than her share of overtime this week and one of her colleagues, who'd recently returned from a vacation, had offered to spell her for a couple of hours. She'd make it up with more overtime tonight.

Rosie had just gotten out the mayonnaise, when she heard a tap on the side door.

Luke's voice came through the screen. "Aha! I've tracked you down." While she stared at him in surprise, he opened the door. "When I called the observatory, they said you'd gone home for the afternoon."

This was the first time Rosie had seen Luke since they'd made love on the beach. He'd phoned her office several times, but she'd had to juggle his calls with interruptions from staff and all the worried people who were flowing in and out of the center these days. Finally she'd agreed to meet him the following weekend to talk over all the decisions they needed to make. Basically she'd been stalling for time because she still wasn't sure how she felt or how she should proceed.

"What brings you out here?" she asked.

"Hopefully, convincing you to have lunch with me. I just couldn't wait until Saturday to see you. I thought we could go for a picnic." He lifted an overflowing basket.

"You're a handy man with a picnic basket, aren't you?"

"Mrs. Waneka deserves all the credit. She packs 'em, I pick 'em up."

Slowly Rosie returned the mayonnaise jar to the refrigerator. She was feeling pretty stressed out from work and not at all ready to discuss Christopher's future. On the other hand Luke, as he stood lounging there with the sunlight from the open door spilling over his tall, lean body and tanned skin, was very tempting. As she surveyed him, she felt her pulse quicken. She supposed she could beg off, pleading work, but it was difficult to refuse the opportunity to get out in the fresh air with this man.

"Luke, lunch sounds great, but I'm not ready to talk about Christopher and all the rest of it yet."

His eyes narrowed slightly, but all he said was "I just want to see you, Rosie." Leaning his wide shoulders against the door frame, he flashed her a smile. All the while his dark gaze surveyed her, seemingly taking in every detail of her appearance, from her long red hair, which she wore loose around her shoulders, to her yellow safari shirt and pants, to her white leather sandals.

Rosie, in turn, couldn't stop herself from looking at him and feeling a rush of heat through her veins as she remembered their lovemaking. Though he was dressed for the construction site in jeans and a dark T-shirt, he must have stopped by Orchid Cliffs to pick up the picnic baskets. From his clean skin and the drops of water sparkling in his dark hair, he'd obviously just showered and shaved. Her fingertips itched to touch his smooth cheek and to explore the contour of his firm chin. She remembered how that mouth, which smiled at her so invitingly now, had felt crushed to hers when they made love.

"I've got a great spot in mind," he was saying.

"I'm sure you do," Rosie murmured. He'd already seduced her twice. Just what did he have in mind for this afternoon? And with her perpetual suspicions about his motives, why did she want to go with him anywhere? She knew the answer.

"I'll be a minute," she said, and went off to tell Liliana she was leaving.

"Since I have to get back to work, I'm going to follow you," she told him when they were both outside in the drive.

For a moment, he looked crestfallen. "Why don't we cruise over to Maile Gardens and leave your car there? I can show you around and then we can head out together to Leilani Overlook for our picnic."

"With all the talk about Maile Gardens, I have been curious," Rosie said. "I'd love to see it."

"Great," he replied, slapping the hood of his truck lightly with the palm of his hand. "I think you'll find it's far from being the devil's den Liliana makes it out to be."

She followed along the twists and turns that meandered back to the main road. A few miles down, his red truck took a right past several black volcanic mounds covered with shell graffiti. "Mary loves George," some lover had spelled out with white shells. "Leslie is my valentine," another graffito declared. Rosie smiled. She'd seen many similar constructions along Queen Kaahumanu in North Chon and they'd never failed to amuse her. Some romantic had obviously transported the idea and spent several days gathering shells.

A few more turns led them to a signpost flanked by carved tiki gods. It read Maile Gardens. Luke's dream development fit so well into the landscape that the houses seemed to nestle into the palm trees, giant ferns and other tropical foliage as if they'd grown wild there.

Luke came to a stop in front of one of the houses under construction and she pulled up behind him. Getting out, he strode over to her window and leaned his elbow on the open ledge. "Want to have a look inside?"

She switched off the ignition. "I'd love to."

They walked single file on the two-by-fours laid across the muddy site. Rosie could hear the sound of sawing and hammering. As they climbed through the opening where the front door would be, she sniffed freshly cut wood.

"There's something special about the smell of a new house," Rosie commented, looking up into the two-story skeleton.

Luke nodded. "Yes, I always feel that way about any building I've designed. But these houses are especially close to my heart. They're passive solar, so they don't burden the environment with power demands. You haven't been back here for several years, so you've missed a lot of the debate about the geothermal power station and the escalating needs for electricity in the islands."

"I've been reading about it," Rosie said, gazing with admiration up at the solar panels. It was wonderful to see houses in sync with their surroundings.

"Even the swimming pools are solar heated."

"This is truly impressive, Luke."

He nodded, pleased by her compliment. "It's as if there's a promise about the future of Hawaii in each one of the houses we've built."

"The future," she said. "Don't you worry about the volcano wiping this all away?"

"Rosie, everyone who lives on the Big Island lives in the shadow of the volcano. But even when Madame Pele has knocked us flat, we've always gotten up and rebuilt. That's as much a part of our heritage as respecting Pele's power."

Rosie understood what he was saying, but she still felt uneasy that he was underestimating Pele's capriciousness.

The eruption they were watching for now could swing in their direction anytime.

As they walked around, he introduced her to each of the workers and his builder, Ky Mahoto.

"Fixed up that skylight in the Hall house," one of the carpenters shouted down. "No more leaks now."

"It's about time," Luke shouted back. "Guess I can put my whip away—for the time being anyway."

"Oh, no, not that!" the workman exclaimed, holding up his hands in mock horror. He gave Rosie a toothy grin. "I want you to know that this guy here is a regular Simon Legree."

Rosie smiled. She could tell by the camaraderie that although Luke was demanding, he was also well liked and respected. He was also designing houses that were not only beautiful but perfectly livable, as she discovered when she met Toshiko Hayakawa and her two children.

"Luke," the petite woman exclaimed, "I saw your truck and I wanted to come and say hello."

"Well, I'm glad you did," Luke replied. He squatted to shake hands with a dark-haired little boy with fat cheeks, who looked about Christopher's age, and a little girl with pigtails, who was, perhaps, a year older.

After Luke introduced the two women, Mrs. Hayakawa invited Rosie in for a tour of her home. Each of the children grabbed Luke's hands and giggled as he swung their arms playfully. Apparently Christopher wasn't the only child Luke charmed.

"We moved in six months ago and we just love it," Toshiko said, showing off her new Japanese-style house with its five spacious bedrooms. The master suite with its sunken green marble whirlpool and private bonsai garden was a haven of tranquil beauty and privacy. And the children's rooms were designed with walls of built-in storage for dolls, toy trucks, puzzles and rock collections.

"This is breathtaking!" Rosie exclaimed twenty minutes later. She was standing in the large open-air living room, with its polished teak floor and dramatic view overlooking the sea. "But what do you do in bad weather?"

"Oh," Toshiko Hayakawa said, smiling flirtatiously at Luke, "this genius of a man has thought of everything." With that, she walked to a corner of the open wall and pulled at a door tucked in the corner. Its glass panels folded out like an accordion. Suddenly the room had a solid wall of window.

Rosie clapped her hands with real admiration. "How clever."

"Yes, even in bad weather we have a marvelous view. It's important to my husband," Toshiko confided. "His job is so stressful. The serenity he's found here is better than a medicine cabinet full of pills."

"I can appreciate that," Rosie said. "It certainly is marvelous to look out at the ocean from your lovely garden. From what I've seen everything about Maile Gardens is spectacular."

And she repeated that to Luke as he drove her along the winding roads of the project and back out to the road in his truck.

"When we're done, we'll have three dozen houses here—all different and all looking as if they belonged to the island."

He spoke with such obvious pride that Rosie was touched. Whatever else anyone might say about Luke Devillers, they couldn't deny that he threw himself into everything he did with passion and dedication. Her cheeks stained and once again she remembered how passionately he'd made love to her on the sand and how galvanizing her response had been.

Luke guided the truck through the black moonscape that skirted the coast. He drove past the blowhole where the ocean spouted like a whale surfacing for air, up to the isolated pavilion overlooking the hard black lava fields.

The white wooden structure was set well back from the sea, but commanded a magnificent view of the surrounding hills and the Pacific. A blue rental car with a family of Japanese tourists had spilled out to inspect some of the rocks. But as Luke and Rosie walked up with their picnic basket, the visitors said a polite hello and piled back into their car and drove off.

Luke and Rosie climbed up the rocks to the pavilion. When they got to the top, they stood for a moment admiring the vast panorama spread out below them. Luke's arm dropped lightly around Rosie's shoulders and she knew he intended to draw her close and kiss her.

"I could eat a whale," she said, breaking the mood and moving away. Avoiding his eyes, she plucked the checked cloth out of the basket he'd set on the bench and shook it out over the wooden table. As she unpacked the food and exclaimed over it, she was conscious of his eyes on her. Was he laughing at her attack of schoolgirl shyness?

"Rosie, stop worrying," Luke said, an amused grin on his face. "I promise, no pressure. I just want to enjoy your company."

Rosie sighed. "I'm sorry, Luke." She met his eyes. "I guess I'm just not sure how I feel about any of this. I need time to think."

"You've had five years to think, Rosie. We both have."

"Not about what happened on the beach the other night."

"Fair enough," he said. He watched her for a moment more, then dropped down on the bench. He picked up a bunch of pale green grapes and popped one into his mouth. "Let's just eat the feast Mrs. Waneka's prepared and enjoy the afternoon."

Letting out a long breath, Rosie took him at his word. And for the next half hour they chatted as they ate roast chicken and tore off crisp hunks of French bread, washing it all down with sweet guava juice.

Inevitably, however, the subject rolled around to Christopher.

"You have to tell him sometime," Luke insisted, leaning back on the bench and planting his palms on the table.

Rosie sighed. "I know. But this isn't the right time, Luke. He's had so many new things to deal with. The move to Hawaii, a new house, Liliana, new friends to make. So much in his life is unsettled now. He needs to adjust to this whole new world before I hit him with something as earthshaking as a father."

"I think you worry too much, Rosie. Christopher is young. I bet he's going to be thrilled to find out he's got a dad just like all the other little boys."

"Yeah, but our situation isn't like other families. How do I explain why we don't live together and where you've been all this time?"

"Good question," Luke retorted.

She could see from the sudden flash of anger in his eyes that despite his charming manner he hadn't really forgiven her for deceiving him all this time. He'd just stage-managed this picnic so that he could try to maneuver her. As she realized that, fear resurrected itself in her mind. *I won't be bullied,* she resolved.

"We've already been through why I kept the secret so long. Christopher needs a little more time to adjust," she repeated.

"I don't want to see this stretch out indefinitely," Luke growled. "Just when do you feel you'll be ready to break the news?"

She held up a hand. Then she stood and walked over to the railing. "Don't pressure me, Luke."

He stalked up beside her and, grabbing her elbow, spun her toward him. "Somebody's got to, Rosie. Otherwise you'll never do it. And I'm not going to stand for that."

They stood regarding each other in stony silence, aware of the animosity and all the other complicated emotions vibrating between them. Then Luke's deep voice shattered the stalemate.

"Rosie, I want to get this thing settled. Just give me a date."

Rosie shook her head. "I need two months."

"Two months?" He took a step back, threw up his hands and paced rapidly back and forth in front of her. "No," he snapped, wheeling on his heel, "that's not acceptable."

She breathed. "What's acceptable?"

"One month."

She was silent, considering, reluctant to concede anything. Then she nodded. "All right. By the end of the month I'll tell Christopher the truth. I'll tell him that you're his father." She clenched the railing. "But I have a condition of my own."

His voice took on a wary tone. "And what might that be?"

"I want no interference, absolutely none, with the way I'm raising Christopher. I'm doing a damn good job."

"I agree. I think you're doing your best."

"My best?" she shot back. "What does that mean? Does that imply I could be doing better?"

He regarded her steadily. "We both know that single parenting is tough—especially with your working all day. Chris deserves two parents. And he has them. So why cheat him?"

Though Rosie deeply resented the implication that she'd been cheating Chris, she couldn't deny that there were times she felt guilty about not being with him as much as she wanted. For a moment she stood sizzling with outrage at Luke's implied criticism. Yet, at the same time, she was too honest to deny it had some validity. As she realized this, Luke continued.

"I'm Chris's father and I should have some say in the way he's raised."

She narrowed her eyes, defensiveness rising up in her. "Not yet you don't."

Luke gazed at her assessingly and she had the feeling he was devising his strategy. For a long while he didn't say anything, and when he did he spoke grimly. "All right, for the time being."

"There's something else. I want you to agree, no matter what, that I keep custody of him." Rosie felt that she was leaping into a chasm by even mentioning the subject, but it had to be done and it needed to be done early in the game before he developed any contrary expectations.

Another long moment passed before Luke replied. "What kind of custody?"

"It means he lives with me. Once we tell him, if it's okay with Chris, you can have him for overnight visits, but he remains in my house."

"I have no plans to take him away from his mother," Luke said shortly. "But Christopher is a Devillers. I'd like him to have my name."

Rosie bristled at this new encroachment. "We're getting ahead of things, Luke. You can't just saunter up and make a demand like that."

Luke's mouth set in a stubborn line, yet when he spoke his voice sounded reasonable. "Okay—to be discussed."

"I also think before we go any further in this negotiation, you need to get to know Christopher better."

"I intend to get to know my son very well. Very well, indeed," Luke declared.

"FAN-TAS-TIC!" exclaimed George McCall, Rosie's colleague at the research station.

"Fantastic and scary," Rosie added. They were hovering in a helicopter over the Big Island's west coast. Below them, the object of their wonder, a stream of molten lava, arched from a tube of black rock, hissing and spitting out over the sea. As it struck the cool water it sent up a gray plume of steam and rock so large it could be seen many miles away. Rosie knew that down the road the omnipresent gaggle of tourists with their fancy still cameras and videocams would be immortalizing Pele's latest show of temper.

"Let's get a closer look," Rosie shouted.

Obligingly the pilot dipped the helicopter so that George could get the best possible angle. The hefty researcher pushed the bill of his baseball cap around to the back of his head and aimed his lens through the side window.

Rosie stared down at one of nature's most incredible phenomena, fire-hose lava. "Pressure must be building," she yelled over the sound of the whirring motor. "Look at the way that's shooting out. The volume on that flow has to be at least twice as great as it was last week."

"Wonder if that means the tube system up north is blocked."

"Let's take a look."

"Definitely."

A few minutes later they were several miles east, seesawing along the mountain ridge. Acres of black rock, leafless skeletons of palm trees and knobs of hardened lava that looked as if they had been pulled like cooling taffy yawned beneath them.

"Let's go down," Rosie said.

As the pilot pulled back on the joystick, Rosie and George donned yellow hard hats. Like a huge alien bug, the helicopter settled on a flat stretch of pudding rock. They scrambled out, careful to avoid the still-roaring rotors, which whipped the hair beneath their helmets with warm, acrid air.

"Over here," Rosie said, and George, weighted down by the forty-pound backpack, followed her to a dip in the lava. Shedding the backpack, George opened the flap and fished out rock hammers, gloves and a thermocouple.

Rosie put on the thick leather gloves. Then, taking the thermocouple, which resembled a long curtain rod with a meter on the end, she gingerly advanced toward the pool of seething rock. Shielding her face from the heat with her forearm, she thrust the rod well into the lava.

Meanwhile George came up behind her, taking notes on a clipboard. "Ooops," he said as his ballpoint pen slipped onto the hard lava shelf where they were both standing. Immediately the plastic writing implement began curling like a cooked noodle.

"Hope you have another one," Rosie said.

"Always have a backup."

As Rosie stood there, holding the rod tip in the molten lava, George stood, recording the temperature in Fahrenheit. "Sixteen hundred... 1,650... 1,675... 1,700."

When the gauge grew still, Rosie removed the rod and stepped back.

"Cool," he said ten minutes later, studying the reading on his gauge. "This came out hotter than hell last week."

Rosie shook her head. "I think you're right about this tube system. It must be blocked farther up." Rosie thought of the magma seething in underground chambers deep below the surface of the earth. It had to seek release somewhere.

"The question is," George said, lifting his hard hat and scratching his thinning scalp, "is the fire hose bleeding off enough pressure, or does Madame Pele have a nasty little surprise in store for us somewhere else?"

Later that afternoon Rosie stood frowning, watching the seismograph. Its needle was shivering up and down the chart. She glanced at her Geodimeter and tiltmeter readings.

George came up behind her. "Lot of earthquake activity."

She nodded. A lot more than usual. I think we're in for some more fireworks."

"I wonder who's going to have front row seats this time," he deadpanned with gallows humor.

BY THE FOLLOWING DAY George's question had been answered. A new flow had erupted along another ridge and begun creeping eastward this time, eating a ribbon of lush greenery and menacing a cattle ranch.

The new direction sent ripples of apprehension through the scientific community and shudders of fear through everyone who owned property downhill from the flow. Early that evening, Rosie and researchers along with the Red Cross, Civil Defense, the BICC and local residents gathered at the community hall of Dove of the Sea Church to discuss emergency preparations. Even a few Pele's Partisans were in attendance.

"Me, I'm not worried," Mr. Fan said, tapping his chest. "Madame Pele, she gonna stop. I'm not afraid. My family's owned this store for one hundred years and Madame Pele, she always leaves us alone."

The meeting was noisy, full of contention as those gathered debated over one another's voices, shouting to be heard in the large, high-ceilinged room. Several times Rosie was called upon. She knew that people were hoping to hear words of reassurance, but in all honesty there was little she could say to calm fears. Through it all, she wondered where Luke was. If the lava flow continued its present downward route, Maile Gardens could find itself a prime candidate for incineration.

Halfway through the meeting, Luke came in the door and took out a folding chair at the back of the room. But if he was worried, it didn't show on his impassive countenance. Liliana, on the other hand, stared challengingly at him. He conspicuously ignored her. As Rosie glanced from one strong face to the other, she put her hand to her brow. With this new assault from Pele, the hostility between Luke and Liliana could escalate into a full-fledged battle.

The meeting went on, and just as fears reached a hysterical pitch, Luke rose to his feet and held up his hands. "I think," he boomed, "we should talk about this calmly." As he faced the crowd and waited, the room grew silent. "Let's use our heads," he said. "The lava flow is nowhere near any of us at the moment. So we have time. We've already developed a contingency plan. Now we can hone it and, if necessary, put it in action."

"That's easy for you to say," one man complained. "You have money. You can start all over again. But what about the rest of us? For some of us, this is all we own."

"What about insurance?" another cried. "Will they cover this—or do they consider this an act of God?"

"My insurance comes up in two weeks," said a woman. "What if my company refuses to renew and the lava swallows up my house the day after? What do I do?"

Rosie felt for everyone. She was only a renter, but she could imagine how she would feel if her life savings were tied up in property that could well be buried under an avalanche of hot rock within days. Her eye caught Toshiko Hayakawa, who looked as though she was going to burst into tears. Rosie thought of Toshiko's beautiful home and how proud she was of it. How sad to have it destroyed, particularly so soon after having it built.

During a potential disaster like this, emotions tended to run high, and they weren't always based on logic. People were eager to blame someone for their predicament. How would Toshiko feel toward Luke if her property was destroyed?

"If push comes to shove we can get together and move houses," Luke was saying. A murmur arose and he held up his hand. "It's been done before."

"Yeah, but our property will be gone," an unhappy homeowner shouted.

"Some people have hurricanes, some have tornadoes, we have Pele," said Mary Burns. "We all knew this was a volcanic island when we moved here. And we were willing to accept the risk to live in paradise. So we can sit around, wring our hands and cry about our bad luck, or we can do something to salvage the situation."

"The important thing is that we not panic," Rosie interjected. "Let's talk action now and discuss some alternatives."

The meeting continued for another two hours. Using a large map and charts, Rosie, George and several other scientists stood at the front of the room, discussing possible scenarios for the eruption and lava flow. At worst, Pele could go on a rampage, cutting a large swath through the developed areas. By the end of the meeting everyone was drained. Dispiritedly they began to file out of the hall.

Luke's head stood out above the crowd and Rosie saw him shoulder his way over to where Toshiko and her Maile Gardens neighbors huddled to commiserate.

Luke put his arm around the Asian woman's shoulders. "Don't give up. A lot can happen in the next few days. And if worse comes to worst, we'll figure out a way to save your house."

Toshiko nodded through her tears and her doctor-husband shook Luke's hand. "We love our home," Dr. Hayakawa murmured. "We don't want to lose it."

As the hall emptied, Liliana went out to the back office to wake Christopher, who'd fallen asleep on the couch. As Rosie gathered up her papers and folded up the large chart, she caught Luke's eye and lifted her hand in a wry salute. He did the same, then turned back to the crowd of home-owners that surrounded him.

Stepping out into the night air, Rosie waited by the front door for Liliana and Christopher. As she stood there she directed her gaze to the mountain in the distance. A thin red ribbon glowed along the far ridge. Right now it was pretty—sort of like an orange neon strip outlining the slope. She shuddered. But what would it mean to all their futures three days, three weeks or three months from now?

Chapter Ten

"This," Liliana declared, holding up a bottle of clear liquid, "is the least we can do. Tell her, Mr. Fan."

Mr. Fan winked at Rosie. "Good insurance. Can't hurt. Might help. Whatevah."

"But gin?" Rosie questioned.

"Madame Pele likes gin."

"What about those *ohelo* berries you threw into her a while back?"

"More insurance."

Rosie shrugged. "At least throwing gin at Madame Pele is a lot better than throwing in virgins."

"Oh, Madame Pele has no use for virgins," Liliana said with a perfectly straight face.

Rosie rolled her eyes. "Okay, one bottle of gin to appease our fiery friend," she said, pulling out her wallet. She looked down at Christopher, who had his nose pressed against the ice-cream case. "Make that one chocolate cone, too."

"Can I get sprinkles on top?" Christopher asked, raising a sturdy arm and doing a little war dance.

While they waited for Mr. Fan to make the cone, Rosie ambled over to two large bulletin boards the shop owner kept by the door. One side was for customers, who pinned up notices of lost dogs, cattle sales, house rentals, home improvement and housekeeping services. The other held a collage of fading photographs and mementos, which Mr. Fan had collected over the years.

"Quite a scrapbook you've got here," Rosie commented as she studied a photo of Mary Burns with long black hair and a miniskirt, which must have been taken in the sixties.

After handing Christopher the cone, Mr. Fan wiped his hands on his apron and came out around the counter over to where Rosie stood. "Me, I'm the island historian," he said with a laugh. "Some of those pictures are ancient history. Here's a picture of me in my soldier's uniform."

Rosie peered at it and wondered if Mr. Fan had suffered much discrimination during World War II. If he had, he didn't betray any bitterness. "What a dashing young man you were!" she exclaimed. "And still are."

Mr. Fan grinned and did a little bow. "These here, they're my sons—Danny and Jack—and guess who that is on the tricycle with them."

As Rosie examined the black-and-white snapshot, Liliana, hands on hips, wandered over and scrutinized it behind Rosie's shoulder. "That's Luke," Liliana said matter-of-factly.

Rosie stood frozen, realizing how much the grinning little boy with the mop of dark hair resembled Christopher. "Well, maybe we should get going," she said, hoping that Liliana wouldn't notice the same thing. To her relief, Liliana said nothing, and after Rosie washed Christopher's ice cream-coated hands with a wet napkin the trio headed out the door.

Moments later as Rosie started up the car, Liliana clutched the bottle against her ample bosom. Silent, a look of determination freezing her broad face, Liliana appeared to be a woman with a mission. Rosie sighed. She herself didn't believe in all the superstition that seemed to guide so much of her baby-sitter's life, but in this case she hoped it would work.

After driving the car up to the lava fields and parking a safe distance away, the trio climbed toward the bubbling new lava flow. Rosie held Christopher's hand tightly and stopped a good fifty yards from the seething river. "No closer," she told him.

"But Mommy, I wanna see."

Rosie shook her head. "We can see what Liliana does just fine from here."

Meanwhile Liliana picked her way up the rocks. Gathering her long skirts up around her ankles with her one free hand, she held the gin bottle aloft with the other.

"Are the rocks hot?" Christopher asked.

The breeze fanning their cheeks felt warm and gritty. And they could hear the earth crackle beneath the flow of magma. A short distance away pools of superheated mud gurgled and sputtered.

"Not hot enough to hurt her feet," Rosie replied. "But you see that river of red up there?" He nodded. "That's very hot, indeed." Two thousand degrees, Rosie thought. "You never go near that. This is as close as you ever get—and only with Mommy."

"But Liliana is going there."

"She's only going there to do something special and she knows just how close she can get without being hurt. So let's just watch her."

Earlier that day Liliana had begged Rosie to drive her up to the flow. She hadn't wanted to go alone because lately, with all the dust in the air, she'd been troubled by asthma. Curious about the ceremony, Rosie had agreed. Now she was having second thoughts about having brought Christopher. She should have realized how fascinated he'd be by this monstrous snake of creeping fire.

At that moment, her attention went back to Liliana, who was standing only ten feet from the flaming river. She had raised the bottle high above her head and was chanting something. The words were lost in the crackle of the magma and the hissing of the wind. All Rosie could make out was "Pele, Pele." With that the stout woman hurled the bottle of gin into the flaming valley, where it exploded and disappeared. Dusting off her hands, she reached into her pocket and withdrew a handkerchief. Holding it to her nose, she turned and came back toward them.

As Liliana's broad sneakered feet plodded down the slope, Rosie remembered the first time she'd seen the Hawaiian. That day she'd been appeasing Pele with the *ohelo* berries. It hadn't worked then and Rosie feared the gin wouldn't work much better.

When they got back to the house Liliana was breathing more easily. Then, after a quick lunch of tuna sandwiches and lemonade, Rosie put Christopher down for a nap. When she got back to the kitchen, Liliana was wiping the last of the lunch dishes.

"Thank you for cleaning up," Rosie said.

"No problem."

"Do you want me to drive you home?"

"My cousin's coming for me." Rosie craned her neck as a rusty pickup swung into the yard. "That's him now."

"I hope the bottle of gin works."

Liliana finished drying off her hands with the towel. "Hope so. But Madame Pele is not always so easily calmed—especially when one of her sons has profaned her sacred places."

"Luke, you mean," Rosie said, suppressing a sigh.

"Yes. Even as a child he was willful and wouldn't listen to good advice." She gathered up the large woven tote she used as a purse. "Your son, Christopher. He looks like Luke." Saying nothing further, Liliana swung the bag over her shoulder and walked out to her cousin's truck.

"See you Monday," Rosie murmured weakly. *Oh, great,* she thought. *Who else has noticed?*

SUNDAY MORNING the church bells woke Rosie. She'd had only a few hours of sleep. When she wasn't worrying about the volcano, she was concerned about who else besides Liliana had put two and two together after seeing Luke and Christopher. She still wasn't ready to tell Christopher the truth, but on the other hand, it would be disastrous for someone else to inform him before she did.

Because of the critical situation at Kilauea, Rosie was scheduled to work. It was Liliana's day off and Luke had promised to keep Christopher while Rosie was at the station. At 7:30 a.m., when she arrived at Orchid Cliffs, Luke was sitting in a cushioned wrought-iron chair on the flagstone lanai at the side of the house. Putting down his newspaper and coffee cup, he unfolded his long length, stood and greeted them.

"What do you think about riding on a horse today?" Luke asked Christopher.

The little boy let out a whoop of joy. "Horsies!"

"Luke, Christopher's never been on a horse before," Rosie said tentatively.

"Don't worry, he'll be right up front on the horse with me. I promise I'll hold him tight."

"I'm just not sure it's safe."

Luke looked annoyed. "Rosie, I'm not going to let Chris fall."

Rosie controlled the spurt of temper that was rising inside her. She knew what was happening. For her, this wasn't about horses. It was about giving up control of Chris. Either she could make every discussion about Chris a battle or she could choose where she wanted to stand and fight. The horse issue, obviously, was not the place to grandstand. She studied Luke's face. He hadn't slept any better than she, judging from the shadows beneath his eyes.

Mrs. Waneka appeared at the side door. "How about some French toast with fresh fruit?" she called out.

"French toast! Yeah!" Chris exclaimed.

"Not for me," Rosie said. "I've got to get out to the station."

Mrs. Waneka's glance went from Rosie to Luke. "Why don't I take this young man out to the kitchen? Maybe he can help me set the breakfast table."

As Chris scampered through the door, Luke shot a worried look up toward the mountain. "Any news?"

"I'm about to find out."

He jammed his hands in his pockets. "I was impressed with the way you fielded all those questions at the meeting last night."

"Thank you. You were pretty good, too. It can't be easy."

Luke shook his head. Then, gazing into Rosie's eyes, he reached out and took her hand. As his fingers engulfed hers, memories of their night together on the beach flooded through her. For a moment, she wanted to slide into his arms and feel them closed around her.

"I've missed you, Rosie."

His voice was warm and suggestive. She gazed at him, drinking in the impressive man who stood before her, his lean hips encased in faded jeans and the muscles of his broad chest outlined by the navy-blue T-shirt. His black tousled hair gleamed in the early-morning sunlight and she itched to run her fingers through it.

"It's not as if we haven't been seeing each other," she said, pulling back. She couldn't let her weakness for Luke cloud her judgment.

"Sure, chance encounters—public meetings and when you drop off Christopher. That's not the way I want to see you, Rosie."

"I'm not sure what you want, Luke."

"They why don't we discuss what I want here and now?"

Disturbed by the sudden intensity in his voice, she shook her head. "Luke, I don't have time for this. I'm afraid Madame Pele is demanding all my attention at the moment."

"My loss," he replied.

"Guess so."

After going in to kiss Christopher goodbye, Rosie made a hasty exit and wended her way up to the center, where she spent the morning monitoring a brigade of quivering styluses. Shortly after lunch, several of the monitoring devices started doing a crazy dance. Moments later damage reports started coming in from the village of Niha. What's more, the area where the readings showed the greatest disturbance was not that far from her own cottage.

For the next two hours Rosie bit her fingernails as she waited for one of her colleagues to come in to relieve her. As soon as one did, Rosie raced out of the station, leaped into her car and headed east toward the beleaguered village. Within a mile of Niha, she squinted and her mouth dropped open. *What is that?* she thought, eyeing an obstruction that hadn't been there the previous day.

It was as if a giant hand had pushed a mountain up and out from the center of the flat earth. Uphill from the fish ponds, a small newly hatched volcano had burst from a field, radically altering the topography. Rosie stopped the car and looked at it. The huge freshly molded mound straddled a plateau. If it decided to spill lava, which way would the flow go—down toward Niha or in the opposite direction, toward the cove where her cottage stood? She swallowed and told herself that if it went in her direction, she'd survive. But what about her neighbors? And what about the Niha villagers who'd lived and worked there for generations?

Rosie got back into her car and drove on to Niha. Several weeks earlier, when she, her mother and Christopher had been there at the luau, the village had had three tidy rows of bungalows at the edge of the fish ponds. Now, from what she could see, the rows were gap toothed. From the damaged houses she spotted, she guessed that the volcanic explosion from the new formation had spewed gases and molten rocks down on them. She saw civil defense workers examining the stricken houses. Red flashing lights from fire trucks and ambulances added to the nightmare quality of the scene. Wailing children were being comforted by their parents, who stood around in tight circles, their faces pale with shock.

Rosie's first impulse was to try to help the villagers, but with the Red Cross, fire fighters and civil defense, she was superfluous. Finally she decided to get out her notebook and make a preliminary survey. As she got out of the Jeep, she caught her first glimpse of Liliana. Arms across her chest, she stood talking to the civil defense workers. Rosie hurried over to her.

"Liliana, are you okay?"

Liliana had a dour look on her face and her uncombed dark hair trailed down her back over her soot-covered muumuu. "I'm fine—my house isn't." She thrust her palm in the air toward her little bungalow. It was no longer a pretty white cottage. Black streaks coated it, its windows were broken and a large hole gaped in the roof. "*Auwe.* Those guys do more damage than Pele," she said, gesturing toward the rubber-suited firemen who were chopping at windows with their axes. "They tell me they have to do that to make sure the fire's out. But I think they're just having fun."

"Was anybody hurt?"

"Not seriously."

Rosie sighed with relief. "If you need a place to stay, you can come home with me," she offered. Then she gave a regretful smile. "That is, providing my house doesn't get the same treatment as yours."

"*Mahalo.* I suspect I will need someplace to sleep," Liliana grumbled. "They've drowned most of my stuff." She scowled. "Are we in for more *pilikia?*"

How Rosie wished she could say there'd be no more trouble. "From what I can figure," she replied, "a great deal of pressure has built up beneath the island, and the places where it's normally vented have gotten plugged up. I'm afraid what we're seeing is just the beginning."

"And what about that thing?" Liliana said. Her black hair whipped as she shook her fist at the newly spawned mountain.

"Get out another bottle of gin. One for all of us."

AFTER THE INSTRUMENT truck and a team of scientists from the station arrived, Rosie spent what was left of the morning taking samples of soil and radon on the new cone and surrounding caldera. She was tired, covered with grime and plagued by burning eyes when her colleagues finally broke for lunch and returned to the village. After washing her hands, she joined the others around an undamaged picnic table to eat a lunch of grilled fish provided by one of Liliana's cousins. The lucky cousin's bungalow hadn't been hit by the fire storm, so he'd been playing good Samaritan.

Tense from a morning of hunching over, Rosie stretched her hands above her head and flexed her stiffened back. Out of the corner of her eye, she caught a glance of a familiar red vehicle that had just rolled up. She was just in time to see Luke and Christopher step out of the truck. Luke hoisted the boy up on his shoulders and walked toward her. The expression on his face was grim.

"We heard the news and decided to come investigate for ourselves. And I sure don't like what I've seen so far," Luke said. His gaze took in the ruined houses and disarray around them. "Not a pretty sight."

"I wouldn't take a stroll around the village just now if I were you," Rosie whispered. "You're not going to win any popularity contests around here today." During the course of the morning, she'd heard several villagers mumbling that this new assault from Pele was Luke Devillers's fault for building too close to the sacred grounds. When people were this distressed, they often needed a scapegoat to vent their feelings. Luke was an obvious target.

As if fulfilling a prophecy, one of the villagers, a slender white-haired man who'd lost his small grocery store, stalked up and shook his finger at Luke. "If you loved your boy there," he said, apparently assuming Christopher was Luke's son, "you would take better care of his future and this island." The man turned to the little boy. "You tell your daddy he must never ever offend Madame Pele again." And with that, the man marched off.

For a moment, nobody said anything. Rosie could feel the curious eyes of George and the other scientists on her and Luke. Impulsively she reached for Christopher, who tumbled into her arms. The little boy had a disturbed expression on his face. Obviously the villager's words had confused him. Rosie stroked his hair and kissed his nose.

He put his arms around her neck and looked searchingly into her face. "What did that man mean, Mommy?"

Rosie colored. "Oh, he was just upset because his store got hurt."

Luke leaned close and tapped her shoulder. "Let's take a walk."

Relieved at getting away from their audience, Rosie nodded and, putting Chris on the ground, took his hand firmly in hers. She turned, and without meeting any of their eyes, she announced to her co-workers, "I'll be right back."

Then she, Luke and Christopher walked in silence toward the fish ponds. Christopher picked up a rock and rubbed it, looking longingly at the undisturbed surface of the water.

"Remember no throwing stones at the fish," Rosie reminded him.

"I got a good look at that volcanic cone on the way in," Luke said as Christopher squatted to examine a lizard.

"Quite something, isn't it?"

"Like a mini-Vesuvius. I don't suppose you can say yet what direction its lava is going to flow in, can you?"

"We can make some educated guesses. It's going to go downhill, that's for sure. And it looks like it's headed eastward."

"Toward Maile Gardens?"

"Possibly."

He thumped a fist into his palm. "It might not go all the way. It never has before."

"No, it might not."

He picked up a stone and squeezed it in his hand as if he wanted to wring blood from it. "I'm looking into moving the finished houses if necessary."

"That's wise."

"What about the villagers here?"

"Well, the Red Cross has set up a relief camp over in Rainbow Falls State Park. There are campsites there and they have some donated tents."

"And their houses?"

"Well, as you could see, a lot of them are damaged already. As for the others, we can't say yet whether the lava will get them."

"I could try to make arrangements to move the ones that are still intact."

"Liliana's probably the person to talk to about that."

Luke made a face. "Great. Talk to Liliana. My biggest fan. She's probably got the tar and feathers ready." He took the stone and pitched it into the pond so hard it sent up a plume.

"Luke! You're not setting much of an example for Chris."

"Right, I'm just totally unreliable."

Rosie stopped and faced him. "Luke, you can't blame Liliana for being angry with you. Her house was destroyed this morning, and rational or not, in her book you're responsible."

"Okay," he said, scowling. "I'm all powerful—the cause of poverty, famine, earthquakes and, certainly, volcanic eruptions. Anything else I should take on?"

She shrugged. "Disease. War. The Black Hole of Calcutta. Mosquitoes."

Luke didn't smile at her humor.

"What's the Black Hole of Cowcuddy?" Chris asked, running up.

Luke ruffled the boy's dark mop. "Something that happened a long time ago and far away. Nothing to do with us, buddy."

A *koi* jumped, breaking the mirror surface of the fish pond. Excited, Chris pulled Rosie and Luke down to the water's edge. "Look, there's another one," cried Chris.

For a few minutes, Rosie and Chris stood peering into the water, pointing at the fat orange-, red-and-black fish. Behind them, Rosie could feel Luke simmering like Niha's new volcano.

She added fuel to the fire by saying, "By the way, I've asked Liliana to come stay with me for the time being."

The news made Luke clench his teeth.

"Liliana again. She's everywhere I turn."

"Well, it was your recommendation that I hire her. And it's been a good one."

He glanced at Chris, who was standing a little way off. "Liliana knows, doesn't she?"

Rosie didn't pretend not to know what he meant. "Not for certain. Although she did mention how much you two looked alike."

Luke smiled wryly. "That's probably where that guy who just read me the riot act got his information."

"Maybe, but all he had to do was look at you and Chris together. And frankly, Luke, given the high emotions running in Niha, that makes me nervous."

Luke whirled around and grabbed both her arms. "Are you saying that you've now got another reason to back off from our agreement?"

Rosie glanced anxiously at Chris. "This just isn't the time."

His voice roughened. "I know. The end of the month."

She said nothing.

"That raises another subject," Luke said gruffly. "It isn't safe for you and Chris to stay at your cottage any longer. You don't live far from here, and frankly, given the instability of the volcano, you'd be a whole lot safer if you were away from all the action and at Orchid Cliffs with me. For all we know that thing could go off in your direction tomorrow—or even tonight." He threw an angry hand in the vicinity of the new formation.

Rosie had been worrying about the same thing and had even considered renting a room out of the range of Pele's anger. But rentals in safe areas were going to be hard to come by now—and any long-term stay at a resort hotel would be prohibitive. "I've been thinking about this. I'm going to call Mary Burns and see if she knows of any place to stay."

"You'll stay at Orchid Cliffs."

Balking at his flat order, she shook her head. "No, living with you would be the same thing as announcing Christopher's paternity."

His mouth set stubbornly. "What's wrong with that?"

"We're not going to go through this again, are we?"

"Looks like we are. Up until now I've agreed to all your conditions. For heaven's sake, I'm even willing to have Liliana come and play chaperone, as if Beatrice isn't enough. But this is a dangerous situation and Christopher is my son. I have the right—no, the duty—to protect him."

Rosie balled her hands into fists. Living so close to Luke, she'd be fighting him for control as well as battling her own desire to make love with him. "I don't think it's a good idea, Luke," she repeated.

"If you're worried about having Beatrice breathing down your neck, you can stay in the guest house. It's private. It's got three bedrooms and a kitchen. You don't ever have to see me if you don't want to."

"Luke—"

His hands tightened on her arms. "You, Chris and Liliana are moving to Orchid Cliffs—and that's that."

"I DON'T KNOW of anything," Mary Burns was saying early the next day. "You're welcome to stay here. It will be cozy—we're taking in the O'Briens and the Landers. All the guest rooms and couches are filled. I'm afraid all that's left is some floor space. I can probably scare up some sleeping bags for you. It's not much, but it's better than being barbecued."

"I'll keep it in mind," Rosie said.

She'd been so mad when Luke issued his ultimatum that she'd stomped off, determined to make her own arrangements no matter what dicta he sent down from on high. Last night and then, after taking the morning off today, she'd glued herself to the phone, calling around the island, trying to find accommodations she could afford. Everything, including a lot of her friend's couches, seemed to be filled.

After thanking Mary, she hung up and went to the window. Luke was still sitting out there in his truck. Early that morning, he'd rung her doorbell and informed her he was moving her to Orchid Cliffs. She'd refused to let him in and he'd refused to go away. Just as he had been every time she'd looked out, he was on his car phone. Who was he calling? she wondered. Well, he could stay out there until his truck rusted for all she cared. Meanwhile she was going to keep dialing until she found a refuge other than Orchid Cliffs.

The phone rang. "Rosie, have you come to your senses?"

"Luke Devillers, why don't you go on home, where you're needed? You're not improving my scenery any." With that, she slammed down the phone.

Seconds later, when the phone rang again, she snatched up the receiver, ready to slam it down. "Luke, I told you."

"Whoa," said the voice on the other end. "It's me, George, friend and co-worker, remember?"

"Sorry, George. It's a long story."

"No time for long stories. I've been trying to get through to you. Civil defense is about to sound the evacuation siren. You've got to get out—we've had a new eruption with a good-sized lava flow. The good news is that it's skirting Niha. The bad news is it's heading your way."

A chill of panic swept through her. "How fast is it moving?"

"Slow but sure..."

At that moment, a fist pounded on Rosie's door. She glanced out the window and saw that it was Luke standing on her porch and that a rental truck had pulled in behind his vehicle. As Rosie listened to George give a discouraging account of the lava's progress, she watched two of Luke's construction workers climb out of the cab. Opening up the rear of the truck, they brought out some flattened wardrobe cartons and began to assemble them.

"I think you should get out as soon as possible," George was saying.

Luke's fist pounded again and she admitted defeat. "I guess my ride is here."

"Pardon?"

"A moving van just pulled up in my drive, so it looks as though I'm on my way."

"You must be clairvoyant."

"Yeah, I inherited it from my mother."

"Let me know if you need anything."

"Thanks. I will," she said. She turned to the door, where Luke was now leaning on the bell. At that moment the bell was drowned out by the louder bellow of a civil defense siren. Luke had won this round. She had no choice now but to go with him to Orchid Cliffs.

Chapter Eleven

"You laughed when I warned you. Now you're not laughing," Liliana declared, thrusting her round face close to Luke's.

His square chin hardened and he stared down at her unflinchingly. "This is an act of nature. Hawaii sits in the Ring of Fire. Volcanoes have made and remade the island for thousands of years." He threw his arms out. "You can throw a whole liquor store into Pele's fire and it won't make a bit of difference. Let's face it, Liliana. Your anger has nothing to do with the eruption. You're angry because of where I built."

"Tell it to *her,*" Liliana retorted with a sharp gesture toward the volcano. Then she retreated to the kitchen to finish packing the last of the groceries.

"This is not about volcanoes," he shouted after her. "This is about changing the island. If it were up to you, we'd still be living in grass shacks."

A "hmmmph" issued from the kitchen.

Luke rolled his eyes. "That woman is impossible."

"If you ask me, you're both impossible," Rosie said, slipping a book into a boxful of scientific volumes. She and Luke had exchanged few words since he'd charged in with his packing crew. Now she scurried around grabbing up the last of her belongings, while Luke and his men trundled the bulging cartons off to the truck. *Orchid Cliffs is only temporary,* she kept telling herself. *Only temporary.*

WELL, IF ROSIE wasn't going to talk to him, he wasn't going to talk to her. The important thing was to get them all to safety. Words would only get in the way. Meanwhile he stepped around her. In fact, the two of them were careful not to be in the same room at the same time.

He walked into Chris's bedroom to check what more needed to be done. "That box 'bout ready to go?" he asked his son.

Chris had been peering into a shoe box filled with rocks and shells. He took a stone from the pocket of his shorts and dropped it in.

"Whatcha got there, buddy?" Luke said as he loosened a strip of tape.

"My lucky rock," Chris replied, and placed the lid atop the shoe box and stuffed it into the larger container. Then he watched as Luke squatted to tape it up. "Chris, do you want to put your monkey in here, too?" he asked, smiling at the worn stuffed animal.

"No," Christopher said. He picked up the toy and clutched it to his chest. "Kong stays with me."

"Let's do a last check." Luke looked around the room and opened the closet door. "What's this?" A multicolored airplane, a fifteen-inch tower and a robot figure lay jumbled in a corner.

"My Legos," Chris said, dropping Kong on the bed.

"Okay, let's get another box."

When all the cartons were packed and Luke had gone ahead to Orchid Cliffs, Rosie made a farewell tour of the house. Each room brought back memories. She walked out to the lanai and pushed the back of the rocker, where her mother had sat when Rosie had admitted Luke was Christopher's father. For a moment, she watched it sway back and forth. Then, with a sigh, she went back into the kitchen and looked around at the cheery room where Luke and Chris first shared a meal. It was funny how attached you could get to a place.

At that moment, her son walked into the room. Before he could say anything, she took his hand. "Come on, Chris, let's go."

With a heavy heart and a last backward glance at the charming pink cottage, Rosie pulled out of the driveway.

"Stop! Stop, Mommy!" Christopher suddenly cried. "We left Kong! We left Kong!"

Rosie jammed her foot on the brake. "Can't do that," she said. They went into the house and found the creature right on the bed where Chris had dropped him. "Animal Rescue League here to save Kong," Rosie announced. She and Chris both grabbed one of the stuffed monkey's arms and walked out with the bedraggled animal swinging between them.

Driving up the winding road a few minutes later, they saw a depressing sight. "What are those people doing?" Chris asked.

Rosie slowed as three men carted a large stained-glass window out to a truck. The window had been the focal point of the Fongs' living room. Rosie sighed and drove on. Another neighbor was out in her yard, digging up her prized landscaping, while her husband and sons emptied the house of furniture. Everyone on this road was taking Pele very seriously.

Once the little caravan arrived at Orchid Cliffs, Rosie left Liliana, aided by Mrs. Waneka, to the unpacking. Rosie had managed to get the morning off, but now, with a chunk of the island exploding under her feet, she had to get back to work. The station was humming as scientists used theodolites, aerial photographs and topographic maps to survey and assess the latest eruptions.

"Looks like your old neighborhood gets the next grilling," George commented.

Rosie stared down at his chart. "The new recreation center will go first."

"Yep, that's the appetizer. The Gleasons' ranch is the entrée—all that tasty beef."

"They are going to move the animals, aren't they?"

"Already have. Otherwise we'd have us one major barbecue."

"And my house is dessert, huh?"

George nodded his balding head. "Looks that way."

Despite the banter, Rosie, thinking of all that destruction, felt a great heaviness in her chest. By the time she left the station late that evening, her temples throbbed.

Back at the Orchid Cliffs guest cottage, Rosie cast a longing glance at the swimming pool as she walked past. It was lit and its turquoise water looked so cool and refreshing. *Maybe before I hit the sack, I'll take a swim,* she told herself. It might wash away the tight coil of tension that had been squeezing at her all day.

Inside the house, she checked on Chris and Liliana, who were sound asleep. Both had good-sized rooms filled with antiques and rattan furniture. She had to admit that the bungalow Luke had provided was even nicer than the one she had left behind.

Finding a bottle of aspirin in the bathroom, she carried it into the kitchen to get herself a glass of water. On the handsome marble-topped table in the breakfast area, she spotted a note propped up on the salt shaker. "CALL YOUR MOTHER" was written in big, red crayoned letters on the slip of green stationery. Rosie looked at her watch. Nine o'clock. That meant it was eleven in Santa Barbara. Not too late to call.

After shaking out two aspirins and washing them down, Rosie picked up the wall phone and dialed.

"Rosalyn Crane Clarke," her mother began, "do you have any idea how worried I've been about you? I saw some perfectly horrifying pictures on the early news of what's going on there."

Rosie massaged her left temple. "I was planning to call you, Mom, but so much has been happening."

"Well, I tried reaching you and I finally gave up and called the observatory, but you were out in the field. So then I tried information and got Luke's office number. Now I find that you've moved to Orchid Cliffs and that there's a river of burning lava about to eat up your lovely little cottage. Thank the stars you're safe with Luke. I feel so much better knowing you're in good hands."

Rosie had listened patiently to her mother's nonstop monologue, but Denise Clarke's last words made her sit up straight. "I'd be safe whether Luke had anything to do with it or not. I'm not about to put Christopher in any danger. I told you that before."

"Rosie, you never think you're in any danger, even when you're strolling along the edge of a fifty-foot drop into a cauldron of boiling lava. Your father was the same way. And look what happened to him. Naturally I worry."

Rosie's expression softened. "I am careful, Mother. I promise. But I want you to know that this arrangement here at Luke's is temporary."

"Of course, dear," Mrs. Clarke said soothingly. "Of course."

AFTER SHE HUNG UP the receiver, Rosie went over to the refrigerator and opened it. *A glass of wine would be nice right now,* she thought. But though Mrs. Waneka had stocked milk, juice, eggs, fruits and vegetables, she hadn't included anything like wine. *Oh, well,* Rosie thought. *A swim will be a lot healthier for me.*

Rosie's clothes hadn't been unpacked yet, so she spent about fifteen minutes digging through cartons before she unearthed a bathing suit. Unfortunately the one she found was an emerald green bikini, not the more conservative maillot that she would have chosen to wear here. But at this hour she wasn't about to tear apart every box in the room.

Outside the air was refreshing. Padding down the flagstone path with its landscaped borders, Rosie listened to the call of a night bird. At the edge of the concrete surrounding the kidney-shaped pool, Rosie knelt and tested the water with her fingers. It was pleasantly cool. Dropping the towel on a lounger, she raised her hands, dived in and reveled in the bracing shock. Surfacing and blinking her eyes clear, she began a lazy sidestroke to the shallow end. The silken water slid over her nearly naked skin. Relaxing, she closed her eyes and lay on her back, letting the water cradle her effortlessly.

WEARILY LUKE PULLED OPEN the front door. It had been a long day. He was glad it was almost over.

"You're finally home, Mr. Luke," Mrs. Waneka said, greeting him in the living room. "I kept your dinner warm for you."

"I meant to call," Luke said. He dropped into a chair and grimaced apologetically. "I grabbed a bag of potato chips and a soda on the way back."

Mrs. Waneka put her hands on her plump hips. "That's no meal. You need all your energy." She took a swipe at an errant speck of dust on one of the end tables. "How did it go anyhow?"

Luke kicked off his shoes and sank back into the white damask chair. "Not well. You can't blame them."

"Yes, but anyone buying a house on this part of the island must know that some risk is involved."

"It's one thing to know it in your head. It's another to watch your dream go up in smoke. Look at all the people who live in southern California—especially the people who build their houses along the seaside cliffs. Even though they know about the dangers of mud slides, fires and earthquakes, they don't believe it will ever really happen to them." He shook his head. "And I guess I'm one of them."

"It's true," Mrs. Waneka said. "We're all living on borrowed time on this island. But it's cruel timing for Pele to act up so soon after these people made their investment."

Yes, cruel, Luke thought. He'd spent the whole afternoon and the better part of the evening visiting with each of his Maile Gardens clients. He'd made proposals, offering several alternatives if the lava headed their way. Right now the flow was moving in the other direction, but in the event it shifted or branched, he wanted them to be prepared to act. And he wanted them to know he'd be there for them if they needed his help. He hoped like hell no one would be needing any.

He followed Mrs. Waneka into the kitchen, where the housekeeper fixed him a sandwich along with a plate of potato salad. As he ate, he asked where everyone was.

"Your aunt Beatrice hasn't come back from her dinner at the Robertsons' yet," she said, naming a prominent rancher family. "Let's see, as for Ms. Clarke, she went off to work and she's been gone all day. I think I heard her car just a few minutes before you came in, but I haven't seen her.

"Liliana and I got a lot of unpacking done and I put some groceries in their cupboards. The little boy—" she clasped her hands "—he's so cute. He helped Shun weed the garden while we worked in the house. When we stopped for dinner, he brought us out to admire the pile of weeds he'd pulled."

As he ate, Luke listened to all this. In his mind he pictured Chris with his sturdy little body and bright, inquiring expression. A wave of pride swept through him. Already he felt that the boy was a necessary part of his life. All these years since Gretchen's death, he'd kept himself busy, but there'd been an empty place in his heart. Now, knowing that Chris existed and having seen so much of him in the past few days, part of that emptiness was filled. Chris belonged here at Orchid Cliffs. How could he ever let Rosie take the boy away?

After satisfying Mrs. Waneka by eating most of her meal, Luke stretched. "Well, I think I'll go over to the office and put in a bit of work."

Mrs. Waneka shook her gray head. "You look bone tired, Luke. Why don't you take a rest and clear your head?"

"I haven't got time."

"Nonsense! You can't shoulder all the problems of the world—at least, you can't do it effectively if you're so tired you can hardly see straight."

Luke grinned and patted Mrs. Waneka's shoulder. "Thank you, Mom."

She took a swipe at him with a dishtowel. "I may not be your mother, but Luke Devillers, I've taken care of you since you were in diapers. And I know what's best."

Luke grinned and rose from the table. "Okay, I promise I'll get some shut-eye, but I really need to put in some work first."

He walked out the side door and stood for a moment enjoying the evening breeze. He couldn't help but feel guilty that his clients in Maile Gardens were worried and the people in Rosie's old neighborhood were panicked. At least Rosie herself and Chris were safe here at Orchid Cliffs. Thank God, he'd been able to persuade that stubborn woman to let him do what needed to be done.

With a small surge of satisfaction, he glanced over at the guest house. Rosie's car was parked alongside it and a light was on in the living room. That meant she was back from work. He heaved a sigh of relief. Whenever she left for the battle zone, he worried that something might happen to her, even though he knew she was smart enough to take care of herself. He thought about knocking just to assure himself that everything was all right, but at that moment the door opened. In the dim halo cast by the porch light, he saw a figure emerge. It was Rosie. And she looked fine. Very fine.

Stepping back into the shadows, he watched her. As she walked down the path toward the softly lit pool, he could see her better. His eyes widened as he saw she was clad in a bikini and had a towel draped over one shoulder. The bikini, though not immodest, showed off her trim feminine curves to perfection. His gaze traveled from her long shapely legs, to her gently flared hips, to her slim waist. Above it her emerald top cupped a pair of beautifully rounded breasts. His eyes lingered there and he had a pulsing tactile memory of feeling their nipples tauten under his fingertips. As she passed him, he followed the twin globes of her firm backside. Again memories of his hands on her body engulfed him.

He sighed. He'd promised Rosie that if she came to Orchid Cliffs he wouldn't hassle her. *Well, Luke, old boy,* he said to himself, arching a black eyebrow, *you lied.* With that, he turned and went back into the house. Unbuttoning his shirt, he strode down the hall to his bedroom, tore off his clothes and quickly changed into his swimming trunks.

His next stop was the greenhouse, where he plucked a red carnation. Then he headed to his office, where he filled two snifters with brandy and set them on a small carved teak tray.

Rosie was floating on her back, her eyes closed, a half smile on her lovely face, when he arrived at the pool. For a moment he stood there, gazing down on her and admiring the picture she presented. Her white legs glimmered as the opalescent water buoyed her up. Around her oval face, her red hair spread in a luxuriant fan. And the half-moon crescents of her wet lashes cast delicate shadows on her cheek.

Reluctantly he lifted his gaze and turned to put down the tray on a glass-topped table. Then, holding the red carnation in one hand, he lowered himself over the edge of the pool, slipping stealthily into the water. Despite his caution, his entry sent ripples across the smooth surface. Rosie's eyes flew open. In seconds he was next to her, playfully brushing her nose with the petals of the flower.

Instantly she righted herself and tried to find the bottom with her feet. But she had drifted into the deep part of the pool. Realizing her predicament, and not displeased by it, Luke slipped his arm around her waist.

"Wait, I've got you," he said as she floundered. He drew her close to his chest so that her breasts and thighs touched his.

Rosie stopped struggling and glared at him. "You seem to have a bad habit of sneaking up on women in the dark of the night," she declared.

"Ah, but if you saw me coming, you might run the other way."

"True, if I had any sense." Then her eyes focused on the flower he still held in one hand. "Isn't this a strange place to do your gardening?" she asked.

"Oh, I wasn't going to plant this. I was going to use this for bait." He waved the blossom at her and a few drops of water fell from it onto her nose. Annoyed, she shook them off.

"I wanted to see what kind of a mermaid I could catch with this," Luke continued. He smiled wickedly. "A blue-eyed, redheaded sea goddess. I think I did very well, indeed."

"Well, this is one 'sea goddess' you're not going to lure with some flower," she retorted. Then, splashing him, she tore away and swam to the side of the pool.

"Hey, is that any way to treat Neptune when he comes calling with a peace offering?"

"I don't see any godlike creature."

He swam over to her. "Even though I come bearing gifts? This is a flower with a mission," he declared, holding the carnation aloft.

"Well, it's mission is impossible."

"All I wanted was to see it in your hair." He cocked his head as he surveyed her face. "It's an old island tradition for women to wear flowers behind their ears."

She looked at him skeptically.

"Now, which of your ears should this go behind? I wonder."

"Does it matter?"

"Absolutely." He pushed a few long red strands away from her neck. "If a woman wears a flower behind her right ear, she's available. But if a woman wears it behind her left ear, she's found a guy she likes and is letting him know she's open to courting." He handed her the flower and closed her fingers around it. "But the lady has to be the one to decide where to wear it."

For a moment, Rosie twirled the bloom in her hand. "Well," she said coyly, "since I part my hair on the right, maybe it will be more becoming if I wear it on that side." Sweeping back her locks, she placed the small stem of the carnation over her right ear.

Luke masked his disappointment with a comical expression of extreme despair. "Still looking, huh? Well, maybe that will change."

"Maybe," she said. She slanted him a sly smile and then pulled herself up out of the water and sat on the edge of the pool. "Now, this island flower legend you just fed me, is it really true?"

Luke hoisted himself up beside her. "Could be. I'm not sure. Actually, I saw it in an old Clark Gable movie."

Rosie laughed. "Then it's really just an ancient line."

"But a good one. It worked with Myrna Loy."

He grinned roguishly at her, enjoying their banter, yet trying to figure out what her attitude toward him really was. Since their lovemaking on the beach, she'd been distant and even contentious. But remembering how she had responded to his touch that night, he couldn't believe that she was so unaffected by him. No, all that standoffishness had to be an act. Maybe she was keeping her distance because she was afraid he'd take Christopher away from her.

Maybe on top of that she was still wary after the way he'd treated her all those years ago. Somehow he had to prove to her that he was different, as was the relationship budding between them.

A slight breeze came up and Luke reached over and took the towel off the lounger and draped it over Rosie's shoulders. He was sorry to cover up all that lovely flesh, but maybe he'd persuade her to stay out a little longer if she dried off.

"I really should go in," she murmured. "It's been a long day and it will be a long one tomorrow."

"Me, too. But before we call it a night..." He stood and lifted the two glasses from the tray. "I don't know about you, but I could use a drink. How about some brandy?"

Rosie hesitated, but then reached out and took the snifter from his hand. He settled back down beside her and they sipped and gazed up at the stars, which filled the night sky like diamonds spread on velvet. The soft breeze ruffled the tall royal palms, making their fronds clatter.

"Liliana asleep?" he asked.

"Yes."

"Good. I can leave my battle armor off for an hour or two."

"Sometimes when the two of you are going at it I feel like an innocent bystander caught in the crossfire between the Hatfields and the McCoys."

"I'm sorry, Rosie. I don't mean to involve you." He took a sip of brandy and grimaced. "The whole battle is strictly a matter of perspective. We're talking about property rights." He took another sip and felt the fiery liquid in his throat. Suddenly he wanted Rosie to understand how he felt. "I've been privileged with seven years of college, and though I know the superstitions that Liliana clings to are not based on fact, part of me is still moved by them."

Rosie looked up at him with curiosity. "Does that mean you believe in all this talk about Pele wreaking vengeance?"

"Not literally. On the other hand, I can't ignore it. I couldn't very well grow up here in the Devillers family with Queen Analani looking down on every move I make and a statue of Pele in the living room and not have some reverence for the old ways. So it really bothers me when Liliana hits me with this 'you don't care about your heritage' spiel.

"Rosie," he said, looking at her, "my heritage is very important to me. I'd no sooner build on a sacred site than I would vandalize a *heiau,*" he said.

Rosie touched his arm. "Luke, I know that. And so does everyone else."

"It's a boundary dispute, Rosie. We just don't agree where the sacred land ends."

Rosie saw his inner torment and cut through it. "Luke, none of this is your fault. You mustn't blame yourself."

"The logical side of my mind doesn't, but I have to admit that there's a part of me that feels guilty—that wonders if there isn't some way that I am to blame."

"Oh, Luke. That's crazy and self-destructive. You can't possibly allow yourself to think like that."

He looked down at his hands. "Ninety-five percent of the time I don't, Rosie. But the past couple of days have been a real test and I have a feeling the pop quiz coming up is going to be a killer."

Her hand was still on his arm. Boldly he took it and brought it to his lips. "I like having you here, Rosie." He half expected her to withdraw her hand, but she didn't. "I know you think I pushed you into coming here, but it was just because I was so worried about you and Chris."

"I know that, Luke. And I know that I was being a little stubborn myself. But sometimes, frankly, you scare me."

That surprised him. "How could I scare a strong, independent woman like you?"

"You wield a lot of power on this island and sometimes you're overwhelming."

That wasn't exactly bad for his ego, but he wanted her to feel comfortable with him. "That's a little like the pot calling the kettle black," he returned with a smile. "Don't you realize how overwhelming you are?"

Rosie stared at him in surprise.

"Oh, yes," he continued in a low voice. "I've been feeling overwhelmed by you ever since we first made love." He began to stroke her hand, keenly aware that something was happening between them. "If it had been just any woman in my bed that afternoon five years ago, it would have been a whole lot easier afterward. I wouldn't have held a picture of you in my mind. I wouldn't have kept wondering where you were and what you were doing. And," he continued in a husky tone, "whether you were thinking of me."

"You mean you were thinking about me when I was in Alaska?" The wariness that had guarded her like Sleeping Beauty's thorny hedge crumbled away from her expression and he felt encouraged.

"Yes. Even though I'd convinced myself that it was better we didn't see each other again, I told myself that the only reason I couldn't get you out of my mind was that I felt guilty for treating you so badly. I knew that minute I saw you back here that I'd been kidding myself."

As Rosie gazed up into his face, her azure eyes seemed to swim and she swayed toward him. "Luke," she whispered. "I don't know what to think."

"Don't think," he said, taking her into his arms. Then his mouth came down on hers.

AS HE HELD HER, she could feel the towel slip from her shoulders. With a splash, it fell into the pool. But Rosie was beyond caring. Her mouth softened under Luke's and her hands went to his chest and stroked the dark whirls of hair around his nipples. With a groan, he deepened the kiss and drew her against his body. She went willingly. Even though she'd been fighting the temptation the past few days, at night she'd been dreaming of this.

As they kissed, all the horrors and destruction they'd witnessed faded and they were lost in a world that belonged only to them. His fingers slipped beneath one thin strap of her suit and he pressed his lips to the soft skin of her shoulder. Rosie quivered and slid her hands around his lean waist to his broad back, so that her breasts were pressed against his naked flesh. A deep heat flamed up between them, and he took the strap he was fingering and let it fall over the edge of her shoulder.

"Rosie," he murmured, "I really meant it when I called you a beautiful mermaid. You could lure any man." With a smooth motion, he tipped her back in his arms and dropped kisses on the side of her throat where her pulse throbbed.

From deep within her, an ache arose, an ache so strong and in need of satisfaction that she was helpless in its grip. Luke seemed to be possessed by an equally fierce hunger. His seeking mouth had found the soft mound of her breast, and pushing the other strap down, he nuzzled the valley between. As she shifted to accommodate him, she felt the concrete beneath them rub coarsely against her bare thighs.

Luke noticed her discomfort. "Why don't we go inside?"

That broke the mood, and conscious of where they were, Rosie shifted. "I don't know," she began to demur, thinking that someone might look out from the house and see them.

"Come with me, Rosie," he said, overwhelming her reticence. He stood and helped her to her feet. Wordlessly he swept her up in his arms and carried her around the back of the house to his private office annex.

As he pushed open the door, Rosie buried her face against his chest. Her whole body was aflame. It didn't seem to matter that this might not be wise. Nothing mattered but being with Luke and satisfying the need pulsing within her.

Inside, steering by the security light filtering through the glass block wall, Luke carried Rosie up the staircase to his private aerie. Gently he set her down on her feet onto the Oriental rug, and for a moment they stood smiling into each other's eyes. Tenderly he stroked her silky hair. "I want you."

The simple words moved her. She wanted him, too. Putting her arms around his neck, she let him draw her close. They kissed lingeringly, their tongues entwining.

Finally Luke pulled away. He grinned. "Maybe we should get out of these wet suits."

Rosie grinned back. "I thought you'd never ask." She rested her arms on his shoulders while he reached around to her back and unhooked her green bandeau top. As the damp scrap of fabric loosened, he kissed the soft skin it revealed. Rosie shivered with pleasure.

As her top fell away, he openly admired her naked beauty, his eyes growing dark with passion. "Rosie, you're so beautiful," he murmured. "After we made love on the beach, I couldn't believe it had really happened. This time I want to savor every moment."

His head bent to kiss the tip of each taut nipple. Again and again he kissed and caressed her breasts. Overwhelmed with pleasure, Rosie closed her eyes. Even the beard-roughened texture of his cheeks as they nuzzled the valley of her bosom heightened her sensual delight. When his tongue licked the aroused flesh, liquid heat streamed to the sensitive area between her thighs. As if sensing the tumult inside her, Luke languorously brushed his hand inside her bikini bottom and stroked the velvety skin of her flat belly. When his knowing fingertips shifted lower and circled her mound of Venus, Rosie sank against him.

Inarticulate with excitement, she gasped as his fingers probed. Feeling her response, he peeled the rest of her bathing suit down to her ankles. Kneeling, he helped her step out of it. While she gracefully balanced herself against his shoulders, he picked up one small foot and dropped kisses on her instep, then the hollow by her tendon and finally the smooth curve of her calf. Shivering in anticipation, Rosie stroked his dark curls as his mouth eased up to her inner thigh, where it fanned the tender flesh with feather-light caresses.

Then his lips found the tender knob of flesh most responsive to his masculine assault. Rosie's legs trembled as waves of pleasure surged through her. He held her soft hips firmly and he worked his tongue up and down, tormenting her with fiery darts of sensual bliss. It was almost too much and Rosie gripped his shoulders to steady herself.

A moment later, he rose and her eyes went to the masculine bulge in his trunks. In seconds they were off. It was then that she saw the commanding erection the suit had concealed. Wanting to give him back some of the pleasure he'd given her, Rosie sensually stroked the shaft with her long fingers. He groaned and tipped his head back, tightening his hands on her waist.

When both of them could wait no longer, he led her over to the large white modular couch that faced the view of the sea and lay her on it. And then he was beside her, kissing her passionately.

"Oh, Rosie," he groaned, and thrust deep inside her. She gripped him with her legs, and they rocked back and forth, struggling toward the fulfillment they both so desperately wanted. They climbed together, higher and higher, and then in a burst of scarlet heat, they climaxed, first Rosie and then Luke.

Afterward they lay in each other's arms, basking in the afterglow of their lovemaking. Though it had been glorious, Rosie realized that there was something more she wanted from Luke. She wanted to hear him say "I love you." But the words didn't come.

Chapter Twelve

Other words came.

"That felt so good." Luke stroked her hair and then the sloping curve of her hip. "You're amazing, Rosie Clarke," he murmured. "I love to hold you. I don't want to let you go tonight."

"Well, you're going to have to," Rosie said, giving him a playful pat. "I have to get back."

"Wait," he said, pulling away slightly and studying her face in the dim light. "Don't run off again."

"Oh, I'm not running off, I've just got to—"

Suddenly Luke looked worried. "Rosie, I haven't said anything or done anything to offend you, have I?"

She looked at him. He'd been the perfect lover and she knew it was unreasonable to expect more, but she couldn't help feeling let down. After they'd found such physical bliss together, she'd needed to know he really cared about her and none of his compliments had been enough to convince her of that.

"Oh, no, Luke," she said, not wanting to let him know how needy she felt. "I should be there when Chris and Liliana wake up. And I do have another long day at work tomorrow."

His head sunk back on the pillows. "Oh, yes, the real world. I'd forgotten about it."

She sat up and bent to search for her bathing suit.

"Why don't I give you my terry robe? I keep one on the back of the bathroom door for when I have the impulse to soak in the hot tub."

She picked up the wet suit and held it at arm's length. "I think I'll take you up on that."

"Be right back." He stood and strolled out of the room. As she watched his naked form disappear, she admired his long muscular legs, his firm derriere and the way his broad back tapered to a narrow waist.

Moments later Luke returned, wearing a pair of jeans and carrying a large terry bathrobe. He helped her slip it on. After she'd belted it, he drew her to him once again and kissed her deeply, exploring her mouth with his tongue. All her resolve to leave faded, and she melted against him. Then once again they were both naked, clasped tightly in each other's arms, this time on the Oriental rug.

Finally, however, they managed to get dressed and stay that way. Not wanting to put on the still-wet bathing suit, Rosie crumpled it in her hand. "You don't need to walk me back," she said when they stepped outside into the starlight. "I know my way."

"Yes, but I guarantee you'll have more fun if I escort you," he said with a cavalier bow.

She arched an eyebrow. "Oh, really?"

They strolled down the flagstone path, talking lightly. A breeze cooled the evening and he slipped his arm around her shoulder.

They had just rounded the corner by the tall yucca plant near the pool, when they both realized they were no longer alone. A large figure emerged from the shadows near the lounge chairs.

"Ah, these must be the culprits now," Beatrice said, holding up Rosie's sodden towel. "The bottom of the pool is a strange place to hang your towel."

Luke took his arms from around Rosie's shoulders and reached to take the soppy material from his aunt. "Guilty as charged."

"You two been swimming?" Beatrice's eyes went to Rosie's hand. Quickly Rosie crumpled the bathing suit more tightly, but she felt sure that Beatrice had seen it and drawn the right conclusion about why it was in her hand and not on her body.

"We had a dip earlier," Luke said, then changed the subject. "It's after midnight. You just get back?"

Even in the dim light, Rosie could see that Beatrice was dressed to the hilt in a flowing embroidered kimono topping a long skirt. Her silver hair was piled high on her head and fixed with jeweled combs. And, as always, she wore her signature pearls.

"The dinner party was wonderful. Sorry you didn't make it, Luke. The Robertsons asked after you."

"Well, the Robertsons always put on a great feast. But I had more pressing matters to deal with tonight."

"I can see that," Beatrice said. She turned to Rosie. "I'm glad Luke is making you feel at home. I hope you're finding our guest house comfortable."

"Oh, yes," Rosie replied, happy for the darkness, which masked her fierce blush. At the moment she felt anything but comfortable. She could feel the other woman's gaze penetrating her robe and felt sure Luke's aunt knew she wore nothing beneath it.

"Well, would you please excuse me," Rosie said, thinking it was best to sidestep any more discussion. "I've got to get some sleep.'' With that, she headed to the safe haven of her little borrowed house. Already living here was getting complicated.

AFTER ROSIE DISAPPEARED, Luke turned back to his aunt. ''What was that all about?'' His voice was low and angry.

''What was what all about?''

''Please keep your voice down, Aunt Beatrice,'' he commanded. ''I'm referring to the way you were talking to Rosie just now.''

Beatrice fingered her beads. ''I was being perfectly civil.''

''I wouldn't call that crack about the towel 'civil.'''

''Come, Luke. Don't you have any sense of humor?'' She took a playful swat at her nephew.

Unamused, he wrung out the towel with his strong hands. ''Let's go inside before we wake up the neighborhood.''

Once on the other side of the door, Luke strode to the laundry room, where he threw the towel in the stainless steel sink.

Beatrice followed him and blocked the door. ''It's perfectly obvious why that towel was floating in the water and why your house guest was wearing your bathrobe. Perhaps you both were a little preoccupied.''

''Perhaps, Aunt Beatrice.'' Luke's dark eyes challenged his aunt's.

For a moment it was a standoff. Then Beatrice raised a hand.

''Very well, it's none of my business. I'm sorry, Luke. It's just that this volcano madness has got me all aflutter.'' She pressed a hand against her substantial left breast. ''That was all anybody talked about tonight. In fact, the

Robertsons are even considering leaving for their place on the mainland."

"And?"

She lifted her shoulders. "They asked me why I don't go back to my place on Maui."

"Well, that's an idea if you're really upset about the new eruption."

Beatrice looked disturbed. As Luke watched her, he guessed part of what was in her mind. The house in Maui, although pleasant, was not as grand as Orchid Cliffs. There Beatrice didn't move in the kind of society circles she did here, thanks to her connection to him. Furthermore, ever since his uncle Charles had died, Beatrice had been lonely. Being here had filled her need to feel important.

"But of course, dear, I'd feel like a rat if I abandoned you," Beatrice went on.

Luke smiled. "You wouldn't be abandoning me. And I wouldn't be alone. I've got Rosie and Christopher here—and a whole house staff."

A worried expression crossed his aunt's face and she began to knead her beads. "But that's not the same as having family around—people who really care about you."

Luke eyed his relative. When she'd first come to live at Orchid Cliffs, her high-society airs had amused him. But lately, especially since Rosie had returned to his life, he'd been thinking how much he'd like his house back.

"Maybe Rosie and Christopher will be family someday soon," he finally said.

Beatrice's eyes widened. "How do you mean that, Luke?"

"Just what I said."

Clearly disturbed, she tightened her grip on her pearls and twisted them into a knot. "Be honest with me now, Luke. You've evaded my question before, but I swear, that boy looks just like you when you were small—and you've been treating him as if he were your son." She paused for emphasis. "Is he yours?"

Luke hesitated. He had promised Rosie that he wouldn't tell anyone, but he was growing impatient with that promise. Besides, Beatrice had already guessed and he wasn't going to lie.

"Yes, Christopher is my son."

Beatrice's face drained. "I'm not sure whether to be happy or upset."

"Try happy."

His aunt was quiet for a moment. "Do you love this woman?"

He looked down at his bare feet and considered his feelings. "I'm thinking about it."

"Oh, Luke," Beatrice implored. "The little boy is adorable. But you're a wealthy man with a lot to lose. Think carefully. Be sure before you make any irrevocable commitments."

"LIKE IT UP HERE?" Luke asked. He held Christopher tightly with one arm while he guided Kameha, his big black gelding, along the shore. The sunlight sparkled on the incoming waves and the sun warmed their shoulders. The little boy's small body fit comfortably against his chest and Luke felt a surge of parental pride.

That morning Luke had persuaded Liliana to let him take the boy riding.

"As long as you're careful," she'd said, scowling at him suspiciously.

Mischievously he'd chucked her under her chin. "I'll treat him as if he were made of glass."

"He's not glass," she'd retorted stoutly. "But looking at him, I'd say he was made of the same stuff you are."

Luke had to restrain himself from laughing out loud. Now, not only did Beatrice know that Chris was his son, but Liliana obviously suspected, as well. Luke didn't mind in the least. It was hiding the truth and living a lie with the boy that bothered him. Tonight he'd discuss the matter with Rosie, he decided.

"Just about time to get back for lunch," he told Chris. "You ready to eat something?"

"A peanut-butter sandwich?" Chris asked hopefully.

Luke chuckled. "I'm sure Mrs. Waneka will have something good for us." He reined Kameha and turned the horse's handsome black head toward the path that lead up from the beach to the ridge where Orchid Cliffs sat. They ambled down the lane, and when they got close to the stables, they dismounted and walked the rest of the way. Lee, the groomer, greeted them and led Kameha back to the stalls.

"Want to help brush Kameha down?"

"Can I?" Chris asked. His dark eyes danced.

"Sure. Every man should know how to groom his horse."

They followed Lee and found him sliding the saddle from Kameha's tall back. Then they watched as he began brushing the gelding down.

"Can I do that?" Chris asked.

Lee grinned, glanced at Luke, who nodded approval, and handed the little boy the brush. Gingerly, with Luke standing close to make sure he didn't get into trouble, Chris stroked the horse's satiny flanks.

"Kameha's a little tall for you. What you need is something more your size—like a pony."

"A pony! Did you have a pony when you were a kid?" Chris asked.

"Yes. I had a great pony. His name was Sundancer. My dad gave him to me for my fifth birthday. Boy, that was a day I'll never forget!"

Chris looked at Luke with adoring eyes. "I wish I had a dad. I wish you were my dad."

Luke felt a tug at his heart. He squatted and took Chris into his arms. "I'd like nothing better myself." At that moment the temptation to tell Chris the truth was overwhelming. It was almost cruel not to tell him.

Liliana's voice saved him from dealing with the dilemma. She came thundering down the fields and into the stable, her hair flying and her skirts whipping around her thick ankles. Huffing and puffing, she came to a halt a few feet away from them.

"Something wrong?" Luke demanded, releasing the boy and rising to his feet.

"Rosie just called from the observatory," Liliana got out. "Good news and bad news. First the good. The lava has turned away from Niha, so Madame Pele," she said, casting her eyes heavenward, "has saved my village—at least for now."

"Well, that's great—" Luke began, but she interrupted him.

"Not so great for Mr. Fan, though. Now his store is in Pele's path. It looks as though she'll eat it up."

Luke frowned.

"Mr. Fan's ice-cream store?" Chris cried out, sounding horrified.

Luke put an arm around his shoulder. "I'm afraid so." He looked up at Liliana. "Has he done anything to get his merchandise out?"

Liliana shrugged. "Don't know."

"We've got to help him!" Chris cried.

Luke knelt in front of the little boy. "I'll tell you what. Why don't you stay here and let Mrs. Waneka give you lunch? I'll go down and help Mr. Fan."

"Mr. Fan is my friend. I want to help," Christopher insisted.

Luke patted him on the shoulder. "Okay, we'll have Mrs. Waneka make us a care package and we'll eat on the way."

"I'm coming, too," Liliana broke in.

"Good idea," Luke said, accepting gratefully the momentary truce that had sprung up between them.

Equipped with bag lunches from Mrs. Waneka's kitchen, the trio hopped in Luke's truck and headed southeast toward Mr. Fan's store. Along the way, the egg-salad sandwiches, soft drinks and apples disappeared quickly. Driving was smooth sailing until they were forced to veer onto the shoulder as a tractor trailer hauling a large bungalow wobbled past.

"We'll be seeing a lot more of that," Luke commented grimly.

"Where are they going with it?" Liliana asked.

"My guess is that they'll park it alongside of the road somewhere and wait to see if there's anything left of the island when Madam Pele gets finished."

As they approached Mr. Fan's place, the traffic thickened. They weren't the only islanders who loved the old man and were concerned about what happened to him. Many of those who came to help were BICC members. The rest, Luke supposed, were curious tourists.

When they arrived at the store, Luke could see the glowing red band of the lava flow way up along the ridge. He wondered how fast it was moving. Often he'd seen lava creep, oozing forward, then seeming to stop, then oozing forward again like living red-hot slime. It could be days; it could be hours.

"Look at that stubborn old goat," Liliana said, gesturing with her head. "A river of lava headed his way and he's sitting on the porch in a rocking chair."

Indeed, she was right. The old man, surrounded by concerned friends and relatives, looked as though he didn't have a care in the world.

When Luke, Chris and Liliana walked up, Mr. Fan stood. "Come for some ice cream, bruddah?" he called out to Chris. "I give you your favorite—double chocolate."

Luke put his hands on his hips.

"We've been trying to tell him, it's time to save his stock and equipment, but he won't budge," Mary Burns called out. She was one of the concerned people on the porch.

Mr. Fan grinned. "That old gal Pele has been threatening me for years. But she never got me and she ain't going to get me this time, bruddah."

Liliana glanced up at the narrow band of fire that seemed to have pushed a little lower during the short time they'd been there bantering with the stubborn shopkeeper. "Don't bet the store on it."

Ignoring her, Mr Fan took Chris's hand and led him inside. "Come on, the cone's on me."

A few minutes later, Chris and Mr. Fan emerged. Chris was licking his fat ice-cream cone, but there was a worried expression on his small face. "I'm scared the fire's going to burn up the store," he exclaimed. The boy and the old man both looked up at Pele's creeping snake of fire.

Luke followed their gaze. The terrain sloped sharply toward the valley where the store sat. Once it reached the drop-off, the lava would flow quickly.

Mr. Fan sighed. "Breaks my heart to think of all da ice cream I've got in there. Should be throwing a party."

"No time for that," Luke told him firmly. "Instead of pretending that this isn't happening, we should be getting all your equipment and stock out."

For the first time, Mr. Fan's brow was furrowed. He shook his head.

Liliana loomed over the small, ancient man. "We need to do this *wikiwiki.*"

"Come on," Luke said, giving him a pat on the shoulder. "I've brought my truck and so have a lot of other people here. We'll save everything we can—maybe even some of that ice cream."

Mr. Fan sighed and muttered *"Auwe."* Then, acquiescing, he and the others set to work. The rest of the afternoon, they hauled loads of groceries, liquor and what furnishings they could fit into their cars and trucks. By late afternoon, most of the store had been packed up.

Proudly Luke had watched Chris, who had proven to be one of the most energetic volunteers, carrying out armloads of candy and magazines and helping Mr. Fan take down the old photographs on the bulletin board.

"Who's this little boy?" Christopher asked, pointing at a snapshot.

Luke, who was dismantling a display case, had turned his head to see what Christopher was talking about.

"Ah," Mr. Fan, said, flicking the photograph with his nail, "dat be a snap of Luke over there when he your age." Mr. Fan stared at the photo and then at Chris. An odd expression came over his face and he opened his mouth to make a comment, but shut it again. Luke sighed. He and Rosie would have to tell Christopher the truth, the sooner, the better.

An hour later, Christopher sat in a corner, his eyelids drooping. "You look beat, buddy," Luke said, rubbing the little boy's head. He turned to Liliana. "Maybe you should take him home. Mary Burns is heading back that way."

Liliana stretched and yawned. "Okay."

Luke glanced out the window. In the hours that they'd been working, the lava had inched much closer. Picking up the binoculars, he studied the simmering fire. He could see trees in its path turning into torches, then falling into its shapeless jaws. Pretty soon, he knew, the very boards he was standing on would be incinerated in the same way. And only hours, after it gorged itself on Mr. Fan's store, it would be at the doors of Rosie's rental cottage.

Once Liliana, Mary Burns and Christopher were gone, Luke redoubled his efforts to save what he could of Mr. Fan's livelihood. He and Joe Rodriguez had just lifted the last carton of groceries onto Fred Myers's truck, when Rosie pulled up. She looked exhausted. Though she'd tied her hair back, loose strands had escaped from her scarf and hung around her face in an auburn fringe. She wore no makeup and her eyes were red from sleeplessness. Even so, she looked beautiful to Luke.

"Any trouble getting through?" Luke asked as he came over to her car.

"The road's still clear, but I don't know how much longer it will stay that way," she said, opening the door and swinging her sneakers out onto the hard packed earth.

Luke turned back to Fred and Joe. "How's it going? You almost done?"

The two younger men nodded grimly. "Think maybe it's time to pull out?" Joe asked.

"Yup," Luke said.

"Not for me." Mr. Fan's jaw set. "I'm going to see this to the end."

"Okay," Luke said. "I'll stay with you. But I'm going to move the truck."

"I think I'll do the same thing." Rosie climbed back into her car and followed Luke out to a safer spot. As they walked back, Luke questioned her about the lava's progress. "You've had a rough day. You look really beat."

She sighed. "It's a madhouse up at the observatory. I stopped at Orchid Cliffs on the way here. Chris was napping and Liliana was dozing in a chair by the pool." She glanced over at the worm of fire that was now within fifty yards of the store and two hundred yards from where they stood off to the side out of danger. The wind carried the sound of its ominous crackling and the pungent sulfur smell burned their nostrils. As they stood next to Mr. Fan and watched the lava surge forward, they lost all sense of time. It was as if they were caught in a moment unconnected to every other kind of reality.

When the lava did reach the edge of the property, a shudder went through the stoic Mr. Fan. "You know, bruddah," he began, "I can't believe Madame Pele, she be so cruel to me." He watched a lick of flame shoot out and torch a palm tree. "Maybe she spare me yet. Sometimes she do that. Stops only one foot away." He held his hands twelve inches apart. "Did dat couple years back—Keary's Furniture Store." His words were brave, but his voice lacked conviction.

Luke and Rosie put their arms around Mr. Fan's shoulders and waited. They both knew a miracle wasn't going to happen this time.

As the lava rushed on, filling the air with sulfur and the crackling of burning plants, Mr. Fan started to reminisce. He talked about the old days when Luke's father and mother were still alive. "They fine people," he said. "Raised fine son." Then he talked about Black Crescent Beach, where Rosie's cottage was, and how his ancestors used to live in grass shacks there until they could afford to build regular houses inland. "Maybe I be living in a grass shack again," he speculated as he eyed the incoming lava that was now just a few feet from the store. "Should have saved some of that gin."

"I'm afraid it will take a lot more than gin to stop Pele now," Luke replied.

And he was right. Fifteen minutes later, Pele's tongue of fire lashed at the wooden frame shop. The air thickened with gray smoke and in minutes the wooden building turned black and crumbled into ash.

Tears streamed down Mr. Fan's face and Rosie's, as well. Even Luke's eyes burned, not only from the smoke and sulfurous gases, but from the charred memories and the sense of helplessness. For a long time they stood there very quietly. Once again, Luke put his arm around Mr. Fan's shoulders. How frail they felt, Luke thought.

"Let's go," he finally said. "I'll take you back to your sister's."

In answer, Mr. Fan straightened his shoulders and strode up the road toward Luke's truck. Over his head, Luke glanced at Rosie, who was staring down the slope toward the sea. Immediately he realized what she was thinking. Her cottage would be one of the next in line. "Rosie," he said, "we'll go home and have dinner. If you want to come back to Black Crescent tonight, I'll bring you."

DINNER WAS a silent affair. Mrs. Waneka had fed Christopher and Liliana earlier and had prepared a large seafood salad for Luke, Beatrice and Rosie. When she'd gotten home, Rosie had spent a good hour answering

Christopher's questions and talking on the phone to people at work. Now, as she sat on the patio, she stared at the candles on the table. Their flickering light was hypnotic, lulling her. For the moment, she felt more like sleeping than eating. Yet there was a wire of tension tightening within her.

"Rosie," Luke said, peering at her after they'd finished their meal, "are you sure you want to go back and see what's happening with your cottage?"

She nodded. Her head felt thick with exhaustion, but she knew she had to see this thing through.

"Oh, the thought of seeing your own house burn. I just couldn't stand it," Beatrice exclaimed. "Can you imagine watching Orchid Cliffs go up in flames?"

"No," Luke replied sternly. "But if it did happen, I couldn't imagine not watching it, either."

Ten minutes later, Luke opened the passenger door of his truck and Rosie slid in. They drove along in silence for a while, then Luke began to speak.

"Look, Rosie, I know this is a bad time to be discussing this." He stared through the windshield. "But it doesn't look as though we're going to find any better time for a while. We need to talk about telling Christopher the truth."

Rosie wrapped her hands around her neck and rubbed at the spot of tension at the base of her skull. "Luke," she said, wearily, "we've already been through all this."

His voice grew gruff. "True, but I'm afraid we *are* going to have to go through all this again. Half the island has figured out I'm Christopher's father. Beatrice, Liliana—even Mr. Fan, for that matter—know what's what. And I think even Chris suspects. Rosie," he said, gripping the steering wheel, "I can't lie to him anymore."

"Chris?" Rosie's head jerked around. "How could he possibly suspect?"

"He's smart—he's your son and mine. Anyhow, one way or another he's going to find out soon. I want it to come from us."

Rosie didn't answer. The truck had rounded the bend and a scene burst on her that left her speechless. Against the dark night sky, the ribbon of lava had rolled over Mr. Fan's store, sweeping away all traces of its existence. Now the magma fell in a viscous waterfall, cutting off the road below as it dripped down like superheated batter and crept toward Black Crescent Beach.

A mile down the road, they stopped the truck at the overlook and got out. "Oh, my God!" Rosie exclaimed, covering her face. "Luke, my house is on fire."

"Sure you want to watch?" Luke asked, putting his arm around her and drawing her close.

She let her hands slide from her face. "I have to watch to really believe it's happening," she said. "If I hadn't seen Mr. Fan's store burn, I would have never believed it had ever existed."

Luke tightened his hold on her and kissed the top of her hair. He wasn't sure what to say, but he felt closer to Rosie at that moment than he'd ever felt before—even when they'd made love.

Palm trees in the lava's path exploded like mined tiki torches, then fell with a swoosh, crumbling like paper held to a match. Nothing could withstand Pele's onward march. Now, as they watched, an ember, then another, lit the gabled roof of the cottage she'd loved. In moments, the little pink house where Luke and Chris had first met was gone—first a flaming shell, then mere cinders, and then it was as if it had never been.

When it was over, Rosie, stressed to the breaking point by the harrowing day, buried her face in Luke's chest and cried. He stroked her quivering back and wrapped his arms tighter in a protective circle. Finally she lifted her tear-streaked face and he stroked her wet cheeks. "We're still here. We're safe and sound."

She sniffed and smiled at him through her tears. "Tomorrow we'll tell Christopher together."

Chapter Thirteen

It was warm and silent inside the truck. Rosie's head lay against Luke's shoulder and her eyes were closed. As Luke glanced down at her, a warm tide of protective feeling surged through him. Right now he wanted nothing more than to be close to Rosie. No, he wanted more than that. Though he knew they were both exhausted, he wanted to hold her in his arms the whole night long.

Back at Orchid Cliffs he helped her down out of the truck and then circled her waist with his arm. He wanted to take her back to his office, where they could be alone. She didn't seem to notice the way he was maneuvering her toward his private sanctum. They were just walking past the pool, when Beatrice came flying out the back door. With the refuge of his office so close, Luke had to suppress an irritated oath.

"Oh, Luke, thank goodness you're back. I just don't know what to do," Beatrice blurted out. "Everyone's talking about what happened to Mr. Fan's store. Even the Robertsons left the island today. With Black Crescent Beach swallowed up, what's next?" She threw up her hands and paced in a circle.

Oblivious to the way Luke held Rosie, Beatrice hurried on. "I know I should stay and help you through this terrible time. But frankly, Luke, my nerves are shot." She pressed a plump hand to her chest. "You know the doctor says I must stay away from stressful situations. Right now my heart is palpitating. That scares me and it makes everything worse."

Rosie had come out of her sleepy fog. Pulling away, she moved off to the side. She put a hand out and touched Luke. "I think you and your aunt need to talk alone. And I'm wiped out. I need to go to bed and get some sleep."

Luke shot her a frustrated look, but what could he say? Reluctantly he wished her good-night and watched her walk off. Then he returned his attention to his distraught aunt. Out of patience, he put his hands on his hips and listened to her list of woes. Finally he interrupted.

"You're right, Aunt Beatrice, all this stress isn't good for you. It would be better for you to go back to Maui, where it's safe. If you want, I'll take you to the airport first thing tomorrow."

Beatrice scrutinized his face, obviously torn. "Are you sure you can manage?"

"I'll miss you," Luke said, patting her arm, "but it will relieve my mind to know that you're safe and sound in your own home. Why don't you get some sleep?"

Beatrice shook her head. "No, my nerves are too stretched. I think I'll just wander around a bit. Maybe I'll sit out here with some nice warm milk."

Luke abandoned all hope of keeping Rosie with him tonight. Maybe it was best anyhow. Resignedly he headed for his own bed.

Once in it, however, he found sleep was impossible. For many minutes he lay reviewing all that had happened. He knew the scenes of destruction he'd seen today would be in his memory as long as he lived. His thoughts, as they always seemed to lately, turned to Rosie. He ached for her.

If only they hadn't run into Beatrice, Rosie would be in his arms right now.

There was so much he wanted to say to her. He'd been proud of her tonight, proud of her strength in this crisis as well as touched by her tenderness. Luke wanted to tell her how he felt, and if she were there crushed against his body he would. But they were apart and likely to remain so, at least for another night. Yet it didn't have to be this way, he thought. Maybe it was time he did something about it.

FIFTY YARDS AWAY, in the guest house on the other side of the pool, Rosie lay tossing and turning. She'd been so tired that she'd expected to fall asleep the minute she'd hit the pillow. Instead she lay wide awake, staring at the ceiling. *Rosie, close your eyes. Go to sleep now. You're going to need all your strength tomorrow.*

But the pep talk didn't work. Sleep wouldn't come. Finally Rosie gave in to her thoughts. Uppermost was the pain and despair she'd seen tonight. However, as she replayed the day's events, the lead role in all of them was held by Luke.

She remembered the way he'd walked her back to her room, and her mind did a little double take. Actually, now that she thought about it, he hadn't been walking her back to her room. He'd been guiding her toward his studio. At the back of her mind she'd known that. But she'd been so shell-shocked that his intention hadn't registered. Now it did.

At first she felt a twinge of regret that Beatrice had short-circuited things. It would be lovely to be lying within the comfort of Luke's strong arms this very minute. Then Rosie thought again. Was that really what she wanted? Already she'd let Luke make love to her twice. Did she want to be his regular live-in lover?

No, she definitely did not want that sort of relationship. For one thing, it wouldn't be fair to Christopher. Already the tongues of the island gossips must be wagging. Now she'd made that worse by moving in at Orchid Cliffs. *What were you thinking, Rosie, when you let Luke talk you into this.* As soon as she could, as soon as things settled down, she'd have to make other arrangements.

THE NEXT MORNING Rosie got up earlier than usual. She had just taken a quick swim and was climbing out of the pool, when Luke came out to the patio with two cups of coffee in his hand.

"I saw you from the kitchen window." He put the steaming cup of Kona coffee down on the glass-topped table and picked up the towel she'd left on the chair and draped it over her shoulders.

"Thank you." Conscious of his gaze on her body, Rosie took a corner of the terry cloth and started drying her hair. As she worked on it, she shot Luke a curious glance. There was something different about him this morning. He seemed preoccupied.

For a few minutes he watched her. Then, when she'd wrapped the towel around her body and tucked in the edges to make a sarong, he handed her one of the mugs.

Rosie cradled it in her hands and savored its warmth. "I really haven't got much time," she said. "I've got to get to work." She took a sip. "Ummm, hot and strong. I really appreciate this."

"Overcast," Luke said, glancing up at the gray pall in the sky. "Smoke from Kilauea."

They stood sipping their coffee and studying the ominous heavens. Then, to Rosie's surprise, Luke reached out toward her and took away her mug. Puzzled, she let it go. As she stood gazing at him, he clasped her hand and held it between his two large ones. With a gentle smile, he brought her hand to his lips and kissed her fingertips.

Rosie's mouth dropped open and she laughed nervously. "Luke... I really do have to—"

"Rosie, I just need a minute."

"If this is about Christopher," she began, "I haven't changed my mind. We should tell him, but we should do it together. How about after dinner tonight?"

"After dinner is fine. But I've thought of something that will make it easier for both of us, Rosie."

"What's that?" Rosie eyed him. He definitely had something up his sleeve, she thought.

He clasped her hand more tightly. "I think we should get married, Rosie."

"Married?" Her jaw dropped and she tried to withdraw her hand, but he held on to it.

"I know you said you weren't interested in marriage. But I hope now you'll reconsider." He gave her palm a squeeze. "I spent the night lying awake thinking about this, Rosie, and it makes such perfect sense. Perfect sense for Christopher and for us. We could all have a great life together—"

With a surge of strength, Rosie yanked out of his grip and stepped back. "Don't do me any favors, Luke."

"Favors? This isn't any favor. Rosie, I'm talking about you and me and Christopher having a life together."

She threw up her hands. "When I marry I want it to be more than convenient. I want the man I marry to be in love with me, Luke. And me in love with him."

Luke stared at her. "Rosie, I really care about you."

"I know you like me, Luke, and that you like having sex with me. But that just isn't enough."

"Now, wait a minute, Rosie—" He went to touch her shoulder, but she drew back.

She couldn't bear standing here any longer. "Goodbye, Luke. I'll see you at dinnertime." And with that, she turned on her heel and strode back to her cottage.

Luke, who clearly wasn't yet ready to give up on this, followed. But just as he was close enough to Rosie to reach out and stop her, Liliana came to the screen door.

At the same time, a rusty green car chugged into the driveway, closely followed by a vintage van. A solidly built Hawaiian jumped out of the car. "Hey, cuz," he shouted at Liliana. "Here's your wheels."

"Damn," Rosie heard Luke mutter under his breath. "Damn."

Rosie stomped past Liliana's stolid figure down the hall to her bedroom. Angrily she slammed the door, then tore off the towel and her bathing suit. Throwing open the closet door, she snatched out a pair of pale blue slacks and a matching rayon shirt. After she'd pulled on her clothes, she stalked into the bathroom and took the blow-dryer down from the wall. Bending over, she aimed the nozzle at her scalp as she ran her fingers through her hair. All the while she grumbled to herself. "The nerve. Thinks he can buy me like one of his wall hangings."

She had just turned the blow-dryer off, when there was a tap on the open bathroom door. Turning, she saw Liliana planted there. With a sigh, she remembered she'd slammed the door. "Did I wake Christopher up?"

"No, but good try."

"I'm sorry, Liliana. I guess I'm just ticked off." She looked over at the tall, heavyset woman who was standing there with her hands on her hips. "I saw your cousin drive up. Is that the car you're borrowing?"

Liliana nodded. "Yep. Not real pretty, but it goes."

"A necessity around here."

Liliana didn't answer. Instead she stood placidly watching Rosie brush her red mane. "Need help with something?" Rosie questioned.

Liliana shook her long, coarse black hair. "Thought maybe you did."

Rosie pulled out her makeup kit and reached for sun block. "Oh? What would that be?"

"I don't mean to listen in. But you looked pretty *huhu* at Luke out there." With a toss of her head, she made a gesture toward the window and then mugged an angry face. "You and Luke not getting along? Means we're going to move out of here soon?"

Rosie's mascara wand stopped midair. "I think it would be a good idea. But I haven't made any plans yet."

Liliana's face took on a stubborn cast. "Moving again would be hard on Christopher. He's just getting used to this place."

"That's true," Rosie said carefully. She replaced the mascara wand in the tube. "But maybe he shouldn't get too used to it. After all the house is only borrowed."

"Why upset the child?" Liliana questioned. "He's happy here. He and Luke have hit it off really well. So well that I'm wondering—" She hesitated.

"What is it you're wondering, or can I guess?" Why not tell Liliana the truth, Rosie thought. The woman obviously already knew it, and Christopher would be hearing it tonight.

Rosie put away the makeup kit, walked into the bedroom and plopped down on the bed. "You know, don't you?"

Liliana's wise dark eyes lingered on Rosie's face. "That Luke is Christopher's father? Yes. Anyone who sees them together would know."

"I was afraid of that."

"He wants to marry you." It was a statement.

"Yes."

"Why don't you?"

Rosie shook her head and then touched her fingers to her temple. "It's very complicated, Liliana."

"What's so complicated? Christopher needs a daddy."

"I know, Liliana, I know," Rosie said, "but there are other things that go into a marriage."

"Like love?"

"Like love."

BEATRICE CRUSHED Luke to her massive bosom and enfolded him in her arms. "I'm going to miss you so much, Luke darling. I'll worry about you every single minute."

Luke smiled and drew back. "No reason to worry about me, Aunt Beatrice. I'll be fine."

She shook her head and then wiped a tear from her eyes. "Promise you'll call me and let me know what's going on."

"I promise."

Nearby the loudspeaker announced that it was time to board. All around them groups of passengers were lining up in the hazy sunlight. Many were tourists. Kilauea's fury had convinced them to cut their vacations short. Others were residents who'd been displaced. Everyone looked unhappy about the situation.

"So much for paradise," one tourist in a loud shirt complained. "Instead of babes in bikinis, we got hell and brimstone."

As the flight attendant began collecting passes before boarding, another tourist turned to his companion and declared loudly, "Goodbye, Pele. I'm outta here."

Luke grinned. It struck him as funny that for every tourist who was leaving because of Pele, more were coming in to get a closer look. Minutes earlier another plane had landed and disgorged a full complement of eager volcano watchers laden with cameras and camcorders.

As soon as Beatrice's plane had taken off for Maui, Luke turned and headed back to his truck. Leaving the airport, he drove carefully, but his concentration was on Rosie. He hadn't handled this morning right. He'd been sure that since they were lovers again she would agree to his proposal—would see how perfect it was for them to marry now and make a real home for Christopher.

But instead of falling into his arms, Rosie had reacted like a scalded cat. For several minutes he replayed the morning scene in his head. Where had he gone wrong? How had he messed it up? Suddenly it was clear to him. *Luke, you fool, a woman needs more than a blueprint as a marriage proposal.* He shook his head. Rosie wanted romance and he'd given her a Marshall Plan. He'd forgotten the L word. But clearly Rosie hadn't.

A mechanical ring broke into his thoughts. Taking one hand from the wheel, he picked up the car phone.

"Luke?"

"Yeah?" Luke recognized his builder's voice. "Ky, is that you?"

"Yep and we got a problem—a big one."

Luke hunched forward. His eyes stayed on the road, but his brows drew together in a sharp crease. "What's up?"

"Nothing good. Maile Gardens is about to go down."

"What?"

"Seems our friendly neighborhood lava flow took another little detour. It's headed straight for the development."

Luke took a deep breath. His worst fears were coming true. Madame Pele wasn't going to spare his dream project, after all. He tightened his grip on the wheel. He wasn't ready to give up yet. "Are the roads still open?"

"So far."

"I'll be right there," Luke said, hanging up.

TURNING THE WHEEL of her car in the direction of Maile Gardens, Rosie saw that the late afternoon had turned even hazier. A yellow sulfurous cast hung over the mountains and draped the valleys, and a light mist of rain was falling.

Rosie shifted in her seat. Late that morning, she'd spotted the change in the lava flow's direction. Ever since, she'd been worried sick about the people in Maile Gardens and Luke, as well. Even though she was still angry with him, she knew what the place meant to him and to the people who had moved there.

What's more, the depth and duration of the seismic patterns they'd been monitoring since the day before yesterday made all the volcanologists' neck hairs stand on end. It was a harmonic tremor—a steady pulsing that told them all that the red-hot magma was coursing through underground tunnels in a steady progress to the surface. The flow would not be stopping anytime soon.

Climbing out of her car, she stared down into the valley, where a spout of white-hot flame shot from a sea of black-topped lava. The crust, dark and lunar, was broken by deep red fissures. A spot of yellow caught her eye and Rosie squinted and grabbed for the binoculars she was wearing around her neck. Focusing quickly, she made out a brightly painted pickup truck that had obviously been abandoned. It had been caught by the creeping fire and now as it sunk below into the simmering stew of lava, it made her think of a bronzed baby shoe.

Suddenly she needed to move on. She needed to know that the people in Maile Gardens were okay.

Luckily the section of road she'd taken was east of the flow and she was able to drive into the development. As she passed the entrance sign, she had to veer around two power company trucks. The men in yellow hard hats appeared to be dismantling the electric lines feeding out of the main supply. Beyond them, Rosie saw what looked like a scene of chaos. But as she drove farther in, she realized that the activity all around her was well organized.

Trucks, trailers and heavy moving equipment littered the roads. Civil defense and Red Cross workers hovered, helping distraught homeowners who were carting their belongings out of their houses. And once again, members of the BICC, who didn't already live in the Gardens, had come to pitch in.

As she wended her way through the tangled mass of movers and homeowners, Rosie heard a few people laughing and joking about their predicament with gallows humor. Others, however, were silent. They stared sadly at prized gardens or gazed mournfully up at houses that she knew Luke had poured his soul into designing.

Halfway down the main road, the car's progress was blocked by a huge flatbed truck. "Uh-oh, time to back up," she said aloud, throwing the dusty vehicle into reverse and maneuvering into a driveway. Stepping out of the car, Rosie got a good look at the house across the street. It was Toshiko Hayakawa's.

It appeared much different from the way it had when Rosie toured it with Luke. The elegant Japanese gardens had been torn out and workmen had knocked off the multilevel decks that had tied it to the landscape. Now, with clanging blows, they were detaching the already-shored-up structure from its foundation. Immediately she recognized the broad back and narrow waist of one of the men in hard hats. When he turned his head, Rosie could see that Luke's expression was grim but full of determination.

Off to the side Toshiko stood forlornly. She was flanked by her husband and two children, whose anxious faces were a mirror of her own. How sad, Rosie thought. And how sad for Luke to see his dream project go up in smoke. At least, from the looks of what was going on, he was probably going to be able to save some of the houses.

Oh, now I see, Rosie said to herself. That's why the power company was out there taking down lines—it was the only way they'd get any of these big houses through the entrance to the main road.

Rosie's eyes were still on Luke. Obviously he wouldn't be around to talk to Christopher tonight. With guilty relief, she realized they'd have to put their plans on hold.

Rolling up her sleeves and ready to help, she walked toward Toshiko. Two hours later when the house was on the truck, Luke came over to Rosie, who was helping the Halls dig up a few of the prized specimens they'd planted in their front yard.

Luke wiped a hand across his dirt-streaked brow. He shook his head. "Time is running out."

Rosie studied the grim expression on his face and nodded.

"And I have three more houses to move," he went on.

She stood and brushed her hands on her jeans. "You'll do it, Luke."

He looked up toward the volcano. "If Madame Pele permits."

FIFTEEN MILES AWAY at Orchid Cliffs, Liliana and Christopher emerged from the swimming pool. "Can I have a banana?'' the little boy asked as he trotted next to Liliana toward the guest house. In his arms he carried a green plastic inner tube adorned with an alligator head.

''A small one,'' Liliana said. ''When you get dressed, I'll make dinner.''

''Is my mommy going to eat with us?''

Liliana shook her head. ''She called. The volcano is plenty *huhu*. Making a lot of trouble for people on the island. Your mommy and Luke are helping out.''

''I hardly see her anymore,'' Christopher complained.

Liliana nodded sympathetically. ''She feels plenty bad about that. Things will change as soon as Madame Pele settles down again.'' Pulling open the door, she ushered Christopher inside to the kitchen.''

''Why is Madame Pele so mad?'' Christopher wanted to know. Liliana had opened the refrigerator to see what Mrs. Waneka had left for them and the little boy came alongside and stuck his head in under her raised arm. ''Mmm.''

Liliana lifted a sheet of aluminum foil. ''Salmon.''

Christopher made a face and pulled out. ''I'd rather have a hamburger.'' He stood on tiptoe and grabbed a banana from a bowl on the counter. Turning back the peel, he looked at Liliana curiously. ''Did you ever meet Madame Pele?''

Liliana got a faraway look in her eyes. ''Once,'' she replied. ''It was many years ago. I was just a little girl, picking flowers outside my village, when I met an old woman. She wanted me to give her one of my flowers. It was lucky I was in a generous mood and I did. Afterward my mother told me that the old woman was Madame Pele testing me.''

''What would she do if you didn't give her your flowers?''

Liliana shook her head. ''Something terrible. Madame Pele has a temper. There is a story behind this,'' she began, pulling out a chair for herself and Christopher. After he was seated on her lap, she continued, "In the old days, long before any of us were born, we had a chief named Kaha-wali."

Christopher giggled at the name, but Liliana raised a stern hand to silence him.

"Kaha-wali liked to sled."

"Sled? There's no snow here."

"Ah," Rosie said with a sly smile, "but Kaha-wali had a sled that ran on grass. The sled had polished wood runners that slid so fast they scorched the grass." She made a swooping gesture. "One day, a very ugly woman came up to Kaha-wali and wanted to borrow his sled. He refused. Now, that was not a good thing to do. The old woman was Pele. When she heard him say no, her eyes became hot coals." Liliana made circles of her thumbs and forefingers and put them against her eyes. "And her hair turned to flame. She stamped on the ground." Liliana made banging noises with her feet. "And," she said, lifting her hands, "lava shot up. Kaha-wali tried to run away *wiki-wiki* on his sled, but Pele is too fast."

Christopher's eyes were wide. "What happened then?"

"Kaha-wali was chased into the sea and the volcano exploded."

"Boy, Madame Pele sure has a temper."

"Yes, she does. You should never do anything to make her angry," Liliana concluded, taking the empty banana peel from Christopher's hand. "Now, let's get into dry clothes before we eat our dinner."

In Christopher's room, Liliana opened his bureau drawers and ran her hand around in search of a pair of clean shorts. Instead, in one of them her fingers encountered a shoe box. "What's this?" she said, taking it out and removing the lid.

"My rock collection," Chris replied, coming over to peer in the box and pick out a prized stone. "Look at this." He held up the translucent chunk. "My grandma gave me this. It's rose quartz."

But Liliana's eyes were focused on something else. With great deliberation, she fished out a large smooth black chunk. She held it up to the light and frowned. "Where did you get this?"

For a minute, Chris looked guilty. "I don't know," he said, rocking from side to side.

Liliana aimed a sharp glance at him. "Christopher, I think you do know. Now, tell me the truth."

Christopher studied his bare feet. "I got it down by the place with big wooden statues."

"The sacred site?"

Christopher shook his head up and down.

"When?"

"You know, when me, Mommy and Grandma went to your big party. We went to the place with the big statues first."

"The luau." Liliana's bosom heaved with a big sigh. "This is not good. This stone is the property of Madame Pele."

The little boy looked stricken. "I didn't know that. Honest!"

"Well, now you know. Lava rocks are *kapu.* You should never take anything that belongs to Madame Pele. It's bad luck."

"Am I going to have bad luck? Is she going to chase me into the ocean?" The little boy's voice began to tremble.

Liliana folded her arms across her chest. "Not if we take it back *wikiwiki.*"

"Now?"

She nodded. "Now."

Christopher swallowed and, clutching Kong to his chest, took Liliana's hand. Together they hurried out to the borrowed old green Chevy.

HOURS LATER, Rosie tiptoed into the guest house. It was past ten and she didn't want to wake Christopher and Liliana. Dirty and bone tired, she headed for the shower. Shedding her grimy blue slacks and shirt, she stepped under the pulsing water and luxuriated in the soothing spray as it beat against her weary body. Helping the families at Maile Gardens had been emotionally draining and physically exhausting.

After she'd towelled off and slipped on her nightgown and robe, Rosie padded over to Christopher's room to look in on him. Quietly she swung open his door and walked in. The moonlight from the open window cast a square of silver light on the empty bed and her heart jumped. She pressed a hand against her chest. *Okay, Rosie, you're just spooked. Maybe he had a nightmare. God knows, this hasn't been an easy time for him. He's probably sleeping with Liliana,* she thought.

Turning, she headed back down the hall toward Liliana's room. A moment later she stood inside it, staring at the neatly made bed. Then she looked out the window and realized the old green car Liliana had borrowed was missing. Had Liliana taken Christopher off in it? But it was so late. Where could they be?

Chapter Fourteen

Rosie looked at her wristwatch. Midnight. She'd spent the past two hours on the phone, calling around, trying to find some trace of Chris and Liliana. Her first phone call had been to the big house, but Mrs. Waneka knew nothing. Then she'd tried Liliana's relatives in Niha. They, too, drew a blank. Next she'd phoned neighbors, including Mary Burns, then the police, the hospital, even the Red Cross station. Again, nothing.

In between she'd kept trying Luke's car phone. All she got was ringing and the mobile operator's recorded announcement that the party she was calling wasn't available. Apparently Luke was still busy with his house-moving. Now, in desperation, she tried again. To her relief, he picked up on the first ring.

"Luke?"

"Rosie?"

"Luke, do you know where Christopher is?" she blurted out.

There was a second of surprised silence. "Isn't he home with you?"

"Oh, Luke, Chris is missing. Liliana is missing. Her car is missing. Nobody knows where they are. I'm worried. It's so late. Where could they have gone?"

Luke was a pillar of strength. "Whoa, back up, Rosie. Look, I'm only a couple of miles away from the house. Hold on, I'll be there in five minutes."

"Please, hurry." Until that minute Rosie hadn't realized how truly worried she was. When she put down the receiver, her hands trembled.

The five minutes seemed like five years. When she finally heard the sound of a car motor in the driveway, her heart leaped. Her first hope was that it was Liliana with Christopher in tow. It wasn't, and when Luke walked in she stared at him tensely. Wordlessly he crossed the room and folded her into his arms. As he held her securely, he stroked her loose hair and then the silky sleeve of her robe. Pushing aside all their differences, she clung to him, taking comfort from the contact with his warm, hard body. Then she pulled away.

"Rosie, start from the beginning and tell me everything."

As she paced nervously, she filled Luke in, including everywhere she'd called. Halfway through the list, the phone rang. Rosie rushed to it and snatched up the receiver.

"Liliana?"

To her disappointment, it was George at the station. "More trouble," he said. "Looks like the lava isn't going to spare the sacred site near Niha. Just as we expected, it's heading right for it."

"What are the chances it will hit the village?"

"Hard to say at this point. I certainly wouldn't plan on planting a garden tomorrow if I lived there."

"Has anybody called about my son?" she broke in.

George was obviously surprised by the abrupt change of subject. "No," he replied slowly.

Trying to keep the hysteria out of her voice, she explained what had happened. Concerned, he promised to call if he heard anything.

When she hung up, she turned to Luke. "I can't just sit here. I've got to go find them."

Luke stood gazing at Rosie, seeing the anxiety on her face. Panic was rising inside him, as well. After the grueling day he'd just been through, he'd felt completely wiped out. Now, knowing that his little boy might be in danger, he could feel his adrenaline surging. Still, he didn't want to go off half-cocked.

"Rosie, where would you start? This is a big island. Do you have any idea where to look?"

Rosie was already running back to her bedroom to dress. She threw up her hands. "I don't know, I'm just going."

"Well, I'll drive you," he declared, striding after her. "If we take my truck, we've got the car phone. I'll write a note for Liliana to call us in case they come back while we're gone."

While Rosie pulled on her clothes, Luke went into the kitchen. For a moment, he stood at the sink, lost. Then, shaking himself, he turned on the tap and got a glass of water. The liquid felt good going down his dry throat, parched from the volcanic ash that hung in the air. He splashed water on his face and tore a paper towel off the roll on the wall to dry himself. The towel came away gray and streaked.

He hadn't eaten any dinner that night, yet the hollow feeling in his stomach came not from hunger but from fear. Where would Liliana have taken Christopher and why? What made sense? Could she have brought him to Niha? Rosie had already called the cousins and they didn't know anything. Wild speculations began to circulate through his brain.

"Did you check the beach house?" he asked when Rosie emerged, dressed in jeans and a sweatshirt.

A light went off in her eyes. "No, I never even thought of that. I just figured when the car was missing—"

"They might be camping out down there. Heaven knows why. But I'll go check."

"I'm coming with you," she said, rushing out the door behind him.

Luke grabbed a flashlight from the glove compartment of his truck and by the thin beam of its light they picked their way along the rugged path through the orchid fields. When they got to the stairs hewn out of the cliff wall, Luke reached for Rosie's hand. He gave it a reassuring squeeze. "Watch your step. This can be a tricky climb in the dark."

Over the years, Luke had taken these stairs countless times and knew every jagged edge. Worrying that Rosie, who'd only been down them a few times, might stumble, he stayed a few steps ahead of her. However, he should have known that a practiced rock climber like Rosie would find the steps no challenge. Fueled by her obvious anxiety, she charged forward and hit the sand before he did.

He hadn't held a lot of hope about finding Liliana and Christopher in the beach house, but when he saw the dark shape of the little bungalow, his heart dropped. "Doesn't look good," he murmured.

Rosie sped ahead anyway. She was standing on the porch, impatiently knocking and calling out Chris's name as Luke fished out the keys and opened the lock. Flinging open the door, they stepped inside and Luke reached for the light switch. He'd been so tied up in his work that he hadn't used the beach house in years. The place smelled dank and the furniture, covered in white sheets, looked like ghosts.

He watched as Rosie ran futilely from room to room. When she came back, her face drained, he once again took her in his arms and kissed the top of her hair. Her shoulders were shaking and suddenly he realized that she was sobbing.

"I know it sounds ridiculous," she said into his chest, "but for some crazy reason when you said 'beach house' I felt certain we'd find him here. Christopher was conceived here, so I thought we'd find him here. I know it doesn't make any sense."

All the while as Luke tried to comfort her he felt a lump rise in his throat. He remembered so well the night they'd been together in this place. There'd been so many mistakes made since that night. He'd hoped they might reclaim them. Were they going to lose the chance? It was too terrible even to consider.

"Don't worry, Rosie. We'll search every corner. We'll find him."

A few minutes later Luke helped Rosie into the truck. While she sat next to him tensely, he reached over and rubbed her shoulder. After turning on the ignition, he picked up his car phone and put a call into Detective Pete Song, a friend of his with the police, and explained the situation.

"Okay, I've got your number," Detective Song said after he'd heard Luke out. "But we've got several missing persons right now. It's a really crazy night, as you can imagine, and my guys are all tied up. The moment I hear anything, I'll be on the horn to you."

"Thanks, Pete," Luke said, hanging up the phone. Then, after glancing at Rosie's pale face, he put the truck in gear and backed it around.

They started by scouting some of the nearby beaches and the little collection of stores up the road from Orchid

Cliffs. Everything was deserted, and there was no sign of Liliana's green Chevy. Next they headed north, checking out some small villages. Afterward they zigzagged south until they reached a spot from which they could overlook the site where Mr. Fan's store had been. It was now a steaming black wasteland seared by the ominous red rivulet of lava inching down the valley.

"I can't believe this is happening," Rosie said as they sat in the truck, looking out at the hellish panorama. "I became a volcanologist because I wanted to help people facing situations like this. Now I feel so helpless myself." She wiped away a tear. "What if Christopher's stuck out there somewhere?"

"Rosie, I can't believe he is," Luke began. "I think you're letting your imagination drive you crazy. Liliana's no fool. She's lived here all her life. I'm sure there's a good explanation for where the two of them are." What it was, however, he didn't know—he couldn't even make a guess at.

"As for your helping people, you must realize you've done that. Thanks to your monitoring the volcano, we've had a lot of warning. All the houses have been evacuated safely—no one's been hurt. And we've been able to save a lot of property."

Rosie wasn't to be comforted. As she gazed at the cataclysmic scene below, her eyes were wide with fear.

"I'll call Pete once more." Luke reached for the phone, then balanced it in his palm and looked at it as if it were a dead mouse. "Uh-oh. It's gone."

"What does that mean?" she asked anxiously.

He shook his head. "Dunno. It's flashing 'no service,' which either means we're out of the service area or there's some interruption in the transmission signal." He sighed. "You know, Rosie, it might make more sense to go home.

That's where Liliana knows to call us, and given my moribund phone, it's probably the only way to reach us at the moment."

She bit her lip. "Okay."

They were silent on the ride back. When they returned to the guest house, the phone was ringing again and Rosie rushed to answer it. A dejected look came over her face. "It's for you," she said, handing Luke the receiver.

"It's Pete," the voice on the other line said.

Luke shot a worried look at Rosie. "Nothing," he told her. He watched with relief as she walked away into the kitchen. When she was out of hearing, he spoke into the receiver. "Go on."

"I didn't want to alarm the lady, so I'm telling you. One of the squad cars found that green Chevy smack dab in the middle of the lava just outside of Maile Gardens, near the sacred site. No sign of anybody, though. One of the copters buzzed it and as far as we can tell it's empty. Looks like it's been abandoned."

"I'll be right there," Luke told him grimly. After he hung up, he made a snap decision. There was no reason to terrify Rosie until he knew what had happened. As much as he hated to, he had to lie.

She was in the kitchen, her back to the counter, when he walked up to her. "Anything?" she asked.

He shook his head. "I've got a few details to clean up at Maile Gardens." He took her in his arms. "I'm going to go out and take care of them. While I'm at it, I'll look around out there. Meanwhile, I think it would be a good idea if you stayed here and fielded the phone. I'll call you in a half-hour."

"How, if your car phone isn't working?"

"I'll find a way."

AFTER HE WAS GONE, Rosie paced back and forth across the tiled floor. Suddenly she stopped. It occurred to her that she hadn't looked closely at Christopher's or Liliana's room. Maybe there was a note someplace, or a clue to where they'd gone.

She reached around and turned on the light when she got to Liliana's room. The wet bathing suit and towel on the floor and the open dresser drawers told her that Liliana had been upset about something. Normally she was neat. So she must have dressed in a hurry and had something distressing on her mind. Then Rosie noticed Liliana's gold sandals by the bed. They were the shoes she usually wore. Had she gone barefoot? A quick look in the closet revealed that Liliana's heavy-soled sneakers were missing. The solidly build leather walking shoes were the ones she'd been wearing when she'd gone to toss the gin into the lava flow. Probably she'd only wear them to do some heavy-duty trekking. At the realization, Rosie's heart thudded.

With a little gasp, she rushed to Christopher's room. His bathing suit and towel, too, were on the floor, and his bureau drawers were open, indicating that Liliana had dressed him rapidly, as well. Still, all his toys sat neatly on their shelves. Liliana would have made him put them away before they'd gone swimming. Chances were he hadn't played with them afterward. Only Kong was missing from his spot on Christopher's pillow.

Then her eyes went to the top of the bureau and narrowed. Christopher's rock-collection box sat open there. She went over and peered into it. Lifting it, she picked through it. It seemed to be full of the usual assortment of Christopher's rocks. Nothing about it brought anything to mind. Yet he and Liliana must have been looking at it just before they'd left or it would have been put away.

A knock at the door made Rosie jump. Luke, she thought. But why would he bother to knock? What if it was the police with terrible news? Taking the box with her, she hurried to the front door, her heart in her throat. She found Mary Burns standing there, looking grubby and exhausted.

"I was driving home," Mary said breathlessly. "I'd been helping out at Maile Gardens and I was on my way back when I heard it on the CB."

"Heard what?"

"What I heard might be nothing, but I thought I should tell you."

"Tell me," Rosie demanded.

"There was a report about an abandoned green Chevy near Maile Gardens."

"Liliana's car?"

"I don't know. I was talking to Bird of Paradise—my gardener's handle. He lives not far from Niha. Anyhow, he heard about the car from the police earlier and didn't make a connection, but later he remembered that he'd seen what might have been Liliana and a child climbing near the sacred site."

Rosie shook her head. "But that doesn't make any sense."

"I know it doesn't, but maybe you should call the police."

Rosie's heart was racing and her mind was buzzing. Somewhere in the back of it, she had the feeling she knew what this was about. "Thank you. I will. Do you know how long ago they were seen?"

"My gardener didn't know exactly. He thinks it was late this evening, but truthfully, he was so wrapped up in what was happening at the Gardens that he wasn't paying much attention." Mary looked at Rosie speculatively. "What are you going to do?"

"I don't know," Rosie replied.

"Is there anything I can do to help?"

"No, but thanks."

"Just call me if you need anything," Mary insisted.

When she had gone, Rosie ran to the phone and called the police and talked to the dispatcher. She hung up with a sinking feeling. The dispatcher had sounded harried. Clearly, with all that was going on, finding Christopher would be low priority. "Well, if he's with an adult, he's probably okay," the man had told her.

Next she tried dialing Luke, but either he wasn't in his car or his phone still wasn't working. She slammed the receiver down in frustration and accidentally hit the shoe box, scattering its contents. Automatically she stooped to pick up the rocks and return them to the container. However, as she scooped up a handful of glittering stone, a small black one caught her eye.

"Wait a minute," she said aloud. She juggled the small black rock in her palm. It was a piece of hardened lava. Her mind raced back to the night of the luau when Christopher had skipped some stones into the ponds. What if he had pocketed some lava rock there or at the sacred site and Liliana had found it? What would she have done? With her superstitious dread of offending Madame Pele, might she have insisted on returning the rock? With fresh eruptions going on all around that area, the thought horrified Rosie. They could be in great danger. She couldn't wait a minute longer. She raced to get her purse and started for the door. Then she stopped short, turned on her heel and went back into the kitchen, where she scribbled a quick note to Luke and left it next to the phone. That done, she headed out the door.

"DAMN! Rosie exclaimed, hitting the steering wheel with the flat of her palm. She'd been sailing smoothly until she'd rounded the corner and run smack into a roadblock. Now, backlit by flares, a Civil Defense volunteer in a yellow hard hat held up a flashlight. She was standing in front of orange-and-white sawhorse barricades.

"Road's blocked, ma'am," the tall brown-haired woman said as Rosie rolled down her window. "Lava."

"But I have to get through."

The woman shook her head and shrugged. "Won't do you any good. You can't go anywhere. The road's cut off."

Rosie stared in frustration at one of the orange pylons flanking the sawhorses. This was the only road to the sacred site. She got out of her car, put her hands on her hips and asked, "I heard a report about a green Chevy stuck in the lava flow out there. Do you know anything about it?"

"Last I heard they thought it was abandoned long before the lava got to it."

"How far from here?"

"Oh, a half mile or so. If it's your car, there's no use trying to rescue it. About the only thing it's good for is scrap metal."

Rosie took a breath. "There's also been reports of a little boy and a tall Hawaiian woman wandering around the area. Have you seen them?"

The woman shrugged. "I've only been out here for the past twenty minutes, but nothing's come through except CD workers and police."

"What about a red truck?" Rosie asked in desperation. Luke had said he was going to Maile Gardens, but there was always the hope that he'd swung this way.

When the woman shook her head, Rosie shuddered with anxiety. She paced back and forth in front of the barrier, trying to clear her head. Then she made a decision.

"Thanks," she yelled over her shoulder, and got back into her automobile. Once out of sight around the curve, she pulled off the street. The nose of the automobile faced a cane field, but the rental car was no all-terrain vehicle. Nevertheless, it was all she had. After rolling up her window, she gunned the motor and plowed into the mass of five-foot stalks.

They scratched at the windshield and cracked and snapped beneath the wheels. Her headlights played weirdly over the thick woody rods going down under her bumper like cardboard soldiers. She knew they were doing terrible things to the car's paint job, but she didn't care. Half a mile in, the cane field stopped abruptly and she hit the brakes just in time to miss driving straight into a ravine.

Breathing hard, she scrambled out of the car. The beam of the headlights lighting her way, she stood at the brink of the ravine. Once again, the terrain was alien and dark, yet alive with the simmering red stew of magma. It was as if the devil were ladling it down the mountain. "God, please don't let Christopher be near this," she prayed.

Desperately she searched for a way to drive the car down. As far as she could see, there was no safe route the car could take. Opening the passenger-side door, she took her flashlight out of her glove compartment. In the dark, with only the limited illumination from the car and her torch, trying to find Christopher and Liliana would be like looking for the proverbial needle in a haystack.

For a minute Rosie stood taking her bearings. Less than half a mile away, from what she could judge, the new lava flow spilled down the ravine to her right. Even from this distance, she could feel its heat, smell its acrid sulfurous odor and breathe its grit. The sacred site lay near it, but if she approached from this angle it ought to still be accessible. Of course her path could be cut off at any moment by a fresh eruption or a sudden forking of the magma flow.

"You're crazy, Rosie," she said to herself. "They're probably home right now wondering where you are." But she couldn't really make herself believe that. Something in her knew that Christopher was out there, in terrible danger.

As Rosie started down the rocky incline, she willed her trembling body to be strong. She'd need all her strength and she'd have to be quick and agile. She lined up a large palm tree in the car headlights to use as a landmark so that if for any reason the headlights went dead, she'd have some guideposts for getting back. As she scrambled over the rocks, tripping and falling but righting herself, she swung her flashlight in a wide arc and called out for Christopher and Liliana.

For fifteen minutes Rosie struggled through the blackened, scorched earth, skirting smoking fissures and small bubbling pools, always noting distinct trees and rocks as landmarks. Her hands and knees were scraped raw and she'd taken a bad bump on her head when she'd tripped on a stump. She was getting close, too close to the fiery lava. Just standing here, she could feel its heat on her face. She wiped her brow and tried to see into the ash-laden darkness.

"Liliana, Christopher!" she shrieked at the top of her lungs. "Liliana, Christopher!"

At first when she heard it she thought it must be her imagination. Then her heart leaped as she called again, "Liliana, Liliana!"

"Mommy, Mommy!"

The voice was very thin, hardly audible. She swung around, listening for the direction. "Christopher, it's okay. It's Mommy. Tell me where you are."

She heard it again, his frightened cry. From what she could figure, it was coming from straight ahead, over the rise.

"Keep talking, Christopher," she shouted, "so Mommy can find you." Where the hell was Liliana, she was thinking as she started to climb.

His voice grew stronger as she ascended. When she reached the top once again she swept her flashlight. It caught the little boy. In the beam, he stared at her like a startled fawn. He was standing, a terrified look on his face and Kong dangling from one hand.

Relief washing over her, Rosie ran down to him and grabbed him up in her arms. "Oh, Christopher, oh, I've been so worried!" She squeezed him as if trying to prove to herself that he was real.

He was crying, and as he pressed his face against hers she felt his wet cheek. "Oh, Christopher, my baby, you're okay. You're okay." For a long moment, she just held him, feeling his warmth and inhaling the familiar fragrance of his little-boy body. She was never going to let him out of her sight again.

"Christopher, where's Liliana?" she finally asked.

"Over there. She's hurt."

Still holding Christopher, Rosie awkwardly maneuvered the light until she found Liliana's prone figure. The large Hawaiian woman was lying full length on the ground. For a moment, Rosie's heart almost stopped as she worried that Liliana was dead. Then she heard a groan. "Thank God," Rosie said quietly. Quickly setting Christopher down but still gripping his hand, Rosie hurried to Liliana's side. "Liliana, are you okay?"

Liliana lay struggling for breath. "Asthma," she gasped. "Trouble breathing."

"Can you sit up?"

"I'll try."

Rosie looked around wildly. How was she going to get Liliana out of there if she couldn't move? "You hold the flashlight, Chris."

Setting down his stuffed monkey, the little boy cradled the torch in two hands and aimed it where Rosie pointed. He held it steady while she helped the woman into a sitting position, but it was difficult. Liliana was heavy and there was no way Rosie could support her weight. "We've got to get out of here," Rosie declared. "But how? Do you think you can walk?"

Liliana shook her head and struggled with her breathing. "Don't know."

"Well, we've got to try."

It took all Rosie's strength to get Liliana to her feet, then shoulder part of her weight. As the heavyset woman leaned into her, Rosie held on to Christopher and the flashlight with the same hand. Several times she dropped it and Chris stooped to pick it up. Finally she let the little boy hold it and aim it toward the beam of her car headlights up on the hill.

They got as far as the tall palm, when Liliana slipped from Rosie's grasp and sank to the ground with a loud wheeze. "Can't go on," she whispered.

Rosie clasped her hands and put them to her forehead. *Think, Rosie, think,* she told herself. They were so close. There had to be something she could do.

"You sure you can't make it any farther?"

"Can't."

Rosie ran a hand through her hair and then stroked the older woman's shoulder. "Okay," she said. "I'm going to take Christopher and go for help in the car. I promise, Liliana, I'll be right back."

Liliana waved in answer.

"C'mon, Chris," Rosie said, taking his hand.

All at once, the little boy, who'd been very cooperative, stiffened and refused to move.

"Don't worry, Chris. We'll come right back."

"Kong!" the little boy wailed.

"What?"

"I want Kong."

"Where is he, where is he?" She pulled Christopher toward her, but he broke loose and went flying back in the direction they'd just traversed so painfully. "Chris!" she screamed, and caught him.

"I want Kong."

Frustration and exhaustion warred inside Rosie. Gripping Christopher's shoulders, she shook him. "Where is he?"

"Back there."

"Back where we were?"

Chris nodded.

Suddenly Rosie remembered. He'd put the monkey down when she'd given him the flashlight. "Look, Chris," she said, crouching to his level, "it's dark now and Liliana needs help. We'll get Kong tomorrow when it's light.'

The little boy let out a screech. "Now! Now! I have to get him now." He struggled so violently to tear away from Rosie, that she could barely hold on to him. Twice she lost her grip and he tried to fly back to where his monkey lay.

She had never seen him so hysterical. For several minutes she tried dragging him back up the hill, but he resisted so strongly that they both kept slipping. Over and over she tried to get him up, and over and over they fell. Finally they landed at the bottom of the hill, where Rosie sat pinning her son against her while she tried to catch her breath and figure out what to do.

A thousand thoughts raced through her mind. How could she possibly get him up to the car and then keep him in it while he was so hysterical? Rosie's heart squeezed with pain. It was terrible to see him in such a state after all he'd been through the past few days. Kong was his security blanket and she could understand why, with the world blowing up underneath his feet, Christopher needed him so badly.

But she had to get the three of them to safety quickly. *If Christopher is willing to stay with Liliana, and I don't have to hold on to him, it might not take me any more than a few minutes to run back and get Kong,* Rosie thought. She had a pretty good idea where he was. Then she'd get back quickly and get Christopher to the car easily. In the long run, it might save precious time.

"Go ahead," Liliana whispered from where she lay a few feet away.

Holding Christopher even more tightly, Rosie put her mouth to his ear so he could hear her through his crying. "Okay, Christopher, I'll go get Kong if you'll promise me you'll stay with Liliana until I get back." She had to repeat it two times before he began to calm down.

"We'll be okay." Liliana gestured for Christopher to come over and sit down beside her.

The boy, still sobbing, allowed himself to be led. "Now, you hold Liliana's hand," Rosie said. "Hold it tight and stay right there." Hunkering down, she put his hand in Liliana's and made sure Liliana had a firm grasp on him. Once again, Rosie shot Liliana a worried look, but the Hawaiian woman only nodded.

"Okay, I'll be right back," Rosie said. Then, with great trepidation, she set off into the dark.

It was not as easy to retrace her steps as she had thought. But finally she was able to steer her way by the landmarks she'd noted earlier. When she was almost where she expected to find the monkey, the ground began to rumble beneath her feet.

"Oh, my God," she said, steadying herself. For a moment, she stood there, hoping that she'd imagined what she'd just felt. If the earth was trembling that must mean it was under great pressure in this spot. Was magma forcing its way to the surface somewhere nearby? She pictured the trapped molten rock squeezing the earth apart as it battered its way relentlessly through the cracking crust. It would carry gas and rock with it. She shivered. This was not a good place to be.

She would have turned and gone back if at that moment the beam of her flashlight had not found the fallen Kong. With a cry of relief, she lunged, snatched the stuffed creature up and cradled it against her bosom. She started off at a run in the opposite direction, but she hadn't covered more than fifteen yards, when there was an explosion. Wisps of steam puffed from a new crack. As she stood transfixed, they gathered into a column of thick smoke.

Orange molten rock pushed apart the lengthening crack. Instinctively Rosie stepped back and whirled. She had to get out of there fast. The smoke, so dreamlike and pretty to look at, could be deadly. Just then, a sudden shift in wind blew a dense cloud of sulfurous smoke directly at her. With the next lungful she sucked in hot sulfur fumes and couldn't breathe. Holding her breath, she ran windward as fast as she was able.

A plume of gas and hot rock blasted from the tortured earth and hailed down like rocket trails. She couldn't hold her breath any longer, and let out a strangled scream as she inhaled the acrid fumes.

Oh, no, she thought as she felt her body go weak. This can't be happening, not now. A moment later, Rosie lay unconscious on the shuddering ground.

Chapter Fifteen

Luke stood with his hands in his pockets, watching police and civil defense workers scurry back and forth, their walkie-talkies blaring. The scene before him was like a nightmare that kept repeating itself.

Detective Pete Song put his hand on Luke's shoulder. "I really don't think the people you're worried about are here. Given the way the eruption went, the car must have been abandoned hours ago."

Luke grimaced. He wanted to believe Chris and Liliana were someplace else. But where?

"Try calling the house again," Pete Song suggested. "Maybe Dr. Clarke has heard something."

With a curt nod of his head, Luke went back to the truck and turned on the ignition. To his relief, the phone was in service again. It had been going in and out all evening. When he called the guest cottage, however, there was no answer.

His mouth going tight, he dialed Mrs. Waneka.

"I saw her car pull out a little while ago," she told him. "I'll go over to the guest house and have a look. Maybe there's a note."

While he waited, he drummed his fingers impatiently on the steering wheel. Now, where was Rosie? He could feel his anger flaring. She'd promised to stay put. But maybe, he thought, her absence meant she'd learned something.

Ten minutes later, Mrs. Waneka called back from the guest house. "There was a note," she told him.

"What does it say?"

"'Liliana and Christopher may have gone to the sacred site. I'm going out there to check,'" Mrs. Waneka read.

For a moment Luke could hardly believe his ears. The sacred site was engulfed in fire. All he had to do was turn his head and he could see the crimson showers of flaming rock shooting up against the dark sky. His stomach tightened and he felt acid rise in his throat.

"Any more?"

"Nothing," Mrs. Waneka said, sounding slightly hysterical herself.

Luke let the receiver down, climbed out of the truck and stood surveying the inferno in the distance. Then he sprinted over to the knot of policemen and told them what he'd just learned.

Pete Song rolled his eyes. "Great, just what we need."

"I'm going to go look for them," Luke declared.

"How?" Pete Song's dark eyes challenged him. "I can't let you do that. You don't know they're there, and it's not safe for anyone to go into that area now."

Luke balled his hands into fists. "This is my son we're talking about. And my cousin—and," he added with a catch in his throat, "the woman I love. Just try to stop me." Before Song could reply, Luke turned and jogged back to the truck. The police lieutenant followed after and caught him just as he was about to climb inside.

"I'm not going to stop you, but take this," he said, thrusting a police radio into Luke's hand. "Call us if you find anything." He slapped Luke on the back. "Good luck and be careful."

Luke headed out to where the road was barricaded. If Rosie had gotten through the police block, chances were he would have seen her. Pulling up to where the civil defense volunteer stood, he got out and questioned her.

"Oh, yeah, I remember her," the woman, who looked dead on her feet, replied. "When I told her she couldn't get through, she turned around and drove away."

"Which direction did she go in?"

When the woman pointed, Luke thanked her and charged back to his truck. He knew Rosie too well. She wouldn't have simply driven off. What would she have done? What would he have done? Look for a place where he could cut through to the site without using the road, he told himself. Could Rosie have done something so crazy? He didn't bother to answer himself. The question was how far could her sedan go on this terrain?

Slowly he drove along the road, looking for places she would have pulled off. "Bingo," he said aloud when he came upon the stand of crushed cane to his left. Swerving, he stopped, shifted gears and started across the field. The truck, considerably higher off the ground than a car, managed the crushed cane with ease. Minutes later he pulled up behind Rosie's car. For a split second he stared at it with a sick feeling in his gut. It was empty, and the beam from the headlights pointed toward Pele's firestorm in the distance.

He catapulted out of the truck. "Rosie," he called out. "Rosie."

To his astonishment, he heard a voice answer. Standing at the edge of the cliff, he peered down into the darkness below. Again he called out. Again he heard an answer too faint to make out. Quickly he ran back to his truck and grabbed the flashlight out of the glove compartment. Just before slamming the door, he remembered the radio and clipped it onto his belt.

Gingerly he worked his way down the cliff, calling from time to time and shining the flash in hopes of spotting something. At the base he found Liliana and Christopher.

Joy surged through him at the sight of the bedraggled little boy. Stuffing the flash in his belt, he swept him up into his arms. "Thank God," he said. "Thank God." Then, putting the child down, he went over to Liliana, who managed to gasp out what had happened.

"You mean Rosie's still out there?" Luke said, staring at the field of lava fountains. They'd be beautiful if they weren't so deadly. And from what he could judge the scarlet fumes weren't far from this spot. No telling how much longer the three of them would be safe here. He cast a quick desperate look at Christopher and Liliana. Before he went to search for Rosie, he had to make sure they were out of danger.

"I'm going to make two trips," he told Liliana. "I'm going to take Christopher up to my truck and call for help. Then I'm coming back for you, Liliana."

"What about Rosie?" Liliana choked out.

"After that I'm going to go get her."

Christopher was easy to carry back to the truck. Liliana, with her bulk, was more of a problem. It took all of Luke's strength to hoist the six-foot woman to her feet and half carry, half drag her up to the cane field. When he had them both safely inside the truck, he gave Christopher a last hug. "The police will be coming soon to take you home."

"I want my mommy," Christopher whimpered. "I want my mommy, I want my Kong."

"I'm going to go get both of them. Your mommy will be home to tuck you in bed." Nice words, but could he deliver on them? Luke clenched his jaw as he descended into the inferno.

The area beyond the slope had turned into the devil's kitchen. Cracks had ripped apart the earth and magma bubbled in pools like cauldrons of fiendish sulfurous stew. The subdued roar from the vents were the gas jets fueling the oven's heat. Above it, he could hear the counterpoint snapping of lava slowly pushing through what had once been a cane field.

Luke's nose and eyes burned from the dense air and his mouth felt gritty. Pulling a handkerchief out of his pocket, he clapped it over the lower half of his face. With his free hand, he swung the beam of his flashlight. She couldn't be here, he told himself. Rosie was a sensible woman. Surely she'd gotten out and found refuge. He wanted so much to believe that. But deep inside, he knew she wouldn't leave Chris alone if there was any way she could have gotten back to him.

"Rosie," he cried. "Rosie." But there was no answer—only the hissing and steaming from the vent and the random explosions that detonated around him like land mines.

For a moment he stood there, squinting toward the car beams, hoping to see Rosie's silhouette somewhere in their light. In the distance he thought he spotted red flashers, which meant the police were close to the truck. At least he wouldn't have to worry about Liliana and Christopher any longer. Now all he needed to do was bring his son's mother back.

Luke pushed on, searching the tormented landscape for some sign of Rosie. Once again he shouted her name. At that moment a flare of red light caught his eye. He flashed his beam in its direction. There was something over there.

Something on the ground. Running, he skirted a crack and leaped across another. "Rosie," he cried out. "Rosie."

She lay crumpled on the earth, flames all around her. With no thought for his safety, he tucked the handkerchief in his pocket. Covering his face with his arm, he dashed through. When he got to her, he lifted her head and shook her. She couldn't be dead, he told himself as he searched for a pulse. "Please be okay," he said aloud. He held her close to him as if he could squeeze life into her.

"Please. Please," he repeated. "I love you, Rosie, and I need you. Don't leave me now."

She was taking breaths, but they were so shallow they frightened him, and even in the flickering red light he could tell her color wasn't good. He tilted her head back to open her air passages so that she could breathe more easily. A moment later he felt her stir. With relief, he kissed the top of her head. He tried getting through to the police with the radio, but there was so much static, he couldn't be sure whether he'd been heard. No matter, they had to get out of there.

Scooping her into his arms, he stood. Something soft struck his foot. Maneuvering the flashlight, he spotted Christopher's stuffed monkey. Crouching and holding Rosie tightly, he stooped to pick up the toy. If Rosie had sacrificed so much to get it, he'd better make sure it wasn't lost. Tucking it down the neck of his shirt, he rose to his feet.

Now as he held Rosie close to his chest, he turned and charged across a black crack that had started to widen. Moments after he'd breached it, he heard an explosion behind him and saw a burst of yellow light. Rocks cascaded, crackling as they were propelled to the ground by the arc of surging lava. The realization of how close he and

Rosie had just come to being incinerated shook him to the core. And they were a long way from being safe yet.

A few yards on a flaming palm tree swooshed across his path, bringing him to a halt. He looked to the right and then to the left, and saw only walls of flame. Straight ahead a fiery rift in the earth had widened so much it was impassable. And behind him magma gushed in a dramatic arc. He and Rosie were on an island surrounded by a blazing sea. Sweat rolled down Luke's neck and saturated his shirt. His eyes burned like hot coals and his lungs struggled for oxygen. In what had to be a hallucination, he suddenly thought he saw Madame Pele herself gazing out at him from the flames. Her hair was shooting streaks of sparks and she seemed to be pointing a finger at him.

"If I've done something to offend you, please forgive me and let us live," he exclaimed. With that the image dissolved in a spray of fireworks.

Falling to his knees, he set Rosie across them and tried the CB again. As he spoke into it, he aimed the flash into the sky. How anyone could see it in this fire storm he didn't know. But what else could he do?

He was trying to make his voice heard through the static on the CB, when the sound of a helicopter penetrated through the roar of Pele's rage. Luke looked up and made out the lights of a rescue copter circling in the distance. Somehow he had to catch the crew's attention. Laying Rosie carefully on the ground, he stood and began waving his flash back and forth, all the while shouting into the portable radio. He didn't even want to think about the copter not finding them after all this.

Then suddenly the copter was overhead, shining its beam down on them. "Gotcha in my sights," a voice on the radio crackled. "Hold on. Sending down a chair."

"Never happier to see anybody in my life," Luke shouted into the speaker as he stared up at the whirling rotors. Moments later a basket swung down toward him. "Move quick. Heat's pretty bad. I can't stay long.'

"Roger."

Dropping the CB, Luke lifted Rosie and grabbed for the basket. He put her in and watched while they pulled her up. At least Christopher would have his mother back, he told himself.

A few feet away an explosion ripped through the earth and involuntarily, Luke ducked. The hair on the back of his hands had been seared away. His skin felt like burning leather and the ground beneath his feet seemed to be melting. It could only have been seconds, but it felt like hours before the empty basket reappeared.

"So close," he muttered. "Just let me make this." As he grabbed for the basket, another explosion detonated near him and he inhaled air so hot it seemed to scorch his lungs. He had to fight to breathe at all. "I get the message, Madame Pele," he rasped as he jumped into the basket and wrapped his singed hands around the rope.

It was an eternity before he made it through the sizzling air into the belly of the copter. The moment he was pulled in, the craft lifted and whirled, then headed back to safety. Luke patted his chest, feeling the stuffed animal, which, miraculously, was still where he'd stuck it. Then he looked over at Rosie, who was being attended by a medic. Chris was one lucky little boy. He would have his mother, his father and his beloved Kong. And Luke intended to make sure he would have them permanently.

Chapter Sixteen

"Yes, Mom, I'm taking it easy," Rosie told her mother.

"Well, you know, dear, I've looked at your chart. Things are going to get really, really good. So, chin up."

Rosie laughed and then looked up. Luke was standing in the open door, grinning at her.

"I think you could be right," she said, and quickly ended the long-distance conversation.

"Feeling better?" Luke asked as Rosie, from her perch on the couch, watched him stride in.

"Much improved."

His eyes roved over her. "You look great to me. No one would ever know you'd left a hospital bed just a few days ago. As a matter of fact, no one would ever guess you've been through such an ordeal," Luke said, sitting down on the edge of the couch next to her.

Rosie made an affectionate face at him. "That's because you took such good care of me," she said, reaching out to lay a finger on one of his singed eyebrows. Though Luke had escaped Pele's fire without any serious injuries, the hair on his arms had been burned off and his skin was still red and sensitive in patches. He hadn't let that slow him down, though. For the past several days he'd been so busy helping his clients reconstruct their lives that she really hadn't seen much of him. Yet she'd known he was thinking of her, because he'd stopped by with little gifts of flowers and magazines while she was on the mend.

Stretching her arms over her head, Rosie asked after Liliana and Chris, whom Luke had dropped off at Niha earlier that morning. They were in the village to help with the cleanup. Rosie had wanted to go, too, but Liliana had insisted she stay home and take it easy for another day.

"You know Liliana. She likes to take charge," Luke said. "I'm sure Niha will be whipped back into shape before tourist season."

"I'm sure it will." She sat up.

"Oh, no," Luke said solicitously, "you rest."

Rosie rolled her eyes. "I don't know why everyone is treating me as if I'm sick. I'm feeling just fine, thank you. In fact, all I need is some exercise to get my muscles back into shape."

"Exercise," Luke said, eyeing her flushed face. He leaned forward and stroked her hair. "God, Rosie, all that smoke you inhaled. All for a monkey. Do you have any idea how worried I was about you?"

Rosie gazed at him. "Luke, I owe you so much—"

He silenced her by putting his finger to her lips. "It's time we got a few things straight between us."

"Oh? Like what? I'm not in for one of your serious 'Rosie, we've got to talk' speeches, am I?"

Smiling, he ran a gentle hand down her bare arm. Then he looked into her blue eyes. "I love you, Rosie Clarke. I think I've been in love with you for a long time."

As Rosie's heart thudded, she savored the words. She put her hand on his cheek. "Luke, I know I've loved you for a very long time."

"Now that we know it's mutual," he said, cupping her chin in his hands and giving her a kiss, "what are we going to do about it?"

Rosie's gaze dropped. "It's time to tell Christopher, isn't it?"

Luke nodded. "That's part of why I'm here. But not the only reason. I'm not a man who gives up easily. Rosie, I want you to be my wife."

She eyed him searchingly.

Taking her hand, Luke held it tightly. "You've turned me down before, but I'm hoping this time will be different. I know you thought I asked you to marry me because I wanted my son so badly." He hesitated, obviously framing his words carefully. "It's true I want Christopher, but believe me, Rosie, even if he wasn't in the picture, I'd still be here on my knees." His hands tightened on hers. "Without you the future looks empty to me. I love you, Rosie. I want us to build a life together here."

Rosie took a moment to gather her thoughts. This was such an important moment—one that she hadn't dared dream about these past five years. But one that in her secret heart she had longed for. Now that it had come, emotions crowded her throat. When she'd returned to the Big Island, she'd been both scared and determined. She'd wanted to introduce Chris to his father and had hoped they'd establish a relationship that wouldn't threaten her. She'd also wanted to work in this place that she loved, even if it was only temporary. But Pele and Luke had conspired to make this a homecoming in a much larger way.

"Oh, Luke," she said, throwing her arms around him. "Nothing would make me happier than for us to be husband and wife and for the three of us to be family."

He took her in his arms and kissed her, savoring the yielding softness of her mouth. Drawing back, he smiled at her, his gaze surveying her face as if he couldn't get enough of her. Then, reaching out, he brushed a few errant strands of the luxuriant red hair away from her forehead. "Rosie, I love you so much," he said. "You have no idea how scared I was. That night I was sure I'd lost you and Chris and everything I'd hoped for."

"Me, too."

For a moment they looked into each other's eyes. Then he was pressing her close to him, so close that she could hear his heartbeat. As he nuzzled the hollow of her neck, burying his face in her silky red mane, she moaned and closed her eyes to savor the sensation. And a moment later when his lips moved to her shoulder and he parted the collar of the white shift she was wearing, Rosie eagerly arched her back in invitation.

In answer, his fingers went to the buttons of her bodice and, unfastening them, found the naked flesh beneath. Slowly he began stroking each creamy white breast. At his touch her nipples grew taut and once again she moaned. Then with his tongue he circled each hard peak over and over until she ached with anticipation.

Pushing the shift from her shoulders, he drew the material down, sliding the fabric over her full bosom and her slim waist. Lifting her hips, she helped him slip it down to her ankles. Then, when she was fully nude, she could feel his gaze on her.

"You're beautiful, Rosie," he murmured. "So beautiful." Now he began to caress her ankles, her calves and knees. When he reached the sensitive skin of her inner thigh, Rosie, compelled by the urgency of her rising feelings, opened to him.

"Please, Luke, please," she whispered.

Then he was standing over her, pulling off his shirt, his eyes never leaving her naked body. In the shaft of sunlight from the picture window, his athletic build was that of a Hawaiian god, Rosie thought—a god who would have tempted Pele herself. Rosie reached her arms out to him, and moments later they lost themselves in the rapturous fires of love.

AS THEY LAY TOGETHER in bed, their arms twined around each other, Luke suddenly sat up and looked at his watch. "It's one o'clock. I told Christopher and Liliana that I'd come get them at two. But before I do, I have something for you."

"You do?" she said, sitting up and drawing the sheets over her naked breasts. She felt warm and loved and so happy that she was almost dazed.

She watched as Luke pulled his shorts on over his lean hips and padded out to the living room. Then she heard the front door open and shut. A moment later he was back. In his hands he held two lush purple-orchid leis. Taking a blossom out of one of them, he stuck it gently in her hair, above her left ear.

Rosie grinned and lifted her hand to touch the delicate bloom. "Does this mean I'm taken?"

"It certainly does," Luke said. "And I want the whole world to know." Smiling lovingly down at her, he kissed her upturned mouth and then draped the leis around her neck.

As their silken petals caressed her bare flesh, Rosie luxuriated in their sensual beauty. She'd never felt so safe and hopeful.

"One more thing," Luke said, reaching into his pocket. "I thought this might look nice with orchids." He drew out a small box and opened it. Inside was a white gold band with a circle of perfect diamonds. "Volcanoes can produce beauty as well as destruction." He took the ring out of its box and slipped it on her slender finger.

Breathless with joy, Rosie held out her hand and admired the elegant jewels. "They're like us," she murmured as she smiled lovingly up at him. "They've been forged in fire, so they'll endure forever."

FORTY MINUTES LATER, Rosie and Luke picked up Liliana and Christopher in Niha. After their traumatic night at the sacred site, Madame Pele seemed to have declared a truce. Once again the lava had skirted Niha and headed for the sea. There'd been no more eruptions and all indications were that the quixotic goddess had decided to withdraw from her cataclysmic labors.

After Luke and Rosie did a quick survey of the cleanup efforts in the village, the foursome climbed into the truck. "If you all don't mind I'd like to check on Maile Gardens," Luke declared. "Are you feeling up to it, Rosie?"

"Sure," she answered. "I'd like to see how things are going there, too."

The road to the development was still cut off, so they parked and hiked in. Sadness hung over the area like a low-lying cloud. They walked along quietly eyeing the torched trees and singed shrubbery. When they got to where Toshiko's house had once stood, they stopped. A blackened swath of steaming rock blanketed her lot and the lots of three other neighbors. For a long while Luke stood with his hands in his pockets, assessing the damage. Rosie came up to his side and linked her arm through his. What was he feeling? she wondered. Was he defeated by this blow to his dreams?

"You know, it's amazing," he finally said. "The people who lost their homes here have already called me about rebuilding. None of them want to leave the island. As a matter of fact, they want me to build a new Maile Gardens, and I'm seriously thinking of doing just that. Already Ky and I have been scouting property."

Liliana, holding Christopher's hand, had walked up behind them. "We Hawaiians have lived with Madame Pele and know how to live with her whims," she said firmly. "And we will go on doing that. Whatever Madame Pele takes away, she gives back something more."

Luke nodded. "I've come to see that, Liliàna. At first I was angry and resentful at all this destruction. But I've come to think that it's just a part of life—that you've got to pick yourself up and build even better than you did before."

"But not too close to the sacred site."

Luke grinned. "Right. Next time I'll pick a spot you and Pele can't complain about.'

Liliana thumped his shoulder approvingly. "You've got a thick head, but eventually you learn."

Christopher and Rosie giggled. "You mean there's hope for this man?" Rosie asked.

"There's always hope," Liliana replied.

For the next fifteen minutes, they walked around, taking in the devastation and the signs of rebirth that were already in evidence. Liliana pointed to a sprig of green that had stubbornly taken root in the charred earth. And as they reached the edge of the plateau overlooking the coastline, they stood gazing down at Pele's handiwork in amazement.

"Look at that," Rosie said. "The beach—it's gotten twice as big." Indeed, the black lava had spilled down and formed a wide ledge. When the lava had touched the cold seawater, the exploded debris had turned into chips of black sand.

Liliana nodded with satisfaction. "It's as I said. Madame Pele destroyed the old beach, but she gives us a new one that will be twice as big and twice as beautiful—that is her way."

At that moment, a ray of sun caught Rosie's ring. The sparkle drew Liliana's eye and she favored Luke and Rosie with a knowing smile. "Let's you and me take a little walk near the new beach," she said to Christopher.

"Yeah!" the little boy exclaimed.

"Careful," Rosie warned. "The lava shelf is still very fresh and it might crumble beneath your feet."

"I know," Liliana said. "We will go carefully." She reached for Christopher, who was clutching the smoke-blackened Kong. With a whoop of joy, he let Liliana lead him down the slope and along the hardened ledge.

Luke put his arm around Rosie's shoulder and drew her to his side. "You know," he said, taking her chin in his hand, "you never officially said that you would marry me."

She lifted her left hand. Luke's ring sparkled brilliantly. "I wouldn't be wearing this if I intended to refuse."

"Still, I'd like to hear the words."

She looked directly into his dark eyes. "I love you, Luke Devillers. And I want to be with you always. I'll be proud to be your wife."

"You won't mind moving permanently to Orchid Cliffs?"

"Not a bit."

"What about your job? I know that your position at the observatory is only temporary and that your work is very important to you."

She smiled. "You're right. My work is important to me. But I have some good news." She put her head on his shoulder and he put an arm around her waist. "George called me yesterday. They want to make my job here permanent."

"Just like me," he said, giving her a squeeze. "I want to make your position here permanent, too."

They kissed, one long lingering kiss, savoring the sweetness of their love. Finally, when their lips parted, they stood, admiring the scene below. In the distance, Liliana and Christopher, stooping to examine some object they'd found in the lava, were outlined against the blue crescent of the sea. Fluffy white clouds floated above them and a gull swooped down to catch a fish.

"It seems like nothing but tragedy and loss a few days ago," Rosie murmured, "but now it seems like a new beginning."

"It's like us," Luke said, turning back to her. "We've lost some important years together, but now that we've found each other again, we're going to build an even more beautiful life." He kissed her cheek and she nuzzled against his chest.

Then Rosie lifted her face to Luke's tanned one. "I think it's time Christopher met his father."

He smiled down at her. "I think so, too."

Then hand in hand they strolled toward the little boy and their future together.

HAPPY
VALENTINE'S
DAY